# CHRISTOPHER BUSH
## THE CASE OF THE MURDERED MAJOR

CHRISTOPHER BUSH was born Charlie Christmas Bush in Norfolk in 1885. His father was a farm labourer and his mother a milliner. In the early years of his childhood he lived with his aunt and uncle in London before returning to Norfolk aged seven, later winning a scholarship to Thetford Grammar School.

As an adult, Bush worked as a schoolmaster for 27 years, pausing only to fight in World War One, until retiring aged 46 in 1931 to be a full-time novelist. His first novel featuring the eccentric Ludovic Travers was published in 1926, and was followed by 62 additional Travers mysteries. These are all to be republished by Dean Street Press.

Christopher Bush fought again in World War Two, and was elected a member of the prestigious Detection Club. He died in 1973.

# CHRISTOPHER BUSH

# THE CASE OF THE MURDERED MAJOR

With an introduction
by Curtis Evans

DEAN STREET PRESS

Published by Dean Street Press 2018



First published in 1941 by Cassell & Co., Ltd.

Cover by DSP

ISBN 978 1 912574 11 7

www.deanstreetpress.co.uk

# INTRODUCTION

## A Mystery Writer Goes to War
### Christopher Bush and British Detective Fiction's Fight against Hitler

AFTER THE Francophile Christopher Bush completed his series sleuth Ludovic "Ludo" Travers' nostalgic little tour of France (soon to be tragically overrun and scourged by Hitler's remorseless legions) in the pair of detective novels *The Case of the Flying Donkey* (1939) and *The Case of the Climbing Rat* (1940), the author published a trilogy of Ludo Travers mysteries drawing directly on his own recent experience in British military service: *The Case of the Murdered Major* (1941), *The Case of the Kidnapped Colonel* (1942) and *The Case of the Fighting Soldier* (1942). Together this accomplished trio of novels constitutes arguably the most notable series of wartime detective fiction (as opposed to thrillers) published in Britain during the Second World War. There are, to be sure, other interesting examples of this conflict-focused crime writing by true detective novelists, such as Gladys Mitchell's *Brazen Tongue* (1940, depicting the period of the so-called "Phoney War"), G.D.H. Cole's *Murder at the Munition Works* (1940, primarily concerned with wartime labor-management relations), John Rhode's *They Watched by Night* (1941), *Night Exercise* (1942) and *The Fourth Bomb* (1942), Miles Burton's *Up the Garden Path* (1941), *Dead Stop* (1943), *Murder, M.D.* (1943) and *Four-Ply Yarn* (1944), John Dickson Carr's *Murder in the Submarine Zone* (1940) and *She Died a Lady* (1943), Belton Cobb's *Home Guard Mystery* (1941), Margaret Cole's *Knife in the Dark* (1941), Ngaio Marsh's *Colour Scheme* (1943) and *Died in the Wool* (1945) (both set in wartime New Zealand), Christianna Brand's *Green for Danger* (1944), Freeman Wills Crofts's *Enemy Unseen* (1945) and Clifford Witting's *Subject: Murder* (1945). Yet Bush's three books seem the most informed by actual martial experience.

Like his Detection Club colleague Cecil John Charles Street (who published mysteries as both John Rhode and Miles Burton), Christopher Bush was a distinguished veteran of the First World War (though unlike Street his service seems to have consisted of administration rather than fighting in the field) who returned to active service during the second, even more globally catastrophic, "show" (as Bush termed it), albeit fairly briefly. 53 years old at the time of the German invasion of Poland and Britain's resultant entry into hostilities, Bush helped administer prisoner of war and alien internment camps, initially, it appears, at Camp No 22 (Pennylands) in Ayrshire, Scotland and Camp No 9 at Southampton, at the latter location as Adjutant Quartermaster.

In February 1940, Bush, now promoted from 2nd Lieutenant to Captain, received his final, and most controversial, commission: that of Adjutant Commandant at a prisoner-of-war and alien internment camp established in the second week of the war at the recently evacuated Taunton's School in Highfield, a suburb of Southampton. Throughout the United Kingdom 27,000 refugees and immigrants from Germany, Austria and Italy (after the latter country declared war on Britain in June 1940) were interned in camps like the one in Highfield. Bournemouth refugee Fritz Engel--a Jewish Austrian dentist who in May 1940, after Winston Churchill became Prime Minister and inaugurated his infamous "Collar the lot!" internment policy, was interned at the Highfield camp--direly recalled the brief time he spent there, before he was transferred to a larger camp on the Isle of Man, for possible shipment overseas. "I was first taken into Southampton into a building belonging to Taunton's School," he wrote in a bracing unpublished memoir, "already surrounded by electrically loaded barbed wire. . . ." (See Tony Kushner and Katharine Knox, *Refugees in an Age of Genocide: Global, National and Local Perspectives during the Twentieth Century*, 1999.)

Similarly, Desider Furst, another interned refugee Austrian Jewish dentist, wrote in his autobiography, *Home is Somewhere Else*: "[Our bus] stopped in front of a large building, a school, and the bus was surrounded by young soldiers with fixed bayonets. We had become prisoners. A large hall was turned into a dormitory, and we were each issued a blanket. The room was already fairly crowded. . . . We were fed irregularly with tea and sandwiches, and nobody bothered us. We were not even counted. I had the feeling that it was a dream or bad joke that would end soon." He was wrong, however: "After two days we were each given a paper bag with some food and put onto a train [to Liverpool] under military escort. The episode was turning serious; we were regarded as potential enemies."

Soon finding its way in one of Bush's detective novels was this highly topical setting, prudently shorn by the author of the problematic matter of alien refugee internment. (Churchill's policy became unpopular in the UK and was modified after the *Arandora Star*, an internee ship bound for Canada, was torpedoed by the Germans on July 2, 1940, leading to the deaths of nearly 1000 people on board, a tragic and needless event to which Margaret Cole darkly alludes in her pro-refugee wartime mystery *Knife in the Dark*.) All of Bush's wartime Travers trilogy mysteries were favorably received in Britain (though they were not published in the U.S.), British crime fiction critics deeming their verisimilitude impressive indeed. "Great is the gain to any tale when the author is able to provide a novel and interesting environment described with evident knowledge," pronounced Bush's Detection Club colleague E.R. Punshon in his review of one of these novels, *The Case of the Murdered Major*, in the *Manchester Guardian*.

For his part Christopher Bush in August 1940 was granted, after his promotion to to the rank of Major, indefinite release from service on medical grounds, giving him time to return full throttle to the writing of detective fiction. Although only one Ludovic Travers mystery appeared in 1940, the year the author was enmeshed in administrative affairs at Highfield, Bush published seven more Travers mysteries between 1941 and 1945, as well as four war thrillers attributed to "Michael Home," the pseudonym under which he had written mainstream fiction in the 1930s. Bush was back in the saddle--the mystery writer's saddle--again.

## The Case of the Murdered Major (1941)

CHEEKILY THOUGH enigmatically dedicated to Scottish artist Josephine Haswell Miller, the first woman elected an Associate of the Royal Society of Arts, "with love, but provided only that she gives us the picture," *The Case of the Murdered Major* is the first volume in Christopher Bush's wartime Ludovic Travers mystery trilogy and the first in the long Travers saga to depart from strict third person narration. (Events are told in the first person by an anonymous individual serving in the British Army—someone who rather resembles the author.) After *Major* all of the Travers mysteries are narrated by Ludo himself, further solidifying the link between the author and his detective and suggesting the influence on Bush of American hard-boiled detective fiction, particularly the contemporary tales of Anglo-American author Raymond Chandler, which are narrated by Chandler's famously cynical and wisecracking PI, Philip Marlowe. (For more on this point, see my introduction to Bush's *The Case of the Magic Mirror*.)

Bush begins *The Case of the Murdered Major* by detailing both Ludo's experience in the Great War (some of which--the time spent in Egypt and in administering a prisoner of war camp--recalls the author's own Great War service) and his life between the wars, up to his recent nuptials with Bernice Haire, which took place sometime between *The Case of the Leaning Man* (1938) and *The Case of the Green Felt Hat* (1939). Aside from the fact that it is a corking detective story, this makes *Major* a good choice for the neophyte Bush reader.

With war having recently been declared on Germany, Ludo and Bernice, who herself is now serving as a Red Cross volunteer, are pleased to learn that Ludo--now, like the author, in his fifties--has been offered an appointment as Adjutant Quartermaster (rank of Captain) at No. 54 Prisoner of War Camp in the city of Shoreleigh. Having accepted his commission, however, Ludo arrives in Shoreleigh to find it "a grim sort of place, with mean and sprawling suburbs and everywhere factory chimneys belching their smoke," and the camp itself "something of a shock"—for Ludo had had in mind "his old camp in Egypt, with its tents and flimsy reed-thatched buildings."

At No. 54 Camp the building Ludo sees before him is "a Victorian monstrosity—a huge out-of-date hospital that had long been the town's white elephant" and now stands forebodingly surrounded by "a double apron of barbed wire." The main entrance of the building, which the narrator likens to a "beautifully set blanc-mange," bears a certain resemblance to that of the main building of the POW and alien internment camp at Taunton's School at Highfield, Southampton, where Bush in 1940 had served as Commandant, with its "semi-circle of regular circular pillars, rising to the top of the first floor, where it supports a semi-circular species of balcony." All in all No. 54 Camp affords a perfect example of the "closed community" setting, which the late modern crime writer P.D. James deemed ideal for a detective novel. "A closed community has a particular attraction for a mystery writer," James once observed. "Apart from its fascination as a microcosm of the wider world outside, the closed community . . . can be a hotbed of intrigue, jealousy or dislike, emotions which can erupt into the ultimate crime."

Tensions at the closed community at No. 54 Camp steadily and ominously increase over the period from September 1939 to January 1940 (the first German prisoners--"the crew and the German passengers of a Hun ship"--arrive in December). Finally they culminate in the murder of the much hated Commandant, Major Percival Stirrop—"a bantam of a man, full of quick and self-important nervousness, with all the jargon of the Service and several of those little ingratiating tricks of manner that appear so charming until discovered to be no more than mechanical and second-rate veneer." Pompous Percival is fond of telling what those who know him eye-rollingly refer to as *The Story of My Life*, but the Major's tedious song of himself reaches a definitive finale when he is discovered dead in the snow outside the main building, with no footprints left around him, though his death most decidedly is an unnatural one.

Suspects in the baffling crime are limited, in the classic manner, by the enclosed nature of the camp setting. How could an outside malefactor have "entered the camp that night," wonders the narrator, explaining: "If he had contrived to mount the wall, and by means of a pole had propelled himself beyond the masses of coiled wire, he would have landed in a six-foot drift of snow which the first winds had blown up from the north. Had he struggled through the snow, a sentry must have seen him and given the alarm. And after killing Stirrop, he had to get outside the camp again. . . ."

Even with outsiders seemingly ruled out of the equation, there are plenty of inside men (and one woman, the memorable Bertha Dance) for investigators to pursue, including Ludo himself, who to work off steam had composed a neat little crime tale, complete with a perfect alibi, called *The Case of the Murdered Major*! (Awkward when that turns up, what?) Then there is the disturbing matter of the prisoner counts which keep indicating that there is an additional unknown and possibly quite deadly denizen of Camp No. 54 lurking within its confines.

Eventually George Wharton of Scotland Yard appears on the scene, looking "more like a patient vendor of vacuum cleaners and less like the tough, go-getting detective of novel and screen." But the unprepossessing appearance of the "Old General," as he is affectionately known at the Yard, deceives, for Wharton remains as keen as ever when it comes to scenting criminals. The Old General enjoys possibly his finest hour in *The Case of the Murdered Major*, though Ludo, who on this occasion is cast in the shade by the consummate professional sleuth, has plenty reason to find personal satisfaction with the outcome.

Curtis Evans

TO
JOSEPHINE HASWELL MILLER,
R.S.A.,
WITH LOVE,
BUT PROVIDED ONLY THAT SHE
GIVES US THE PICTURE

# PART I

# GETTING ACQUAINTED

# CHARACTERS

*(a) Administrative Staff of No. 54 P.W. Camp*
    Major Stirrop, Commandant
    Captain Travers, Adjutant/Quartermaster
    Captain Winter, Interpreter
    Doctor Dulling, Medical Officer
    R.S.M. Ramble
    R.Q.M.S. Mafferty
    Provost-Sergeant Ebbing
    Provost-Sergeant Stamp
    Sniffy Brown, Batman
    Private Timms, Batman
    Miss B. Dance, Shorthand-typist

*(b) Guard. Company of 2/5th Midshires*
    Captain Byron
    Lieutenant Dowling
    2nd-lieutenant Pewter

*(c) Others*
    Captain Tester, Late I.A.
    Captain Lading, M.I.
    Colonel Caithby, Shoreleigh Garrison H.Q.
    Supt. G.N. Wharton, New Scotland Yard

*These characters are not in the order of their appearance, but there should be no difficulty in making their acquaintance*

# CHAPTER I
## TRAVERS ARRIVES

Did you soldier in the last war? Do you regard yourself as conversant with the old army routine—its maligned quartermasters, its grim adjutants, its splenetic colonels, its ramrod sergeant-majors, its orderly-rooms, stores, drills, and a score of other things which are a part of memory? Suppose, for instance, that you—old-stager as only other people call you— were offered a job of work in this war. Would you jump at it like a shot and assume you could soon pick up the old threads, and in less than no time be an oiled, efficient cog in the dear old machine?

If so, you might get something of a shock, which brings us to this story, and the experiences of Ludovic Travers.

Perhaps you have met Ludovic Travers before. You recall his six-foot-two of lamp-post leanness, his huge horn-rims; his diffident, attractive smile, dislike of conventions, insatiable curiosity, eccentricities that never concealed good breeding, and the whole man permeated, as it were, with a likeableness that never lost a friend or made an enemy.

In the Great War private influence managed to conceal queer eyesight, and Ludovic Travers became a full-blown private of infantry. As a sergeant in 1915 he won a Military Medal at Loos. Then he accepted a commission and 1917 found him a Company Commander in Egypt. Then dysentery knocked him over pretty badly, and when at last he left a convalescent camp he was offered the job of adjutant to a Prisoner of War Camp. There, until the end of the war, he stayed.

It was not till the winter of 1919 that he came home, At the death of his father he came into a considerable sum of money, but his way of life remained the unobtrusive same, except perhaps that he liked to drive a really good car. He wrote those well-known economic essays—pills of shrewdly informed innards with whimsical chocolate coating—and was recognised as a financial expert of some importance. Something in that line brought him into contact with Scotland Yard, and, both before and after his marriage with Bernice Haire he was one of those unofficial experts whom the Yard has always on tap.

But it needed no special prescience on the part of Travers to recognise long before it came that war was inevitable. Like millions more, he was unsettled by perpetual crises, moved to fierce indignations, and anxious to do something about it all. The call for ex-officers gave him his chance. He passed his medical—bateyes and all—and was esteemed fit for any home service. Then came the great day when he came back to the flat to find Bernice flourishing a letter.

"Darling, they've offered you a job!"

Travers hooked off his horn-rims and began polishing them—a trick of his when at a sudden loss or on the edge of discovery.

"Who's they?"

"The War Office, darling!"

Travers beamed fatuously, took the letter, and had a look at it. The look became one of reproof.

"But, my dear it's addressed to me and smothered all over with *Secret and Confidential*."

"That's why I simply had to open it," she told him disarmingly. And then, quickly, "What's Qmr. stand for?"

Travers read the document slowly through. What he was being offered was the appointment of Adjutant/Quartermaster at No. 54 Prisoner of War Camp, Shoreleigh. He was asked to state whether or not he would accept the appointment, and he was further confidentially informed of the method by which he would be apprised of the imminence of war and his orders to move.

"What rank will you have, darling?"

"Rank?" said Travers, and blinked. "Oh, yes—rank. Captain, of course. An Adjutant's always a Captain, except when he's a Major." He gave a reminiscent smile. "Not a bad job when you come to think of it. What I was doing in the last show."

"But, darling, that was twenty years ago!"

"Well?" said Travers, with a smile of some condescension. "I can do that job on my head." Then a slight frown. "Of course I don't know a lot about the quartermastering side, but that ought to be easy."

Travers let his moustache grow and proposed trimming it to a toothbrush, and for some days after that he might often have been seen in his leisure moments, long legs stretched out from his favourite chair, the tips of his fingers pressed lightly together, and on his face the look of a benevolent Buddha. What he would be thinking of was that old camp of his in Egypt, the quiet, smooth routine in the office tent, the companionship of the Mess, the old Turk with his shifts and wiles, and likeable personality, and, above all, he would be recalling his old Commandant, Major Brand. A great chap, Brand. Knew his job from A to Z and left other people to get on with theirs, and above all blessed with an impish humour and a withering scorn of red tape.

And so to the end of August, when at breakfast one morning the 'phone went. It was a friend—and also a personage—giving confidential news, and ending it with the somewhat flippant remark that if Travers had not bought his uniform he had better do so.

That last evening in August it was the wireless at nine o'clock that gave Travers, with others, his orders to go. Next morning Bernice saw him in uniform for the first time.

"Darling, you look lovely!" she said. "Do let me kiss you."

Then there were inquiries as to what the ribbons were, and a dozen other things. And before the train went everything that had been rehearsed overnight was gone through once more. Shoreleigh, a fine seaside town, shouldn't be a bad billet. Bernice could come down on leave from her Red Cross work, and when Travers's own leave was due, he could come to town, and one of these times he might bring his Commandant with him.

"That would be rather jolly," Bernice said. "Except, of course, that you mightn't like him."

"Not much risk of that," Travers assured her largely. "Mind you, he mayn't be a tip-topper like old Brand, but you bet your life he'll be all right."

"Darling, now you're a soldier you must use the correct terms," Bernice told him with mock reproof. "What you mean is that he'll be a sahib."

Travers laughed. "That's it. Absolutely pukka. He may even be Poona."

At the station there was something of a thrill—presenting his free warrant and finding the clerk passing out a ticket without demur. It was a kind of symbol that sent him back twenty years and in some curious way bound him to the Army again. More than ever he knew he would have no difficulty in picking up the old threads. The job was going to be easy, as he told Bernice.

"No, darling, not easy—cushy. Isn't that the word?"

Travers laughed again. Cushy was indeed the word.

It was Travers's first visit to Shoreleigh, and in the falling rain of that early afternoon he found it a grim sort of place, with mean and sprawling suburbs and everywhere factory chimneys belching their smoke. He was somewhat perturbed, too, that the taxi-driver had not immediately known where the Prisoner of War Camp was situated, and indeed it took a good five minutes of inquiry before it was discovered to be four miles out of the town.

Do you know what a Prisoner of War Camp is like? If you think you do, you may be wrong, and for the very simple reason that such camps have about only one thing in common—a solid surround of barbed wire. The building itself may be a school, the grandstand of a racecourse, a huge private house, or empty mansion—anything, in fact, even huts, where prisoners can live in confinement under the conditions which Geneva has laid down for minimum decency or comfort. As Travers was nearing that Prisoner of War Camp which was to be known as No. 54, he was thinking of his old camp in Egypt, with its tents and flimsy reed-thatched buildings and the first sight of his new home was therefore something of a shock.

The building he saw was a Victorian monstrosity, a huge out-of-date hospital that had long been the town's white elephant. Two good things about it were that its walls looked mightily substantial, and that it lay in several acres of parkland. Round the actual building a double apron of barbed wire had already been erected; and everywhere contractors' men were swarming like ants; wiring windows, erecting huts, draining here and sand-bagging there, and generally transmogrifying the landscape.

Travers paid off the driver, hunched his shoulders against the rain, and looked round for someone to question.

"Any military about here?" he asked a lineman.

"There's an officer in that building there," the man told him, and hollered to a navvy to help with the luggage.

That building there was a palatial kind of outhouse, two-storied and rather like a coach-house that had been made into tiny flats. A door was open and seated at a table, busy with an *al fresco* sort of lunch, was a Captain with a couple of ribbons. As he got to his feet he looked taller than he had been when seated, for his shoulders were immensely broad. His jaws were square, his hair a badger grey, and his eyes a cold blue. His smile and his manners were charming.

"Hallo!" was Travers's greeting. "You belong here? I'm Travers, the Adjutant, so I'm told."

"I'm Winter, the Interpreter."

"Interpreter? That's a new one on me. In my old show we used to make do with Armenians."

Winter smiled at that, then looked inquiringly.

"Had any grub? There's plenty here."

Travers made sure there was, then set to. He was going to like Winter, he was telling himself. He was obviously the quiet sort, and he looked as if he knew his job.

"So you're a German expert?"

"In a way yes," Winter told him diffidently. "Practically bi-lingual, really."

It turned out that he had been brought up under a German governess, and as a young man had spent years in Germany, where his father had business interests. His war experience had been interesting, for he had fought with Smuts in Africa. Like Travers, he had applied for a job and had promptly been booked as an interpreter. That, as he and Travers agreed, was a miracle, since the War Office had put a round peg in a round hole.

"What's the Commandant like?" Travers asked.

A curious look flashed across Winter's face, and then was gone.

"Not too bad," he said. "He's only been gone a few minutes, as a matter of fact. Stirrop's his name. Major Stirrop. A local man. I mean he lives about twenty miles away. I expect he'll spend the day here and pop home every night till we get really started."

"And when's that supposed to be?"

"We're actually Z.21," Winter said off-handedly.

"What on earth's that?" Then Travers's fingers went hastily to his glasses. Rather dropping a brick for the one man in the show who was always supposed to know everything, to be confessing ignorance.

"The fact of the matter is," he explained, "it's twenty years since I was in this sort of game. Things must have moved on a bit since my time."

"Moved on?" Winter smiled. "My dear fellow, you won't know the job. A man I know tells me there're fifty times as many Army Forms and red tape as there were in the last show."

"I'll get the hang of it," Travers told him confidentially. "I mean, the adjutant side of it. I will own up that this quartermastering business is bothering me rather."

"That'll be all right," Winter assured him. "When the Administrative Staff gets here, you'll have plenty of help. You get a full-blown regular regimental quartermaster-sergeant. He'll know all the ropes."

Travers had felt another shiver at the mention of an Administrative Staff, and when Winter handed him a list—which he had copied from the official one in Stirrop's possession—he read it with an aplomb he was far from feeling. Compared with the old free-and-easy administration, effective enough too, the list was terrifying. There was to be a regimental sergeant-major, provost-sergeants, a civilian doctor, and a regular R.A.M.C. staff with an equipped hospital for both prisoners and guard. There was office staff, cooks, batmen, and the Lord knows what.

"Talking of that Z.21 business," Winter was saying. "All it means is that Z is the date when the balloon really goes up and twenty-one days after that we've got to be ready to receive prisoners."

Travers nodded sapiently as he handed back the list.

"What about guards?"

"A company of the 2/5th Midshires, so Stirrop says. They'll march in as soon as their huts are ready. Would you like a quick look round, by the way, or would you rather go along to the hotel?"

The Mess Room and sleeping quarters for officers would not be ready for a few days, so Winter had installed himself at an hotel about a mile away. He had conveniently brought his own car down to Shoreleigh, and they piled Travers's luggage in.

That night Travers insisted on celebrating, or christening, the new show with a full bottle at dinner, and to his great surprise Winter turned out to be a man who couldn't stand a great deal of tipple. That taciturn tongue of his became gradually loosed, and Travers learned a whole lot of things. One other thing should be said about that comparative loquacity on the part of Winter.

Several things about Ludovic Travers would become obvious before you had been long in his company, and Winter had had some hours in which, if he wished, to study him. For one thing, Travers's manners were always delightful and unforced. He was the perfect listener and supremely well-informed. For all his disregard of diehard convention and his occasional quaint mannerisms, one knew one's self assuredly in the company of a man of rare sympathy and insight; with whom confidences would be implicitly safe and to whom sharp practice would be more than an abomination. Travers himself, often puzzled why people should make him the depository of their secrets, was wholly unaware of the qualities that invited them. Once more he was to be surprised when Winter began to talk so freely.

"What's Stirrop actually like?" Travers had asked.

Winter shrugged his shoulders. Travers raised his eyebrows.

"Like that, is he?"

"He's got his points, I suppose," said Winter. "Too much of a damn' windbag for me. Can't get a word in edgeways with the man. Knows everything and done everything. And a hell of a lot of the dear old regiment."

"Fighting soldier?"

Winter grimaced. "Not so's you'd notice it. Makes out he knows everybody in the Service. You know: talks about Freddy So-and-so who used to command the So-and-so's, and Tommy Somebody Else who's got a damn' good job at the War House. You know the palaver."

"I know," said Travers. "Blimps in the making. Still, it takes all sorts to make a world."

There was a whole lot more Travers learned about Major Stirrop. After the last show he had got a job in Burma, and he'd now been retired for about ten years. His civilian activities were connected with a local brewery, of which he was a director. He was married and had a son in the Service, and so would be fifty-ish, which was the age of Travers himself and Winter.

That night as he lay waiting for sleep, Travers was not so happy as he had been about the cushiness of the new job. Some-how he was beginning to suspect that in twenty years things had moved and he himself had stood still.

"All of which," said Travers to himself, "is damn' puzzling. When we fought the Boer War we started where we left off at the Crimea. Then in the last show we started off at the Boer War. If we're not going to start off this one where we left off in 1918, then there's been an earthquake at the War House. Beg its pardon, the War Office. And as I haven't read about it in the papers, we'll take Master Winter with a grain of salt."

The following morning Travers met his new Commandant, Major Percival Stirrop. He was a bantam of a man, full of quick and self-important nervousness, with all the jargon of the Ser-vice and several of those little ingratiating tricks of manner that appear so charming until discovered to be no more than me-chanical and second-rate veneer. For instance, he came bound-ing forward to Travers with outstretched hand.

"How are you, Captain Travers? So glad to see you."

Then the spate of words began. Travers heard what was later to be known as "The Story of My Life." He gathered that the Major had for a short time been in a Prisoner of War Camp during the last show, and that this new camp would carry on from there. This new war, which was bound to break out officially at any second, was obviously going to take place on the special behalf of Major Stirrop. There was a lot of talk about the "old Bosche," and various So-and-so's who had commanded this and that, or had been in Rangoon. There were also some subtle questions about Travers's regiment and his connections, and there the impish mind of Travers deliberately refused to flourish the old school tie.

"Well, I suppose we'd better talk business," Stirrop said at long last. "You'd better be getting on with your indents. Have you got any Army Forms?"

"I can soon have 'em," Travers told him craftily, and then changed his mind. "One thing I'd like to say to you, sir, point-blank. I told you the experience I've had as Adjutant, but all this Quartermaster business is new to me. You'll have to allow me a little time to pick up the job."

"That's all right, my dear old chap," Stirrop assured him. "If it comes to that, we're all new to the job."

But deprecating as that last remark was, Travers could see that Stirrop had been therein included for purposes of politeness only. What's more, he had not liked that quick, petulant look in Stirrop's eye at the mention of straight talking and limitations. The new Commandant, he was rapidly becoming aware, was going to be something more than a handful.

The rest of that morning was infuriating. Stirrop pranced round the camp with Winter and Travers at his heels, and all the time he talked and talked and talked. If it were not to his two satellites, then it would be to foremen or workmen, while the satellites cooled their heels and begun to feel more and more hungry. Then when at long last the three returned to the office, Stirrop had an enormous list of things for Travers to get on with. Office furniture and stationery must he indented for at once, and all the lists had better be drawn up of stores required, and equipment, medical supplies, and heaven knows what.

It was almost three o'clock when he announced his intention of returning home. He gave Travers his telephone number.

"Ring me up if anything happens. I don't suppose it will. Good-bye, old chap. See you in the morning."

"Blast him!" said Winter. "Doesn't he think we ever want to eat?"

That early evening Travers went off on his own, announcing that he would not be in to dinner. What he had come to realise was that the job he had so gaily bitten off was likely to be more than he could at the moment chew. Moreover, if there was the likelihood of argument with Stirrop, then the sooner he knew that job, and his own rights and duties, the better.

He had noticed troops in the town, and what he now did was to hunt up their headquarters. There he found a warrant-officer of the good old type, and after a few confidential words took him off for a meal with suitable liquid refreshment. When he returned to the hotel, the taxi brought a more than respectable bundle of Army Forms, all duly noted for uses and occasions.

And he had learned a good many things—that people like regimental sergeant-majors and regimental quartermaster-sergeants were nowadays the virtual equivalents of subaltern officers, for instance, and should be addressed officially as "Mr.," and by the troops as "Sir." He learned where to indent for stores and equipment, and how to do it; what returns to make and where to render them; what sort of orders were likely to be published, and the nature of Army Council Instructions. Above all, he was furnished with a fairly recent copy of King's Regulations, which is the soldier's Bible, and the whole evening left change out of a couple of pounds.

One thing particularly pleased him.

"This adjutant's job of mine. Any alterations from my day?"

"No change at all, sir," the old boy told him. "The Adjutant's the most important man on the job. He's the one who's got to know. Between you and me, sir, that Commandant of yours will be the usual figure-head. He signs on the dotted line, where you put your finger."

There was no perturbation in the mind of Travers as he waited for sleep that night. In a week's time he'd know that job endways and backways. And he'd show Stirrop as much. And without blethering about it. All the same, he had the vaguely uncomfortable feeling that Stirrop wouldn't go through life content to do nothing but sign on the dotted line.

# CHAPTER II
# TRAVERS FINDS OUT

OCTOBER ARRIVED. Shoreleigh itself had undergone a tremendous transformation, storming as it now was with troops and defences. As far as concerned the Prisoner of War Camp, the most important happening in the town had been the early establishment of Shoreleigh Garrison Headquarters, which—for the benefit of the uninitiated—may be described as the parental and ruling military authority of the whole area. It had its Brigadier and Staff, who were everywhere abroad on tours of advice and inspection. Such, of course, were the official descriptions of its activities; those advised and inspected preferred to describe them as blue-pencil Nosey Parkering and ruddy interference.

Then, of course, it was the duty of Garrison Headquarters to disseminate War Office, Command and other Orders, and to collect the innumerable weekly and monthly returns. Stirrop found that Headquarter Staff a godsend. He was always round at their Mess standing drinks and receiving them, relating the *Story of My Life* to such as cared to listen, and ingratiating himself generally. In his own camp he would be constantly quoting the opinions of Headquarters, and, nearly always, against those of his own staff; and, even more infuriating, there was nothing too trivial for him to ring them up about. At all hours of the day he would announce that he would have to go round and consult Headquarters, and off his little bantam legs would scurry him, while his cold little eyes would be everywhere as he went through to the main gate, looking for causes of complaint.

"What's his idea?" Winter asked Travers once. "You and I both know he's in this war for what he can get out of it. Is he trying to scrounge a better job, or get made up to Colonel, or what?"

Travers shrugged his shoulders.

"Don't know," he said warily. "Perhaps he wants a little intellectual relief. After all, you and I are a couple of pretty boring cusses to spend one's days with."

That month brought tremendous changes in the camp. Dulling, the civilian doctor, had turned up early, as had all his R.A.M.C. staff. A prisoners' hospital had been equipped inside the main building, and there was an annexe outside the barbed wire for troops. Under him were also such people as sanitary men and cleaning fatigues, and within his jurisdiction was the huge kitchen which would deal with prisoners' food. All troops had their cooking headquarters outside the barbed wire.

It was a great day when the balance of the Administrative Staff arrived, and as Stirrop happened to be away shooting, Travers received the party. There were two batmen. One named Brown, alias Sniffy, he would share with Winter. The other, named Timms, was for the Commandant. There were two provost-sergeants, whose principal work would be with the prisoners. Their names were Stamp and Ebbing, and each was an old-timer.

And so to the two warrant-officers. Mr. Ramble, the Regimental Sergeant-Major, was short and sturdy, and, independent of his ribbon record, was obviously a fine soldier. Travers took to him at once, and was to rely on him much. What Travers liked was his quietness of manner. No crisis could flurry him, and, above all, he not only knew his job from A to Z, but was blessed with a strong sense of humour.

Regimental Quartermaster-Sergeant Mafferty was cast in the same mould, but yet vastly different. He was to be Travers's right-hand man, and, indeed, the man upon whom the whole camp depended, so it might be as well to look at him rather closely.

In height he would be about five-foot-ten. He was lean, his complexion was brick-red and his cheek-bones high. His dark moustache was waxed to points of needle sharpness, and his back was straight as the familiar ramrod. In repose his face had an expression of grimness and taciturnity, but when he smiled, which was rarely, at once the whole man changed to something exceedingly likeable, and one remembered the smile and forgot the taciturnities. His ribbons showed him to be a first-class fighting man.

Travers interviewed the two warrant-officers in his own room, and decided to be frank from the start. He confessed his own ignorance compared with their knowledge, said that he expected them to stand by him and that, for his part, he would never let them down.

"You needn't worry about the work here, sir," Mafferty told him with that warm smile of his. "That'll be cushy, sir."

"That's right, sir," said Ramble. "You leave it to us, sir, and we'll see that everything goes O.K."

When Mafferty had gone, Ramble stayed behind.

"May I say something to you, sir?"

"Why not?" smiled Travers.

"Well, sir, I much appreciated, and Quartermaster-Sergeant Mafferty did, the way you spoke, and I'd like to mention something in confidence."

"Well?" invited Travers, still smiling.

"I've known Tom Mafferty for years, sir. He's the best man at his job in the whole Midland Command. I'd go further than that, sir. He's the best in the country."

Travers' eyes narrowed slightly.

"Then where's the catch?"

'Catch, sir?"

"Yes. If he's all that good, why hasn't some big show collared him? Or why hasn't he got commissioned rank? Why's he been side-tracked down here?"

"Well, sir, that's what I was coming to," said Ramble, slowly recovering from the rapier astuteness of Travers's questions. "The fact is, sir, he's his own enemy."

"Just how?"

"His temper, sir. He's been broken twice on account of it, and been made up again because he was too good a man to be kept down."

"Does he drink?"

"No, sir. He's fond of his glass the same as I am, and he's the quietest living chap you know. But if he knows he's right about anything, sir, he sticks to it, and that's when he's likely to lose his temper."

"His Irish temper, shall we say?"

"That's right, sir. The fact is, sir, he can't stand being interfered with. He knows his job and—well, to put it bluntly, sir, he won't stand mucking about."

"And not a bad point of view either," said Travers heartedly. "The trouble is apparently that the Army hasn't thought the same."

Ramble gave an impeccable salute.

"'Well, thank you very much, sir. And now, if you'll excuse me, sir, I'll go and see to my men."

It was another great day when the guard marched in: "D" Company of the 2/5th Midshires, comprising three officers and a hundred and twenty men. Stirrop announced that he would take the salute, and Travers had never felt such a fool in his life as he and Winter—twin satellites—stood behind the fussy little man trying so hard to look like a hairy-chested soldier.

The Midshires were a Territorial battalion, and their officers took their job most seriously. The junior was Second-lieutenant Pewter, then came Lieutenant Dowling, and a Captain Byron was in command. Byron, a solicitor in civil life, was about thirty years old; very tall, very thin, and very earnest. What he didn't know—which was an enormous deal—he made up in enthusiasm, and his men were said to adore him. His manner was diffident and nervous, but like Mafferty he had a really attractive smile.

It was the duty of that guard company to furnish all outside duties and fatigues, as well as the guards themselves. The latter were not too onerous. The windows had been so heavily wired that no guards were needed inside the building itself, but a provost-sergeant with a runner would sleep there when prisoners were in camp, in case of any disturbance, and there was quite an elaborate system of alarm bells. All that the guards did, therefore, was to hold the main entrance gate, and to patrol by day and night between the wire aprons. To get from the building to anywhere outside, one went through a heavily wired series of gates, furnished with padlocks, the keys to which were issued only to certain responsible officers.

Officers' quarters and Mess, as well as all administrative offices, were outside the wire, and so communication between them presented no difficulties, and required no keys. But there were many other keys for all that—keys to admit to the main building, for example, and keys that locked the prisoners' rooms.

Is all this boring you? I hope not, but if it is, be assured in mitigation that it is all essential. And if you think you are getting something of a conception of what a Prisoner of War Camp may be like, then perhaps you have forgotten two vitally important things. Ludovic Travers had never taken them into his calculations, and they were two more signs that the world had moved on while he had been standing still.

First was the question of the black-out. How could one guard prisoners and prevent escapes when the whole camp, in common with the rest of Shoreleigh, had to be inkily dark? Well, it just couldn't be dark, so between the aprons of barbed wire there was a modified system of flood-lighting. On receipt of an air-raid warning yellow, this lighting was immediately turned out, and all guards were doubled.

Then there was the general question of A.R.P. Not only, mind you, the provision of respirators for troops, and suitable trench shelters, and covered posts for sentries, but the finding and training of rescue parties, fire pickets, decontamination squads, and demolition groups. There was a gas decontamination centre to equip. Fire points had to be made all over the main building and in the various huts, each point with its sand and water buckets, stirrup pump, shovels and gloves, and all the rest of it.

No wonder that one of the largest rooms on the ground floor had to be taken over as a store. You know the song—

*There is Ham, there is Jam,*
*In the Quartermaster's stores . . . !*

Well, in Travers's stores there were things which even that flippant ditty does not mention. There were blankets by the thousand, everything for the re-equipment of troops, spares of this and that from dining-room crockery to razors, safety, and cleavers, cooks'. And in case prisoners should arrive wounded, filthy or lousy, there were hundreds of sets of clothing. And towels, soap, disinfectant, latrine paper, bed-boards and trestles, tables, forms, chairs, bedding and the Lord knows what, all to be indented for, ledgered and frequently checked, and you have some idea of why Travers made a slight miscalculation when he so blithely assumed that quartermastering should be easy.

There is one last preliminary to mention—the arrangement of staff rooms. The guard had their own offices among the hutments, but the camp headquarters was in that building where Travers had first met Winter. Apart from it, a few yards away, was a smaller room which had been comfortably fitted up as the Commandant's office, but it is the main room that matters.

It is an easy room to visualise. Imagine a building the shape of a matchbox standing on edge. Two rooms are downstairs and two correspondingly up, with a staircase as you enter the right-hand downstair room. In that right-hand room was Winter with a clerk, now, since there were no prisoners, acting as officer in charge of P.A.D., or, as the civilian might prefer—A.R.P. In the larger room upstairs was Mafferty with two clerks, one on general work and the other principally concerned with rations. In the smaller room was Ramble, who, according to the administrative lay-out, was the Commandant's right-hand man.

In the larger room downstairs was Ludovic Travers, or the Adjutant, or Captain Travers, whichever way you like to look at him. His room had a wash-up and lavatory, as had Winter's, and since the chimney ran in the middle, there was a fire in each of the four rooms. In the Adjutant's office was the main telephone, with extensions to upstairs, to the Commandant's office, to the guard at the main gate, and to the guard company office. Travers, in either words, had to have his finger on the pulse of things, though there were to be times when he would curse the day that telephones were ever invented.

The staff of his room consisted of two people—a runner, though only occasionally, and a shorthand typist. When the Administrative Staff turned up it was discovered that there was no shorthand-typist among the clerks, so authority was obtained from Garrison to engage a civilian. The result was Bertha Dance.

Miss Dance was of the tallish, willowy type; a mistress of personal embellishment and with an excellent control of the hips. If Nature had been left to itself she might have been really good-looking; as it was she might have been described as not without attraction. At her work she was absolutely in the first class, but the trouble was she was none too fond of work and her chief anxiety seemed to be to ingratiate herself with the Commandant. Though she was consistently late, Travers gave up reprimand, for she had the hide of a hippo.

"You certainly know how to pick 'em!" was Winter's comment to Travers after her first interview.

Travers smiled and left it at that. What he had almost said was, "You ought to know," for he had more than a shrewd idea that Winter was very much of a ladies' man. He was very rarely in Mess of an evening for one thing, and at least two women would occasionally ask to speak to him on the 'phone. Also he was very much of an immaculate in the manner of get-up and appearance. One quite amusing thing Travers discovered for himself when he and Winter one day were leaning over a document—that the handsome black of his colleague's hair was due less to Nature than to art.

And now that we know practically all we need about No. 54 Prisoner of War Camp, what about a quick look round, with a rough diagram as guide?

Three miles out of Shoreleigh you leave the Green Man on your left and where the road forks take the left hand. Soon you come to a ten-foot brick wall, spiked on top, and on its inside—which of course you can't see—are huge entanglements of barbed wire.

At the main gate you are halted by a sentry. If you have a Government pass, signed by the Commandant or Adjutant, you are admitted and you find yourself in the pleasant park whose trees you have seen as you approached by the road. Outside the inner gate, opposite the main building, another sentry halts you by day, though at night you would not have been allowed to enter the camp at all without reference direct to an officer.

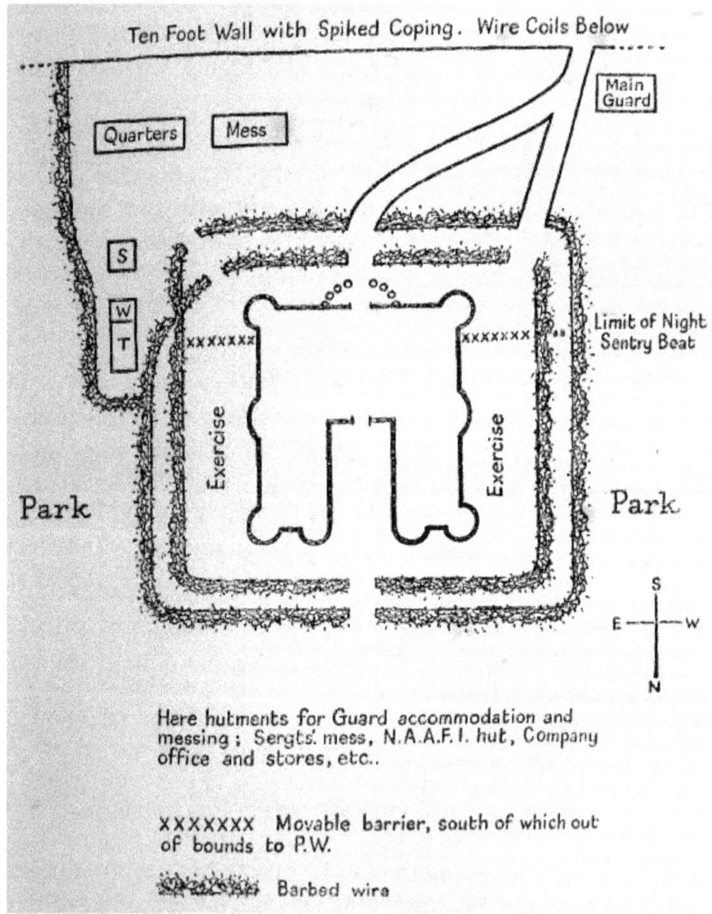


Here hutments for Guard accommodation and messing ; Sergts'. mess, N.A.A.F.I. hut, Company office and stores, etc..

xxxxxxx  Movable barrier, south of which out of bounds to P.W.

Barbed wire

You run your eye over the building. It reminds you of a beautifully set blancmange. Funny little crenellated towers balance all the corners, but it is the main entrance that fairly staggers you, for it consists of almost a semi-circle of regular circular pillars, rising to the top of the first floor, where it supports a semi-circular species of balcony. Two other floors rise above it, making four in all.

You are taken, perhaps, to the Adjutant's office, and as you near it you see a sentry patrolling between two thick aprons of barbed wire. If it is a fine day and there are prisoners in the camp, you may see them at exercise in the pretty considerable spaces between the barbed wire and the main building. Farther north, beyond the barbed wire, you see long rows of huts, and troops moving about, and a lorry or two, delivering rations perhaps, or stores, or collecting swill or camp rubbish.

The Adjutant's office you enter by the second door of that old coach-house building. It is a well-furnished room as far as offices go; there is an air of peaceful activity, and there is a cheerful fire. An even more homely touch is the teacup by the side of the typewriter which is being manipulated by a languorous-looking lady with well-defined lips and the loveliest red nails. You tell yourself that there are many worse jobs than that of an adjutant, and you certainly wouldn't mind changing his for your own. There, perhaps, you are right, but more likely you are wrong.

The dice are weighted in your favour for the simple reason that it would be far too tedious for you to wade through even an ordinary day in Captain Travers's life. But each morning Sniffy Brown brought a cup of tea at 07.45, and at 8.15 Travers entered the Mess for breakfast. At 09.00 he was in the office, and from then till 19.00 hours, except for a break for lunch, he was hard at it. Sometimes the rush of work would drive him frantic. The 'phone would ring incessantly, Garrison would pester, the War House would want to know, and something was bound to go wrong with rations or laundry or boot repair of troops. Mails would come and go, the Commandant would clamour for this and that; pow-wows had to be attended, and practices for air-raids, fires, and prisoners' escapes. A dozen people would have to be interviewed and the camp inspected. There would be wordy and windy conferences with Stirrop, and often brass hats would call. All the cash accounts would have to be made up, and if it was the end of a monthly pay period, the extra work would be as long and trying as that which confronts a bank at the end of a quarter.

In those first few months of the camp's existence, all days were alike, and Travers got accustomed to getting his weekly bearings by the arrival of Friday, which is pay-day and meant more work, but also a visit to the Shoreleigh bank. In the evenings he was rarely out of camp, for the rules had it that either the Commandant or his second-in-command must always be on tap, and since Stirrop came somehow to assume that Travers wished for no leisure, he was rarely in Mess himself. Often, indeed, Travers would return to the office and work there till late, while Mafferty, slogging unavailingly at catching up with the vast accumulation of before his arrival, would be working upstairs too.

But at 22.00 hours to the dot, Travers would move along to his camp-bed, though not always to sleep. As the weeks went by he would often he awake for hours, so full of anger and indignations that the very whirl of his thoughts would frighten him. When he awoke in the night, the maddening thoughts would again start their circling, and it would often be dawn before he could fall asleep again.

The reason of all that, of course, was Major Stirrop.

# CHAPTER III
# THE GOOD SHIP 54

THERE ARE SHIPS that are happy and others not so happy. No. 54 Prisoner of War Camp was a damnably unhappy one. Travers's own private description of the place was "hell with oases." And the perfectly infuriating thing was—as both Ramble and Mafferty were one day to point out—that the camp might not only have been an exceedingly happy one, but a place where one could have done good work and yet had a reasonably good time.

Travers first saw the red light clearly in that short period before Mafferty's arrival, when all the work was on his own hands. After a comfortable night at his home, and lined with a good breakfast, the Commandant would reach camp at ten-thirty or later. He would be genial enough; address his Adjutant as "old chap," and Travers would hope for a quiet day. That something would happen.

"Have you indented for those fire-buckets? I think you ought to."

"I've already indented," Travers might say patiently.

"How many?"

"I can't say off-hand," Travers would say. "I'll look it up for you if you wish."

"But, damn-it-all, man, you're the Quartermaster. You ought to know. Fancy indenting for buckets and not knowing how many you indented for."

The first time that kind of thing happened, Travers made a stand. He pointed out that he was indenting for thousands of things on scores of forms, and that to carry everything in one's mind would be to have the memory of a Datas. Stirrop refused to take it like that, so Travers pointed out something else.

"If the Brigadier or anyone else comes here, sir, and asks you a question, you can't always answer point-blank. You have to look things up, or refer to me."

"That's nothing to do with it," Stirrop said. "You're the Quartermaster and you ought to know. Damn-bad staff work. Damn-bad."

Thereafter Travers was never free from those infuriating challenges—"You're the Adjutant!" or, "You're the Quartermaster!" The trouble was that once Stirrop was crossed, he flew into a rage, and he would sulk for hours. Never once did Travers hear him admit an error, though if something he did was too patently wrong to be disowned, he would make it a joke.

"Extraordinary of me doing a thing like that. Not like me at all."

But no sooner did the camp get settled down than Stirrop found the niche of his darlingest imagination. He became the hub of things, and liked to see himself as the great controlling brain of some mighty organisation. He was always asking for the 'phone to be put through, and for Miss Dance to be sent in to take down letters, and in the meanwhile Travers himself or Mafferty would want to ring up about something vital, and instead would be kept hanging about for hours. And, of course, while he had the 'phone through to him, various departments would ring up from outside. Then Stirrop would settle himself comfortably in his chair, one vast importance.

"Commandant No. 54 Prisoner of War Camp speaking."

It might be an inquiry about troops' pay, or rations, or clothing, but he naturally liked to handle it himself, and since he lacked the most elementary knowledge of methods or procedure, Travers and Mafferty would find themselves with errors to remove and mismanagement to put right, or would discover they had been committed to something that broke every regulation of the Service. Or letters would arrive which were Greek to them, till they discovered that they arose out of some wordy and windy effusions that Stirrop had taken on himself to write to all and sundry without reference to a soul. Mafferty was sometimes livid with rage.

"The fact of the matter is, sir," he told Travers bluntly, 'you're being treated like an office boy and I'm just a ration clerk."

"No point in taking it too seriously," Travers told him. Once the camp had really settled down, he kept on assuring himself, then Stirrop might settle down to something decent too. Perhaps Stirrop was worrying because that Z.21 business had gone phut, and prisoners might really arrive before the camp was ready.

In those first few weeks Travers managed to retain somehow a sense of proportion and a sense of humour, for until repetition staled them and they became actually menacing, many of Stirrop's little ways were genuinely funny.

His impatience, for instance, and the way he imagined—or at least acted—as if he were the one person in this world who was right, but that the rest of the world was not only wrong but in a conspiracy against himself. As soon as he arrived in the office of a morning, Travers would be there with the necessary correspondence, and would invariably hear and witness something like the following.

"Sign this, do I? Now where's my pen? What the hell's happened to my pen! Would you believe it? One can't leave anything on this desk without some bloody fool has to go and touch it."

Meanwhile he would be picking up this and that and throwing it down and working himself up to a fine little rage. Then Travers might discern the pen.

"Oh. There it is, then. Now the bloody thing won't write. Who the hell's been tampering with this ink!"

It would be the same with poor Timms, his batman, or even with Ramble, his supposed-to-be right-hand man. He would come dashing into Travers's office.

"Have you seen my batman? Where the hell's that bloody fellow got to? Would you believe it! I saw him only a minute ago, and now he's gone and disappeared."

But to accompany the Commandant in his car from the camp to town was the titbit. Travers would rarely say a word, but would be listening to something like this.

"Damn these cyclists. Why the hell they let 'em on the roads I can't make out . . . Now is that fellow going to stop, or isn't he? Make up your mind, you bloody fool! There! Would you believe it! Didn't give a signal of any sort! . . . There we are. Lights against us again. Why the hell they have the lights I'm damned if I know . . ."

Then there was another side which Travers earlier found most amusing. When Stirrop spoke in a quiet voice and addressed him as "old chap," then some favour was about to be asked. It might be could Travers spare him if he took a day off for a shooting trip, or to see old Charles So-and-so "who used to be my Company Commander at So-and-so." Or he would ask if Travers minded if he made the week-end last out till Tuesday morning as this and that really must be done at home. Travers always urged him to take every spot of absence he could. After all, Stirrop's absences were holidays for all, and were later to be the oases in hell.

Once Stirrop lost a page or two of camp standing orders, later to be discovered under an old newspaper in his office. But in he rushed to Travers, and all the clerical staff had to be assembled and questioned. When he had gone, Miss Dance remarked in her languid voice:

"If I do find it, how shall I know if it belongs to the Commandant?"

Winter grunted.

"Easy enough. Every page'll have about ten 'What the hell's' and a dozen 'Would you believe it's.'"

Towards the end of November there was a first-class row. Travers had seen it coming. Ramble and Mafferty had been getting more touchy and on the jump, and the former was losing his sense of humour. Then the balloon went up—twice.

The first ascent was at an air-raid test. Stirrop forgot as usual the very orders he himself had issued, and imagined that this was taking place, when something else was laid down. The point was that Ramble was not just where he expected him to be. First came mutterings and stamping of feet, then the temper was lost altogether. In front of all the assembled squads Stirrop was rushing furiously about.

"Ram-BLE! . . . Ram-BLE!! . . . Where the hell's the bloody old fool got to? . . . RAMBLE!!! What the hell do you think you're doing!"

So much in brief for that. The second event was when the Commandant paid a visit to Mafferty's room on some business or other, and on coming down went straight to Travers. In his cold little eyes was that narrowing look that meant trouble.

"Are you aware that Mafferty writes letters?"

"Of course I am, sir."

"What! You allow a quartermaster-sergeant to write letters!"

"You'll pardon me, sir, but he's not a quartermaster-sergeant. The world's moved on since our time. Mafferty's a second-class warrant-officer . . ."

"Are you telling me my own business? Haven't I been a Company Officer?"

"Excuse me, sir, but let me speak. This isn't a company, and this isn't twenty years ago. It's expressly laid down in K.R. that Mafferty can and should write letters . . ."

"But, good God, man! A quartermaster-sergeant! What are *you* here for?"

Travers sighed. "If you'd have allowed me to go on, sir, I'd have said that the same para. of King's Regulations lays down safeguards, which I follow. Mafferty writes letters about things which concern his particular department, but it's I who read them and sign them."

Crossing him was the final straw, as Travers should have known.

"I don't wish to hear any more about it. It's got to stop. You understand that? It's got to stop."

Travers knew the time had come to make a stand.

"What you mean, sir, is that I'm to inform Mafferty that he isn't to write any more letters?"

"That's it. As a matter of fact, I've already told him so."

"Very well, then, sir. I'm telling you here and now that I shall countermand that order. If you wish to take disciplinary action, then I shall fight. I shall go straight to the Brigadier with that para. of King's Regulations in my hand."

A vicious little sneer came over Stirrop's face, but there was also a wariness as Travers could see.

"I'd sleep over that if I were you. It wouldn't be easy, perhaps, for you to get another appointment."

But Stirrop refused to force the issue. Travers had won, but to know that Stirrop, who never forgave a defeat, would be well on his tail from then on.

Those two happenings, which took place in the same week, had a sequel. Ramble and Mafferty approached the Adjutant and asked for a private and confidential interview, to which, as men having a grievance, they were entitled. The camp was too dangerous, and that early evening they met in the saloon bar of the Green Man.

Something else should here be mentioned first. It would have been tedious to rehearse all the rest of Stirrop's little tricks, though it should be remembered that they were at the back of those two warrant-officers' minds. That he was grossly selfish may have become apparent, but there remains also the fact that he was a liar who believed his own lies. He was a hogger of the limelight, and what could be more galling to those who had sweated, improved, and reorganised, than to hear someone else throwing his weight about over the 'phone or in the presence of some brass hat, with: "I soon found out what was wrong here, sir. . . . It took me a long time to work this out, sir. . . . Do you think I've done right, sir, in . . . Now this is something I was rather pleased about, sir, when I thought of it. . . ."

To put the whole thing bluntly, therefore, Stirrop had the implicit obedience of the whole camp. Discipline was good—Ramble and Travers saw to that—but men see, hear, and talk. What Stirrop had lost was every man's respect, and he was to be dangerously near losing their loyalties.

"The truth of the matter's this, sir," began Ramble, when the drinks were on the quiet corner table. "Mafferty and I are thinking of asking to be returned to our units."

"We can't stick it, sir, and that's the end of it," Mafferty said.

Travers smiled. "Now, now, now. You mustn't talk like that. You're not the only people who have to put up with things—"

"We know that, sir, and if we were you, sir, we wouldn't put up with it either."

Travers listened to a very long list of complaints, and knew that a first-class scandal might burst on Shoreleigh Garrison at any minute unless there was careful handling. He argued and persuaded, and even asked what he should do if they, his two essential men, should go and leave him in the lurch.

"That's the only thing that's kept us back, sir," Ramble told him. "If it hadn't been for you, sir, and the way everybody likes you, we'd have made these complaints days ago. You don't mind us talking like this, sir?"

"Not at all," Travers said. "I wish, perhaps, you hadn't brought me in personally, but there we are. But I'll tell you what I'll do, and what I think you both ought to do."

The upshot was that the two agreed to carry on. Travers reminded them of their promise to stand by him, and his own never to let them down. Now, as soon as they had a very real and definite grievance, they should come to him, and at once he would insist on an interview with the Commandant. And, to start with, he would have an interview the following morning, and try to get things on a new footing.

Stirrop was forgotten for a few minutes, while new drinks came and the corner grew hazy with tobacco smoke. Then Ramble mentioned something specially confidential which Travers ought to know. He approached the matter sideways by asking if Travers had heard anything about Miss Dance.

"Yes," said Travers dryly. "I did gather that the camp name for her was The Whore of Babylon, and I'd meant to ask you to jump down hard on anyone you caught using it."

Ramble made a wry face.

"It wasn't that exactly, sir. She's been seen out with the Commandant, and the men are talking about it."

"What do you mean by out?"

"Well, once it was walking out in a lane pretty late at night."

Travers thought for a moment, then shook his head.

"Better leave that alone. It's dynamite."

"All the same, sir," went on Ramble doggedly, "I thought you ought to know."

"You never know what's safe in your own room, sir," put in Mafferty, "if she goes in the other room with tales."

"True enough," said Travers. "All the same, hasn't she got a bloke of her own? I've rather gathered that impression."

Travers, as a matter of fact, had gathered more than an impression. Recently a man's voice had asked for Miss Dance on the 'phone, and by her attitude he had judged who the caller was. Young Pewter of the Midshires had mentioned going to a dance and how he had seen her there with a cove called—what was it now?—Tester—that was it. A Captain Tester, who had been in mufti.

As for the quiet work that Stirrop was putting in, Travers could now understand a good many things. Once he had tapped quickly at the Commandant's door and gone in, only to be aware of certain quick movements, and a strange scarlet on the face of the shorthand typist. But, as he had told the warrant-officers, that business was far too dangerous to be even aware of.

The following morning he requested a few minutes of the Commandant's time, but was unable to state even a case, for as soon as the purpose of the interview became apparent, Stirrop refused to discuss the matter. Travers, he said in so many words, had his remedy. If he was dissatisfied, all he had to do was resign. Travers gave him a straight, level look, and then walked out of the room.

Resignation was a thing he had thought of, but it would mean leaving his successor to suffer the same treatment, and it would mean desertion of Ramble and Mafferty. Moreover, to run would be cowardly. And yet to fight would be merely to rat on one's senior officer, and he more than suspected that Stirrop had dug himself so well in at Headquarters that to fight him would be a forlorn hope.

One afternoon in the following week the Commandant walked into Travers's office with a stranger, As usual, when in the company of others, he was most genial.

"May I introduce Captain Tester. This is Captain Travers, the Adjutant."

Miss Dance had got to her feet. Travers had scrambled up to be aware of a blond young fellow of about thirty, in a really immaculate lounge suit.

"I've heard of you a good deal, Captain Travers," he said.

"And not all to my good," Travers said.

Tester laughed. "Not to your bad, if that's the right word."

Stirrop actually patted Travers on the back.

"Make out a pass for Captain Tester, will you, old chap? We've just been having a look round the camp." He was off again as he spoke. "See me before you go, Tester, will you? And you might come in a minute, Miss Dance, if Captain Travers can spare you."

While Travers made out the pass to the camp, Tester told all about himself. He was Indian Army, but a shot through the belly in Wazirstan had nearly scuppered him altogether. As it was he had been invalided out.

"Tough luck," Travers told him.

"It was, rather," Tester said. "Still, I'm hoping to get back. Working the good old influence for all it's worth."

Meanwhile, he said, he was staying at the Royal, where Travers must come and dine with him some time. Travers said he would be delighted. Then before Tester went on for a farewell word with Stirrop, the two inspected Tester's rakish-looking car.

After that—and contrary to every regulation—Tester was always looking in. Stirrop and he were much together, and Travers could make neither rhyme nor reason of it all. Which of the two was the *ami complaisant*, he did not know. What he suspected was that Tester was the one in ignorance, but as he had never cottoned to him, he didn't give a hoot either way. What he did object to was Tester's popping in and out of his own room at all hours, and it was on his account that he made a habit of seeing that both the outer door and that leading through to Winter were locked when he himself was out.

Winter, too, expressed a dislike for Tester. As for Travers's relationships with Winter, they were very vague and shifting. Winter was a queer cuss. He never stood up to Stirrop, and though Stirrop had rapped his knuckles more than once in public, he said very little behind his back. Sometimes he would even make excuses for him, and to his face he was the very model of correctness. Travers felt in fact that all the weeks he had known Winter, he had never really yet visualised the man as a whole or assessed his real personality. Not that he disliked him. Far from it. Winter in many ways was a good sort—though even there he sometimes seemed just too anxious to please.

* * * * *

The second week in December word suddenly came from War House that prisoners were coming. They turned out to be the crew and the German passengers of a Hun ship—sixty in all. Then there was panic. Stirrop was making arrangements, forgetting them and making others, rushing round like a madman, bawling here and bellowing there, and working himself up to such a state that the whole camp was on edge.

When the hour of arrival came, it was too much for him to keep out of the limelight, and, contrary to standing orders, he rushed off to the station to supervise, instead of leaving matters to the guard as laid down. There he fell foul of Byron, for he began ordering the guard about before the gaping crowd, and ticking Byron off for doing the very things he was supposed to do. Byron came to Travers afterwards simply seething with rage.

"I think I ought to tell you I'm going to my Colonel to make a protest. I've had about as much in this camp as I can stand."

Travers placated him.

"Right-ho," Byron said. "I'll take your advice, sir. But any more cracks like I've had recently, and there's going to be a hell of a row. Only yesterday, sir, he was about as rude to one of my officers as he could be—and in front of the Colour-Sergeant."

In spite of the fact that having prisoners made even more work, Travers enjoyed the break in routine. He also saw Winter in a new light, for the Interpreter certainly knew his job, and it was a joy to see him having a few homely words with a truculent Hun. But what Travers enjoyed most was the visit for interrogation purposes of a couple of Intelligence men from the War House. They knew their job if ever men did, and with one of them, a Captain Lading, Travers got quite pally. He even fixed up a meeting with Bernice in town.

Ten days after the prisoners arrived, word came down to move them forthwith to another camp. The panic was on again, but at last the camp was empty once more.

"I don't know about you," Stirrop said to Travers, "but I feel absolutely worked out. Isn't it time some of us had a spot of leave?"

"What about you, sir?" Travers asked cunningly. "You'd like seven days at Christmas?"

"Well, I would," Stirrop said. "What about you and Winter?"

"My wife's coming down for ten days," Travers said, "and I thought of putting up at the Royal. No reason, sir, why you and Winter shouldn't both get away."

A few days and Christmas came, and peace descended upon the camp. Life was to be like that. When the Commandant was there it was as if men worked in a fog, over a delayed-action bomb. When he was away, the fog lifted, there was no bomb and upstairs Mafferty could actually be heard humming. And it wasn't that people took it easy. More work was done in less time, and time was left for leisure.

And now, after all these preliminaries, the decks are, as it were, cleared for action. But one question you may be asking yourself. How is it that you—the author—knew all about that camp and what was in Travers's mind?

Well, there's such a thing as giving information to the enemy, and being guilty of conduct prejudicial to good discipline, so I shall have to hedge. But you may remember that the camp took a long time to make, and it would be the Engineers in charge of most jobs. I might have been the head wallah known as the D.C.R.E., and so have been very close to Ludovic Travers.

In fact, to own up frankly, once I ran across him when he was very much down in the mouth, and he told me a good deal. Some of it I had guessed for myself. And when he mentioned that he'd stand a poor chance of being heard at Headquarters if he made a complaint, I gave him some news which ought to have cheered him.

"Don't you believe it," I said. "Stirrop isn't *persona grata* round there. I happen to know that they think he's just a chatty little nuisance."

Unfortunately, both for his own sake and for that of Stirrop, I don't think Travers quite believed me.

# PART II
# THE MURDERED MAJOR

# CHAPTER IV
# WHO WOULD BE AN ADJUTANT?

IT WAS COLD that January. Some people said such cold had never been known, and if No. 54 Prisoner of War Camp was anything to judge by, the statement was close to the mark. Three foot of frozen snow covered the park, and the provosts were out all day with fatigue parties, clearing paths. Pipes burst everywhere, and R.E. plumbers virtually lived on the place. Icicles hung like stalactites from eaves and sentry shelters, and the bitter wind cut like an Antarctic blizzard. Fuel entitlements and blanket allowances went by the board, but though the troops had half a dozen blankets per man instead of the regulation four, the hutments were still too cold for sleep. Men off duty would crouch round the stoves like broody hens, and each morning there was a sick parade like a theatre queue. The main building with its central heating was not too bad. Somewhat ironical that, that if prisoners came they would sleep better than troops.

Travers was awake that January morning long before his batman arrived, for the oil-stove had gone out, a keen blast was coming through the open window, and he was shivering beneath the piled blankets.

"Hadn't you ought to sleep with this window shut, sir?" Sniffy ventured when he came in with the tea and caught the blast.

"Better be frozen than poisoned," Travers told him. "What's it like outside?"

"One o' them silver thaws, sir. So slippy you can't stand. May I have your Sam Browne, sir?"

"Sorry, I left it in the office," Travers told him. "The telephone orderly will give it you."

Travers gulped the hot tea, then lay on thinking. The usual Monday depression was at once in his mind. At ten o'clock Stirrop would be back from his usual week-end, and he was wondering what particular balloon would go up during the day. And, of course, there might be some more news about those P.W. coming. Gawd! how smoothly things might go if somehow

Stirrop didn't turn up after all. Why the devil someone hadn't cracked him on the head long ago was hard to fathom. If it had been the front line, Stirrop would have had a bullet in the back long ago.

Travers smiled to himself at something he remembered, though it had been far from a smiling matter at the time. There had been some argument about rations, and Mafferty had been summoned to the Commandant's room. There had been high words on all sides, with Mafferty finally losing his temper.

"My God! Don't you answer me like that," Stirrop had yelled at him. "You do as I bloody well tell you, or neck and crop out of this camp you go."

Travers was just in time. He saw Mafferty's clenched fist and the whitening knuckles, but it was he who stepped forward first between the two. Stirrop had noticed nothing, but he had had a narrow squeak. Afterwards Travers had cursed hell out of Mafferty for losing control. To be broken, and maybe given six months in military clink, was too big a price for personal satisfaction or even pleasure. Later Mafferty thanked Travers, but that same day he had taken French leave and wandered off somewhere with a mind too maddened for work.

The tea had brought a pleasant warmth and Travers snuggled down in bed. Once more he was busy with something that had vastly cheered him of late—a perfect scheme for the murder of Stirrop. Academic it might be, but there was something vastly pleasing in the mere prospect of seeing Stirrop dead only in imagination. And Travers had a dozen cunning alibis on which to draw. That one of the air-raid test was his favourite. Now suppose there was an imaginary incendiary in the roof and Stirrop could be induced—

The door opened and Sniffy reappeared.

"Here's your things, sir, and it's nearly a quarter past, sir."

"My hat! So it is!" said Travers, and scrambled out of bed.

Young Pewter was the only one in the Mess, and at the marmalade stage of breakfast.

"Morning, sir."

"Morning, Pewter. You Orderly Officer?"

"Yes. sir," grinned Pewter. "Not a bad job either, these days. Better than being on parade."

Then in came Byron.

"Morning, sir. Any news about those P.W.?"

"Divil a word," Travers told him. "All the same you hadn't better let any men out of camp."

"Commandant coming back?"

"Why not?" Travers asked dryly.

Byron flushed sheepishly. "Oh, I just wondered."

Travers clapped him on the shoulder. "You keep your thoughts well under your hat, young feller-me-lad."

He finished breakfast and was having a quick look at *The Times* when Winter appeared. He was spruce as ever, and showing only the least trace of a hangover.

"How's tricks, old-timer?" asked Byron, who was a great pal of his.

"Oh, about the same," Winter told him in that quiet, almost taciturn way of his. "Any news about P.W., Travers?"

"Nothing new, but they're still on the menu."

Then Doc. Dulling put his nose through the door, spotted Travers, and came in. He was a quiet little cove, always landing himself in hot water through his utter ignorance of military procedure. Travers liked him, though rather irritated by the persistence of the bedside manner even when Stirrop was at his most objectionable.

"Ah, here you are then," Dulling said. "Can you spare me a minute?"

"Spare you half a dozen," Travers told him. "Have a cup of our delicious coffee. Or was it tea?"

"I've just had one at the cookhouse," Dulling said.

"Come along then," said Travers. "We can talk on the way to the office."

Dulling thought the fug in the huts was highly dangerous. Better open windows and issue more blankets still rather than have cerebro-spinal. And could the huts be regularly sprayed? The R.A.M.C. sergeant would be responsible.

"Give us a list of what you want to indent for, and we'll try to rush it through," Travers told him. "If it isn't available, buy it yourself and bring me the bills and I'll pay you out of either camp account or contingent. Anything else?"

"Any news about prisoners?"

"Nothing new," Travers said. "As soon as anything comes through I'll ring you at your house."

The two parted outside Travers's office. Inside, the room was red-hot. The night telephone orderly and his runner had seen to that. Travers got down to the morning's mail, and was soon frowning as he glanced at the clock. Miss Dance late again.

The telephone went. Travers mechanically picked up the receiver, then winced as he heard the quick, impatient, high-pitched voice.

"Hallo, hallo! What the hell's the matter with the 'phone? . . . Hal-LO! Ah, is that you, Travers? Would you believe it? For ten minutes I've been trying to get hold of you . . ."

Five minutes of that and he came to the point.

"What I wanted to ask you, old chap, was about coming in this morning. You wouldn't believe the muddle there is here. Burst pipes and every other bloody thing."

"No earthly need for you to come in, sir," Travers assured him.

"You sure? Nothing about those prisoners?"

"Even if the prisoners do come, sir, there're plenty of us here to look after a tupp'ny-ha'penny job like that."

"Well"—a little titter—"I suppose there are—really. You don't mind then if I don't come in? I shan't turn up unless I hear from you, then it might be late."

"I think you'd be unwise to come in late," Travers said. "The roads are pretty bad. Why not take a day off and come in in the morning?"

"Well, I hardly like to. Suppose some brass hat comes round?"

"There's such a thing as your being under the weather," Travers suggested diplomatically. "I don't think there're any questions a brass hat can put up that I can't find an answer for."

The 'phone was replaced and Travers was nodding to himself with well-earned self-congratulation. Then in walked Miss Dance.

"Good morning, Captain Travers."

"Good evening, Miss Dance."

She laughed, "But it isn't so late as that, surely. And my alarm clock went wrong."

"There was a certain American President, I think it was, who once remarked that either his secretary must get a new watch or else he'd get a new secretary."

"But you're not the Commandant," Miss Dance said pertly.

Travers's eye narrowed.

"I don't think I'd say that again if I were you," he told her frigidly. "You're working in my office, and being late is bad discipline. And if you imagine it's a question of your going or my going, then work out the chances for yourself. And now, please, get on with copying this Army Council Instruction in quintuplicate."

Before he could settle again to the morning's post, the 'phone bell was once more ringing.

"Is that No. 54 Prisoner of War Camp?"

"Yes. The Adjutant speaking. Who's that?"

"This is War Office—Major Vince."

"Oh, yes, sir."

'Is the Commandant there?"

"No, sir, he's rather under the weather this morning. Anything I can do, sir?"

"Those prisoners you were told to expect. They'll be coming some time to-day. Midland Command will telegraph arrangements."

"Very good. sir. A's or B's, are they?"

"Oh, treat 'em all as B's. You won't be keeping them more than a few days."

"Numbers, sir?"

"Numbers? Midland Command will tell you all that."

Travers replaced the receiver, then leaned back in his chair and stoked his pipe. He half rose as if to go through to Winter with the news, and then in came an orderly.

"Telegram for you, sir."

It was the one from Midland Command. Seventy-four crew and enemy aliens ex *S.S. Grossenfeldt*, with one officer and thirty other ranks escort arriving Shoreleigh station twenty hours. Escort to return immediately on completion.

Travers got through at once to R.T.O. at Shoreleigh station. He had heard about the move, and confirmed train times.

"Right-ho," said Travers. "We'll be there with necessary transport. You ask civilian police to be there and keep back Nosey-Parkers."

"Not many of them at that time of night," he was told. "And you can bet the trains will be running late."

Travers went into action. Ramble and Mafferty were called down to Winter's room, and Byron was sent for. Inside a quarter of an hour, everything was cut and dried. Mafferty would see to rations—B. class rations, which were those of Prisoners of War—-and would have a hot meal ready from twenty-one hours onwards. Ramble would have the necessary rooms ready, and warn provosts and their squads. Byron would take additional guards to the station, and arrange hut accommodation for the arriving escort. He would also have imaginary day and night practice with sentries forthwith.

"That's that then," Travers said. "All that remains to do is to warn the doctor, and arrange transport. You might ring the doctor, Ramble, will you? Captain Winter, you'll be responsible for your own show. I'll count the prisoners as they come in, and lend a hand with the reception."

"What'll the Commandant be doing?" asked Winter.

Travers had been somewhat amusedly noticing the growing perturbation, and now he sprang his pleasant surprise. The air lightened with relief.

"You'll pardon me, sir," Ramble said, "but do you really think the Commandant will expect to be warned?"

"The Commandant agreed that we could handle the situation," replied Travers officially.

"I can certainly handle my end," Byron said promptly.

"Everyone can," put in Mafferty bluntly. "There's nothing to handle, sir, if you go about it the right way."

Travers was going back to his office when Winter gave a precautionary little cough.

"Too busy, are you, to spare a minute or two?"

"Good Lord, no," Travers said.

Winter sent his clerk off on business, then listened at the communicating door for the sound of Miss Dance's typewriter.

"The Commandant's been up to his old tricks again," he told Travers quietly. "About you, to me, this time."

Some weeks previous it had been discovered that Stirrop was in the habit of discussing members of his staff with others, behind their backs, and at Winter's request principally and primarily it had been understood between him and Travers that if Stirrop discussed either, each, unless secrecy had been requested, should at once communicate with the other. Some of the disclosures were annoying and some ironically amusing, as when, for instance, Stirrop had plaintively said with regard to Travers: "He likes being a martyr, that's what it is? What's the fellow doing? Nothing at all. Every time I go in his room he's sitting there smoking that filthy pipe."

"Yes," went on Winter. "It was on Friday. You knew he'd sent for me?"

"I think it was after I left," Travers said.

"Oh, yes, you'd gone. He'd got some stranger in there, telling him *The Story of My Life*, and kept me hanging about till best part of half-past six. Then he began talking generalities just for an excuse, and then dragged the conversation round to you. Asked all sorts of questions about your private life. Most interested in knowing if you had any private influence. I told him damn all."

Travers grunted.

"I think his idea was to find out if he could give you the push," went on Winter.

Travers smiled grimly. "He'll have a scrap on his hands."

"My God, he will!" He hesitated for a moment or two. "I suppose he hasn't been chattering about me or my enormities lately?"

It was Travers's turn to hesitate.

"Well," he said at last, "as a matter of fact there was something—and on Friday—which I didn't like to repeat for fear of hurting your feelings."

Winter shot him a quick glance.

"Don't worry about me. I've got a hide like a rhinoceros."

"Right-ho, then," Travers said. "He was most anxious for me to tell him all I knew about you—which also was damn-all. Then he said that ever since he'd clapped eyes on you he was sure he'd met you somewhere years ago, and for the life of him he couldn't remember where."

Winter gave a sniff.

"He told me that himself one day. As I said, the world's a small place. What I was certain of was that I'd never met him. He's unforgettable."

"But that isn't all," went on Travers. "He wanted to know how you'd managed to get this job. I told him the same way as he and I got our jobs. Then he hinted the W.O. was very slack these days, and all sorts of what he called riff-raff could get in."

"My God! What a dirty little tyke he is." He shook his head bewilderedly. "And what'd you tell him?"

"I said he'd be able to see your whole record and family history in your B.199A."

Winter's mouth gaped.

"What's that?"

"Just a minute," Travers said, "and I'll show you."

He nipped into his office, passed some more work to Miss Dance, and then was back with half a dozen Army Forms. Two were handed to Winter.

"Here you are, young feller. Came by this morning's post. To be filled in according to King's Regulations, para. so-and-so.

One copy to be certified and then sent to W.O. by me and the other's retained by the Unit."

"It looks a regular dossier," said Winter, staring at it.

"Just what it is, and a pretty complete one at that."

"Any hurry for it?"

"Lord, no. We've all three got to do them, so I'll collect them sometime when the rush is off. Say in a week's time."

"I'll attend to it," Winter said, "and I hope it makes the old man's eyes pop. I wouldn't mind having a dekko at his when it's filled in."

Travers smiled non-committally. Winter halted him at the door.

"Thanks for spilling the beans about our friend. Rather important, don't you think, that we should keep each other promptly informed?"

"Yes—perhaps it is. But it's a dirty game all round."

"But necessary?"

"Maybe," said Travers, and shook a sad head.

He was nodding to himself as he went through the communicating door. Dirty it was, and it was doubtful if the best way of countering underhand work was to go underground one's self. Far better be a master of one's job, and do it, and leave the treacherous little swine no possible genuine complaint.

Travers rang Transport and arranged for meeting that train just before twenty hours. Then he finished the morning's mail, gave out letters to various departments, and dictated more letters. Then while Miss Dance was typing them he noticed something strange about the fourth finger of her left hand.

"Hallo! What's all that?"

"Oh, that," she said promptly, and out went the ring at arm's length to be surveyed. "Just an engagement ring."

Traven raised interested eyebrows.

"Captain Tester?"

"Perhaps."

"Early wedding?"

"Plenty of time to think about that," she told him archly.

Travers settled down to the compilation of a couple of returns, and then all at once there was a slam that fairly shook the room.

"Damn Winter!" he said. "The fellow's always slamming doors. Why the devil can't he go out quietly."

Then Travers smiled sheepishly. He was giving a perfect performance of Stirrop at his petulant best. Not that he wouldn't have a word with Winter. Damn-bad manners slamming doors.

His eye caught the clock. Midday already, and he hadn't had his morning inspection of camp.

Ramble was waiting with the medical sergeant and the orderly provost, and the four made the usual round. Then just as Travers had dismissed his parade and was coming out of the main door, he caught sight of Tester waiting on the steps. During Bernice's Christmas visit, the two had naturally seen a good deal of Tester at the Royal. Bernice thought him charming, but Travers had still never quite cottoned to him, maybe because Tester was of a generation with which it was hard at times to find points of contact.

Tester that morning was wrapped up to the eyes in a handsome coat with a fur collar, which gave him the look of a rakish Russian. He had come, Travers imagined, as he often did—to take Bertha Dance out to lunch.

"Well, how's things?" Travers asked him.

"Not too bad," Tester said, and then somewhat diffidently: "Could you possibly spare me a minute?"

"Come along in, then," Travers told him. "It's too nippy to stand out here."

They kicked the snow off their shoes and Travers unlocked one of the prisoners' rooms.

"And now what's all the trouble?"

"I hardly like to tell you," Tester said hesitatingly. "The fact is, I'm in a devil of a hole."

"What sort of hole?"

"Well, it's this." He looked round as if afraid of being overheard. "I've been frightfully worried. Driven nearly off my nut, in fact. Then this morning I made up my mind to confide in you. It's about Bertha. Miss Dance."

"But I thought—"

"No, it's something different. The fact is I had an anonymous letter a few days ago. I can't show it you because I chucked it on the fire."

"The best place for it."

"I don't know. I'd like you to have seen it now. What it said was that the Commandant here was well, a bit too friendly with my girl, and I'd better look out."

"I see," said Travers, and grunted.

"Yes, and the trouble is I've been putting two and two together, and I know there's the devil of a lot of truth in it. And what can I do? I can't have a stand- up row with him. That'd queer my pitch with Bertha. What the devil am I to do?"

"Have you spoken to her?"

"My dear chap, how can I? Acting on an anonymous letter! That'd properly send the balloon up."

"It's difficult," Travers said, and shook his head. "Mind you, I'm not committing myself in any way, but entirely without prejudice I'd suggest that you keep your ears and eyes open and if you see really good cause, then you can act. But it's a rotten situation—if there's any truth in it.'

"It is a bit," Tester said mournfully. Then he cheered up somewhat. "Thanks a heap for what you've said. But I'm warning you that if I catch a certain someone up to any monkey tricks, I'll knock his block off."

"You'd better keep that to yourself," Travers told him, forcing a smile. "And you'd better forget that you've been here at all. Which reminds me. This will be your last visit for a bit. We've some boy friends coming to-night."

"Prisoners?"

"That's it. It's as much as my tunic, or the Commandant's, is worth to let you in here when there're prisoners."

They moved back to the main door, and there Travers was just in time to dodge back out of the sight of Miss Dance who was coming towards the Bentley. A minute later Travers emerged to see the car going out at the main gate, and he stood for a moment or two shaking his head over the new situation. Much as he would have liked Stirrop to be the recipient of a thick ear, even at the hands of Tester, he knew the danger of scandal in the camp.

Suddenly he was aware of a curious sort of depression, only to realise at the same moment that it was the covering oppression of that huge entrance porch with its Christmas cracker pillars and vast flat top. Then he smiled as he remembered one of Stirrop's earlier, windy ideas, how that since that top concrete veranda could be reached from the corridor on the first door, it might make a good machine-gun post in the event of a prisoners' mutiny.

The alarums and excursions of the morning had put Travers well behind with work. The afternoon post was heavy and just when he was about to knock off at eighteen hours for an early dinner and a breather before the next excitement, Mafferty came down to the office, wanting to know if Travers had any details about the port of departure of the expected prisoners.

"I don't know a thing except what I've told you," Travers said. "There'll be the ship's officers—which reminds me. They'll have to be given the chance of buying extras, and we must find them waiters and batmen out of their rank and file. They'll have their meals first, as was done last time. The crew and their so-called passengers can all be lumped together."

"Yes, sir, but where do they all come from?"

"West Coast of Africa," Travers said.

"That's what I want to know, sir. Won't they all want an issue of clothing?"

"Good Lord, yes," said Travers. "Fancy this climate, after Africa."

"What I was thinking was, we'd make an issue in the morning, sir, when things are a bit easier. What shall I give them?"

"Thick pair of trousers, shift, vest, pants and one of those woollen pullovers. Let me see now. We've no authority for payment, so we'll make each cove sign for what he has and pass the account to whatever camp they go to next."

"Any Intelligence people coming, sir?"

"Haven't heard any," Travers told him. "Perhaps they've been interrogated this time on board ship."

By 19.30 the buses had gone to the station taking Byron and his additional guard, and Travers had the briefest of pow-wows with seniors of departments in his office.

"Everything all right with you, Mr. Pewter?" He ticked off the list. "Quarters for the escort? Reception guard? All posts manned? Main Guard know about lights? . . . Good. Then I needn't keep you any longer."

The medical sergeant, Mafferty, and last of all Ramble, reported all correct, and Travers was left alone except for a telephone orderly and his runner. The R.T.O. rang to say the train was running late—about half an hour, he thought. Travers cursed the trains and the War House. Why it couldn't have been arranged that prisoners arrived during daylight was something he couldn't fathom. For one thing they could have marched the four miles and saved public expense.

Dulling arrived and reported. Then earlier than Travers expected, the R.T.O. rang again to say the train was in and the buses were being loaded.

"Might as well cling on here for another quarter of an hour, doc.," Travers said. "A bit more cosy than hanging around at the main door. Unluckily it's a dark night."

"The snow helps, don't you think?" Dulling said. "Oh, and by the way, any of those Intelligence people coming this time?"

"Not that I've heard," Travers said.

"What was the name of that youngish fellow—the captain? Awfully smart at his job."

"You mean Lading," Travers told him. "Awful nice chap, as you say. Did you know his father was a Bosche?"

"Really?"

"Yes, but a decent sort of Bosche. The mother was English and that's why young Lading went to Rugby. Then the father died and the mother came back to England."

Then suddenly he gave a look of surprise, for Dulling had gone a most peculiar red, and was like a man with something on his chest and unable to get it off.

"I ought . . . I mean . . . Well, I think I ought to tell you something. Between ourselves." He lowered his voice and glanced round at the two orderlies at the other end of the room. "I'd rather you didn't mention it to the Commandant."

"I certainly won't," Travers told him, and waited.

"*My father was a German, naturalized a few years ago, just before he died. The name used to be Dufleheim." He smiled, rather feebly. "That was long before I came to Shoreleigh."

"I shouldn't worry about that, doc.," Travers said. "And you can rely on my keeping it well under my hat. And I suppose, by the way, that you speak the lingo?"

Dulling shook his head. "It's an amazing thing but I've completely forgotten every word of it. And I did it at school too. Honest to God, I don't believe I could count up to ten."

At a quarter to nine—or twenty-forty-five—the first bus was seen at main gate. It came through and slowly crawled towards the main door. Other buses followed and then the line halted. Pewter's guard lined the road and Ramble gave the order for the first bus to unload. Winter hollered in German that every prisoner must be responsible for bringing his own luggage into the building, unless it was too heavy to carry. Travers moved on through a double line of guards to the lighted reception-room. The doors were open, and with one of the provosts as check, he prepared to count the new arrivals.

They marched through in single file, and a mixed lot they were, with about only one thing in common, which was that they all made exaggerated shivers to indicate the excessive cold. The officers were well clad, but some of the rest seemed to have the thinnest of clothes, and a good few were still wearing topees. They were of all ages and all sorts. One or two of the younger officers were as truculent as they dared to be, and of the rest, some looked tired and indifferent, some were chattering among themselves as if to keep up courage, and one fellow, as he passed

Travers, actually gave a curl of the lip. Travers called Winter over. Winter blasted hell out of him in a few well-chosen words, and the line moved slowly through again. Then something really peculiar happened. A good many of the Huns wore beards, and it was a bearded one almost at the end of the line who, as he passed, bestowed on Travers *an unmistakable wink*!

After the first shock, Travers wondered if it were some nervous affliction, for another wink followed it. Then the blinking of the eyelid stopped, the man looked straight ahead again, and Travers passed him through.

"How many do you make it, Sergeant Stamp?"

"Seventy-three, sir."

"Correct," said Travers. "Seventy-three it is."

The prisoners lined up in the hall, each man with his hand luggage in front of him. Boilers of tea appeared, and each man was given a mug. While Travers dismissed the buses and interviewed the officer of the escort. Winter harangued. The prisoners were told camp routine, and what was expected of them. When the tea was drunk they were marched off under escort to relieve nature, then assembled again, and this time in their categories of ship's officers, ship's crew, and more or less genuine passengers. The heavy luggage had meanwhile been brought in, and the following day the prisoners would be allowed access to it under supervision to remove necessaries only.

The search and the medical inspection began. Each man stripped to the skin and, while the doctor examined him, the provost staff under Ramble went through belongings. Impounded articles went into a bag, giving the number which at the same time was allotted to the particular prisoner, and all papers and documents were brought to one of the two long tables at which Winter and Travers respectively sat. Names were taken and checked against the Nazi membership cards which every prisoner had. Money was counted and a receipt given, and then as soon as a room total was completed, that room was marched off under escort, and cookhouse orderlies brought each man a hot meal of good old army stew.

All that may sound a fairly rapid procedure, but it was well after midnight when the last room was locked up and the last light out. Travers, Dulling, and Byron adjourned to the Mess for bread and cheese and hot coffee.

"Gawd, but I'm tired!" Travers said. "Still, I expect we all are."

"Captain Winter's going on all night, is he?" Dulling asked.

"Not quite," Travers said. "He likes to get his papers in order before he turns in. He'll be along later. By the way, Byron, there were only seventy-three boy friends. The escort officer said one had gone sick way back, so you'd better warn Pewter in case he gets the wind up when he takes the count."

The three ended up with a whisky for night-cap, and then Travers would wait for Winter no longer, but decided to turn in. After all, he could tell him in the morning about that extraordinary cove with the wink. Someone slightly mental, probably, or else that extraordinary rarity—a Bosche with a sense of humour.

# CHAPTER V
# THE WINKING MAN

TRAVERS WAS IN the Mess rather earlier the next morning. Dowling, who was Orderly Officer, was just going out. Winter was just beginning breakfast.

"Hallo!" said Travers. *"Quelle mouche te pique?"*

Winter was a first-rate French linguist, and he and Travers would often talk French when it was a question of secrecy. Miss Dance, for instance, knew no French at all. And here is a convenient place to state that Travers's German was more than ragged, consisting as it did of a few pat phrases and no more.

"I'm not really late," protested Winter. "As a matter of fact, I've been in the camp for an hour already."

"And how did our boy friends sleep?"

"Not too bad. They're full of complaints, though. Asking for no end of favours, and wasn't there some back-chat when they learned they'd got to clean out their rooms and do latrines!"

"They won't get much change out of Ramble," chuckled Travers. "Did you ever see him march into a room and holler 'Achtung!'"

"He's a good fellow, is Ramble," Winter said. "Oh, and before I forget it. Young Pewter's entered up the Count Book wrongly. He's got it down as seventy-three."

"There are only seventy-three," Travers said. "I signed a receipt for the bodies and property of seventy-three. There were to have been seventy-four, but one cove was taken ill before they started. He may be along here in a day or two. Don't forget, too, that the doc.'s got two under observation in hospital."

'The escort officer came in. He was going back with his men in about an hour's time. Travers asked him how he had slept.

"Gosh, it was cold!" he said. "I seemed to spend the whole night turning from one sore hip to another."

"About time you young fellers learnt the horror of war," Travers told him. "Good luck to you in any case if I don't see you again. I shall come along and lend you a hand, Winter, as soon as the Commandant gets here."

Everything had been so carefully planned out that Travers would not be needed for a couple of hours. All the same, he was early in the office and was well on the way with the mail when Miss Dance arrived. She seemed the least bit upset, and Travers wondered whether Tester had spoken after all. But the engagement ring was still in place.

It was after ten o'clock and Stirrop had not arrived. It was too much to hope that he would take yet another day's leave, but Travers could congratulate himself on the smoothness and even gaiety with which that arduous yesterday had passed, and contrasting it with the panic and frayed nerves that had marked the previous arrival of prisoners. Now for a few days everybody was going to be overworked, Winter in particular, though a spot of real work for a change would do him no harm. Then when the prisoners had gone there ought to be a spot of leave for himself. Seven days in town was something to look forward to.

"The Commandant's here," announced Miss Dance.

"So he is," said Travers, and grabbed the pile of urgent correspondence. "If I'm late you might see if Quartermaster-Sergeant Mafferty has finished that fuel return, and then get on with the B.158's."

He entered the Commandant's office to be greeted with a grunt and a look of thunder.

"I think you might have let me know that prisoners were coming?"

"When I spoke to you on the 'phone, sir, I didn't know they were coming. Everything's gone perfectly smoothly."

"That isn't to say something mightn't have gone wrong."

"Nothing did go wrong," said Travers curtly. "I told you on the 'phone that we could handle any situation—"

Stirrop rapped the table with his knuckles—a trick that always infuriated Travers.

"I'm not talking about that. What I say is that if prisoners are coming again, I'm to be informed at once. What's all that you've got there?"

"Various things for attention and signature."

Stirrop waved them impatiently aside.

"I don't want to see that damn' rubbish now. How many prisoners are there?"

Travers made a full report as far as interruptions allowed. Stirrop grunted.

"Who's the Orderly Officer?"

"Dowling."

"And who's Orderly Provost?"

"Stamp."

He grunted again, just the least bit more irritated because he had not caught Travers out. Then he got to his feet and reached for his British warm.

"I'd better go along and see them. Do they speak English?"

"Some of the officers do, and all the passengers," Travers said. "The crew speak it very little."

Outside the Commandant slipped up on a frozen path and but for Travers's quick hand would have taken a purler. That was more than enough for an outburst.

"Why the hell hasn't Ramble had these paths cindered? Would you believe it, and I told him myself. .. . And what's that man doing over there. Look how he's holding his bloody rifle! Did you ever see such a lot of bloody fools to send here as guard. Where's Byron?"

"He may be in the main building," Travers said.

But Byron wasn't there, and Stirrop forgot that particular indignation at the sight of the busy hall. Winter and his clerk were preparing a questioning table, and Stirrop went across to him.

"What's this for?"

"For interrogation, sir."

"You mean to say you haven't begun interrogating yet?"

"The men are being re-sorted and some haven't finished fatigues," broke in Travers.

"Then they damn-well ought to have done. Damn' bad staff work. Damn-bad."

Travers kept a stiff upper lip and said nothing. Winter, from whom a straight left would have sent Stirrop for six, was taking it lying down, and the passivity infuriated Stirrop still more.

"Well, haven't you anything to say?"

A look came into Winter's eyes which Travers had never seen before. Then it went.

"If you say what you want done, sir, then I'll do it."

"Want done! Good God, man, haven't you got any ears!" He shook his little head in a mad, childish sort of rage. "My God, you'd drive me into an asylum. Where's the Captain?"

"Captain Friedemann?"

"Who the hell else should I mean?"

"He's in Room 5," said Winter evenly.

"Then I'll speak to him." He tossed himself about again, then changed his mind. "I'll see him in my room. This blasted place is like an ice-house. Why the devil doesn't Mafferty see it's kept warm?"

Off he went at a furious pace, so that Travers's long legs could hardly keep up with him. But no sooner were the two in the Commandant's room than Travers's fingers went to his glasses.

"There's something I must say to you, sir."

"Well, what is it?"

Travers's anger was beginning to rise.

"This, sir. That if Captain Winter cared to report that you'd spoken to him as you did just now in front of N.C.O.s and men, there might be trouble."

Stirrop shot him a look, then turned away.

"I don't need your advice as to how to keep discipline, Captain Travers."

When he turned, that crafty look was in his eyes, and he spoke with an exaggerated slowness which was evidently meant to convey some irony.

"Somehow I don't think we shall be troubled with our friend Winter very long." Then he broke off as if he had said too much. "Better let me look at those papers before that blasted Bosche gets here."

And yet, when Captain Friedemann did come in with Ramble, even in front of him Stirrop had to pose. With much ceremony he introduced Travers as if he and his Adjutant were the warmest and closest of collaborators.

"I shan't need you, Sergeant-Major," he said to Ramble. "I'll bring Captain Friedemann along when we've finished our talk.'

"Tell Captain Winter I'll be with him in exactly ten minutes," Travers said to Ramble, and then went on to his office. Already in the Commandant's room yet another stranger—and more than a stranger—was about to hear the *Story of My Life*.

Officers, and even high-up brass hats, often remarked to Travers that prisoners in their estimation were too well treated. One particularly bloodthirsty specimen of the latter class said that if he had his way the whole of the misbegotten unmentionables would be put up against a blue-pencil wall and ruddy well shot.

Now since this story depends largely on the doings of prisoners as well as of camp personnel, you should know in broad outline how No. 54 Prisoner of War Camp was run. First of all, the camp was really a clearing station, and not a standing camp, but main principles still held good. They were based on this incontrovertible fact. Prisoners of war of all belligerents in all countries must be subject to universal rules as agreed at Geneva. The British abide by those rules and expect the enemy to abide by them too. If we did not, then the enemy would have a pretext for ill-treatment of our men, which is something we wish above all to avoid. As for our safeguards—well, there are a good few. Officials of the Red Cross have access to camps in all countries, and prisoners may write letters of complaint to specified neutral embassies or legations.

No. 54 Camp catered for all ranks. Officers were better fed and slept on real beds with a chair for each. As there were ten of them in camp, they just occupied one large room, which was handy for administration. They were liable for no fatigues, but were expected to help with the discipline of other ranks.

All other prisoners were given the regulation ration, which is less in quantity than that of British troops, though if heavy fatigues were done, then extra food was allowed for. Prisoners had right of access to the Commandant, right of reasonable recreation and exercise, and were allowed to write letters and receive them when duly censored.

Those are merely indications which just about touch the edge of the subject, but as such they will do. Now look at a daily routine card for January, copies of which in German were in all rooms.

## CAMP TIME-TABLE

07.00 Reveille and Count.

07.15 Personal and Room Fatigues.

08.00 Breakfast (Officers).

08.15 Breakfast [Other Ranks).

09.00 Fatigues. Sick Parade.

12.00 Commandant's Count.

13.00 Dinner (Officers).

13.15 Dinner (Other Ranks).

17.30. All Ranks.

18.15 Black-out.

20.30 Count.

21.30 Lights Out.

Now to see precisely what those orders mean. The first count was done by the Orderly Officer, accompanied by a provost-sergeant. Then prisoners cleaned out their bedrooms and removed the latrine buckets which had been in the locked rooms all night.

Officers had breakfast first because it was brought to them by their batmen in a special room. After any meal there was dining-room fatigue and squads in rotation swept corridors and cleaned other rooms which prisoners used. As for sick parade, it was held under Dulling in the main hall, after which time—once the prisoners had settled down—the hall was used as a recreation-, reading-, and writing-room for all ranks, though prisoners still had access to their bedrooms, which were left open all day.

At 20.15 at night, the Provost cleared the hall and all prisoners went to their rooms, where the Orderly Officer again took the count. In the rooms the prisoners remained, but at 21.30 lights were turned off and all rooms locked. Since the Orderly Provost and his runner occupied a central room all night, they were available if a prisoner was taken sick, or if suspicious sounds were heard. All round the building the modified lighting gave sentries sufficient view of the wire, and from Lights Out the camp would be in silence, except at changes of guard. One exception in guard-mounting should be pointed out. At night no sentry patrolled in front of the main building, which was particularly strongly wired, and, moreover, Stirrop objected most vehemently to being disturbed in the night by changes of guard.

Naturally, on the morning after the arrival of prisoners, things could not go according to the timetable. Profiting, however, by the mistakes of the camp's first experience, the staff had worked out a routine which was calculated to make the delay as short as possible. When Travers got back to the main building that morning everything—thanks to Stirrop's being safely in his room—was going as smoothly as could be.

Every enemy alien had a large official card—ultimately to be made out in quadruplicate—embodying the information which is primarily required. Dulling took over first, weighing prisoners, recording height, weight, and description, and giving any special medical history. From him they went to Winter. He once more checked names and numbers, and articles which had been confiscated temporarily, and he made sure each man knew camp rules.

Then came Travers. He checked money, told prisoners how they would be allowed to spend it, and, if they had only foreign currency, obtained their written authority to change it at prevailing rates. Each prisoner was then given a cash card—a kind of summarised Bank Pass Book—which he signed.

Ramble next took over. Every article in a prisoner's heavy luggage was checked in his presence, and the prisoner was allowed to remove necessary clothing and comforts. Then Ramble used his judgment as to what warmer clothes he was likely to need, and gave him a written chit which would be handed to Mafferty and his storeman. In the store, then, the prisoner was fitted out, and having signed a receipt would make his way to his room, arms full of new and old belongings. When the check was made it turned out that no less than forty-two prisoners were given complete outfits.

Travers settled down to his own particular job with a couple of assistants. It was a job of work that he very much liked, for it gave him a personal contact with every prisoner. Later, of course, Winter's researches would divide prisoners into three rough categories—fanatical Nazis, pro-Nazis, and not so very pro, and Travers was always interested to see how his own judgments, unbacked by official evidence, would coincide with Winter's groupings. Nearly always he was wrong. The Hun is a peculiar creature. The most dangerous can be the most suave and amenable and grateful, while apparent surliness or even obstruction may simply be due to nervousness—and that not only of guards and staff, but even more of the prisoner's Gestapo-minded companions in confinement.

A runner suddenly appeared in front of Travers's table.

"The Commandant's compliments, sir, and will you take the count for him, as he's busy."

Travers looked at the clock and saw that it was well after midday. Another quarter of an hour and all prisoners were in their rooms, and accompanied by Ramble and the Orderly Provost, Travers took the count. Nine officers—correct, provided that Captain Friedemann was still with the Commandant, and a runner confirmed that he was. Fifty-eight other ranks in rooms and five in hospital—correct. Grand total for the count book, duly signatured—seventy-three.

It was too late to resume work before lunch, but at 13.30 a fresh start would be made, and it was confidently expected that everything would be finished by tea-time. Travers nipped back to his office to see what had been happening. The Commandant was seen making his way back in camp with Friedemann, voice never ceasing while he was in earshot. Winter came in and Travers told Miss Dance she might as well get away to lunch.

"I wish to heaven the Commandant wouldn't make himself so cheap with people like Friedemann," Winter said. "It lowers everybody's discipline, and not only that, you never know what privileges he's been giving him which we'll never hear about till something happens."

"Why don't you have it out with the Commandant yourself?" Travers said, and smiled somewhat drily. "A hefty bloke like yourself ought to start off with some pretty good advantages if the argument got a bit warm."

"Life's too short," Winter said. Then, as an afterthought, "Besides, what sort of version would he give if there was a stand-up row? Army discipline's a queer thing, you know. He might charge me with the devil knows what, and then swear black was white to support it."

"You must know," Travers said, and then suddenly made up his mind to speak. "By the way, did you say anything about chucking this job?"

"No," said Winter, surprised. "Why?"

"Only that the Commandant made a very cryptic remark this morning after that little fracas in the hall. He hinted you mightn't be here much longer—then he shut up."

Winter's eyes narrowed.

"Oh, did he? He may be right and he may be wrong. I shall be the one to decide that."

"Got any good friends?"

"Plenty," Winter said. "I don't want to boast, but when my application went in it was backed by Lord Stroude."

"Sounds good." Travers said, as the two made their way towards lunch. And yet he wondered. Stroude was the perfect Blimp—a product of the dear old school who had been found jobs by pals in many ministries. Somehow Travers could hardly see him rolling up his shirt sleeves and wading into a scrap on behalf of Winter. At the first sign of trouble Stroude would be far more likely to disown his protégé entirely, and make for the nearest long grass.

At 13.30 work began again. Stirrop expressed a desire to lend a hand, and attached himself to Ramble, where he held up proceedings by engaging in protracted talk to such prisoners as could speak English.

Travers was getting on well, with no queue waiting at his table. Sometimes, indeed, he had a minute or two to wait, which gave time for a quick smoke and a look at other people. In that none too certain light at the hall he couldn't help noticing for the first time how much Dulling had of the Teutonic in his appearance. Then he thought he must be wrong, and it was only that Dulling's confidences were making him imagine things. After all, a good many people had something German in their make-up. Winter often looked like a Hun, and he had the trick— of which he was quite unaware—of making an occasional bow from the waist up. And what about Stirrop? If ever there was a little Prussian bantam, it was Stirrop.

It was almost at the end of the job that Travers looked up from the table to survey the next man, and there was the gentleman with the wink. He had not yet received an issue of warm clothing, and he was looking none too clean and his beard would have done with a trim.

"You speak English?" Travers asked.

Beckner—the card showed his name—shook his head in a rather stolid way.

"A leedle I spik," he said very slowly.

"Never mind," said Travers. "Do you speak French?"

His face lighted. *"Oui, m'sieur. Un p'tit peu."*

"Well, it'll be better than my German," Travers told him amiably, "so we'll stick to French."

Beckner's money was in French and Belgian francs, and he readily signed the authority to change. Everything else was in order, and Travers waved a friendly hand to indicate that he might go. But Beckner gave a quick look—first round the room and then at Travers's two clerks—and then quick as lightning had put an envelope on the table under Travers's nose.

"What's this?" Travers said. "I can't receive any letters or petitions now."

Beckner shook his head violently. Then, to Travers's complete stupefaction, the left eye—farthest from the clerk—closed itself in two deliberate and ornate winks!

Travers's fingers went to his glasses, then fell. When he looked again, Beckner had moved on as he had seen others do, in the direction of Ramble. Travers picked up the envelope, felt that there was a document of sorts inside, and then with a shrug of the shoulders put it into his tunic pocket.

But for the fact that he went to the office before tea, he might have told the whole Mess about the peculiarities of Beckner; as it was, he remembered the letter and opened it when Miss Dance had just gone. A glance at the signature and his eyes popped out of his head. A frantic polish of his glasses, and then he was reading:

DEAR TRAVERS,

Burn this when you have read it. I wonder if you will recognise me, I hope not. At the moment I would rather you said nothing to a soul. I have been given a free hand

and would rather your Commandant knew nothing—at present.

Please see I have key to open prisoners' rooms, and to get out of the main building, as a situation might arise when I have to leave hurriedly. Will find excuse to-morrow for private interview.

MAURICE LADING

# CHAPTER VI
# THE EXTRA PRISONER

TRAVERS PEEPED into Winter's office to see if he were there, but the room was empty. Ramble was just coming down the stairs.

"Everything go smoothly with you?" Travers asked him.

"Very well indeed, sir," Ramble said. "The Commandant didn't help a great deal, but we got on all right. I'm a posh German spouter now, sir."

Travers smiled. "Your *Achtung!* is one of the best I've heard."

"You're out of date, sir," grinned Ramble. "I've got a whole lot more now. You ought to have heard me this afternoon."

"Well, let's hear a sample."

"All right, sir. *Stille stehen*, that's when you want them to keep still and not keep moving about.*Vorwarts*, that's when you get 'em on the move. *Dass ist verboten*, that means you can't do that there 'ere."

Travers laughed. "You're a regular linguist."

"There's yards yet, sir, if only I could remember them."

"And where'd you get them from? Captain Winter?"

"No, sir. I happened to be talking to the doctor and saying I wished I knew a spot of German so he said, what do you want to say, and I told him, and before I knew where I was there was me spouting German."

"Well, keep up the good work." Travers told him. "And before you go, have you got a prisoners' room list made out?"

"Here it is, sir."

He produced his notebook, and Travers ascertained that Beckner was in Room 9. Outside the door the two separated, Ramble bound for the Sergeants' Mess and tea, Travers for a short drink before changing for dinner.

Winter was about to begin an early scratch meal. What he was proposing to do that evening was to go on working in an unoccupied room near the hall, so that the prisoners would be handy if he needed one of them for interrogation. He particularly wanted to have a talk with Captain Friedemann, whom he suspected of being an out-and-out swine.

"The Commandant dining in?" Travers asked.

"No," said Winter. "He left word he'd be round at Garrison. What about a drink to keep me company?"

"Don't think I will," Travers said. "About time I had a spit and polish."

But he did not go to his room. With Stirrop going out and Winter safely in the Mess, he had a chance too good to be missed. And as he made his way towards the camp, he could not help thinking once more about Dulling. What did he mean when in those volunteered confidences he declared he knew no German? Was the expression a relative one, meaning that compared with, say, Winter, he knew no German at all? Whatever it meant it was surely indiscreet of the doctor to volunteer German to Ramble when he was anxious to keep secret the fact that he was of very recent German descent.

But Dulling soon passed out of Travers's mind as he neared the main entrance and thought of a possible meeting with Lading. Something extraordinary must be going on for Intelligence to have planted him there. As for the question of secrecy, there was something which Travers found not unpleasing—that it was himself and not the Commandant who was to be made the confidant of Lading's purpose. Lading had evidently summed up Stirrop on his last visit and was only too aware that a confidential word to him would soon be the property of all Shoreleigh.

He let himself through the wire gates, through the main entrance door, and then through the special door that led to the hall where the prisoners would be spending their early evening.

There were so few of them compared with the number the camp could hold, that only the ground floor was being used, and even there some rooms were unoccupied.

Travers blinked as he came in from the darkness outside. Just inside the door to the left were the officers, some reading and others playing cards. Captain Friedemann rose politely at the sight of him, but Travers smilingly waved him down again. Everywhere in the hall were groups of other prisoners, reading, playing games, or promenading about the room. In one corner some sort of a class was assembled, and it turned out to be a group of enthusiasts having a lesson in English from one of their number.

Almost at the first Travers had caught sight of Beckner, and there was no doubt about Beckner's having caught sight of himself. That slow progress through the hall had brought Travers nearer and nearer to the right-hand side door which led to a corridor. Occasional prisoners were going in and out on the way to and from their rooms. Travers made a slow way along the dimly lighted passage till a glance back showed that it was at the moment empty. Then he inserted a key and whipped open one of the unoccupied rooms, and just inside the door he waited. Faint footsteps were heard. A second or two and another dark figure slipped inside. Travers turned the key and left it in the lock, then pulled a straw palliasse towards him.

"Better squat down here in case anyone flashes a torch," he whispered.

Still, for a faint moment, he wondered if it really were Lading, then the reassuring voice came.

"Bit of a shock for you, what?"

"Yes," Travers said. "And what's it all mean?"

"First of all, this," Lading told him. "Everything contrary to Geneva, so officially M.I. know nothing about me. I was asked if I'd do the job, and then I was disowned. If I'm spotted or anything gets out, then I just chance my arm. And you'll have to swear on a stack of Bibles that you knew nothing about it. That suit you?"

"I dare say I can be just as good a liar as you," Travers said cheerfully. "But what's back of it all?"

"In the very strictest confidence, all sorts of things. One of 'em's this. We're dead plumb certain that some mighty dangerous coves are among the gang you've got here. The French were pretty slack about everything on the West Coast, but we're sure that in this collection are some very important agents who'd just gone out from Germany. Some of the real top-wallahs. Don't ask me how we know. My job's to find out who they are."

"But if they're here they can't make trouble," pointed out Travers.

"We'll come to that," Lading told him, "I was rushed by plane and otherwise to Accra, popped into clink, and then taken aboard with one or two other coves from there when the boat called in, and I've got the most perfect set of papers you ever saw. You ought to have seen me taken on board, by the way. Handcuffs and all!"

"Yes, but now we've got your papers."

"That's what you think. Feel this pocket. There's some you didn't get. And what I'm supposed to be is an ostensible German planter from French Equatorial Africa, who was really a high-up Nazi agent—sort of wandering Gauleiter. The French got on my track so I slipped across the border and down to the coast where the British nabbed me. That's why I speak practically no English, but good French."

"I get you," Travers said. "And what else do you hope to find out?"

"It's just a bit vague. This shipload was sent here deliberately because various things have been going on. There've been a whole lot of leakages about sailings from the port here. There's been sabotage in one or two local factories, though nothing's been allowed to leak out. What the idea is, is that the coves in this camp will try to get into communication with the coves outside, who are the ones we want to grab."

"But, my dear fellow, it's impossible. We take the most stringent precautions. How can there be any communication with outside?"

"Don't make me laugh," Lading said. "You fighting soldiers are so trustful. You don't know half the ingenuity of the coves you've got in this camp. Look at the last war. I've only read about things, but there were French prisoner officers who'd guarantee to produce a key for any lock within twenty-four hours, and if I told you some of the things I heard aboard ship, your hair would stand on end."

"Good Lord, you scare me stiff!" Travers said. "We don't want any escapes from this camp. The War House'd have the tunics off us."

"No panic," Lading told him blithely. "There won't be any escapes. People who want to escape have to do a whole lot of spade-work first. Learn a camp and get their bearings, for a start. And that's where I come in. All you people have to do is to watch out for anybody who has to leave camp lawfully. Some cove, for instance, who gets toothache, and has to go to an outside dentist under escort. You take damn-good care he has a good escort. You keep your eyes on that sort of thing and I'll do the rest. Have you got those keys?"

"All labelled," Travers told him, handing them over. "Two to get you outside, one for the wire gates, and one for the towns. Anything else you want?"

"I don't know that there is," Lading said. "I may fake a spot of insubordination with one of your provosts. If he reports it, you can have me hauled up before the beak. Any likelihood of your Commandant being away?"

"Every likelihood," said Travers dryly. "The weekend, for instance."

"That may be a little late," Lading said. "Tell you what. If the Commandant is away, you come into the hall with no cap. That'll give me the tip."

"Good. Want any money?"

Lading chuckled. "I've got fifty pound-notes on me at the moment. Feel this other pocket. Here, under my armpit. Another thing your search-party didn't get wise to. Now I'd better slip out. Oh, and just one bit of information. Friedemann's a first-class swine. Regular tough guy. By to-morrow morning this camp will be organised, Gestapo and all complete. Any cove who isn't a hundred per cent Nazi is due for a very thin time."

He got to his feet, gently turned the key, and took a peep out. "Good luck, old-timer, and, Heil Hitler!"

In the same second he was gone. Travers waited a full minute and then slipped out too.

He had intended looking up Winter in whatever unoccupied room he happened to be at work, but a lucky glance at his hands showed him they were so grubby after squatting on that floor that if Winter had seen them he must have wondered. So Travers went straight through to the outer door and so to his room. Sniffy was waiting anxiously.

"Sorry I'm late," Travers said. "You were going to the pictures, weren't you?"

"It doesn't matter, sir," Sniffy told him with no great heartiness. "There's a darts competition in the N.A.A.F.I. hut, sir, instead."

"Right," said Travers. "Bring me a pail of hot water and I'm finished with you."

He had a stand-up bath, changed into his best slacks, and made his way to the Mess. Not a soul was there.

"What's happened to everybody?" he asked the orderly.

"Captain Winter's over at camp, sir, and Captain Byron and Mr. Pewter at the Royal, if they're wanted. A sherry for you, sir?"

"I think I will," Travers said. 'What's on the menu?"

"A rare nice bit of steak, sir, and some chips. Then baked apples."

"Right," said Travers. "I don't want my steak too underdone, and I'd rather not have any of your famous gravy."

He had a few minutes with that great stand-by of his tired hours—*The Times* crossword—and then the meal came in.

"Mr. Dowling's late," he remarked.

"He is, sir, isn't he? He ought to've done the count before now."

The meal was finished, with a spot of cheese as bonne bouche, and Travers had once more settled to the crossword before Dowling came in.

"What's happened to you, young feller?" asked Travers. "Been lost in a snow-drift?"

"The most amazing thing happened, sir," Dowling said, and he sounded really excited. "We couldn't get the count right."

That was something which had happened before, as Travers remarked. Occasionally the medical people would bring a man into hospital and forget to warn the Provost or Ramble, and there would be a prisoner short until he was run to earth.

"Oh, but this is different, sir." Dowling said. "We went through the rooms and ended up at the hospital, and there was a prisoner too many!"

Travers sniffed.

"Well, and how'd you straighten it out?"

"We didn't, sir. Ebbing said it was—"

"Wait a minute. Why was Ebbing on duty?"

"He arranged it with Stamp, sir. They often do change about if one wants to get off suddenly. And, as I was saying, sir, Ebbing said it was damn-funny and he was sure he'd got the figures right, so we kept them in their rooms and started all over again. You wouldn't believe how careful we were, sir, and when we'd finished we still found there were seventy-four!"

Travers sat up and look notice.

"Well, *are* there seventy-four? What'd you do about it?"

"Well, sir, Ebbing said we ought to report it and have some-one else take the count as well—"

Travers clicked his tongue annoyedly. Ebbing had always been very much of a fool.

"So I sent him to see if he could find you, sir, but you weren't in Mess—"

"Why on earth didn't he look in my room?" Travers asked plaintively. "Well, go on."

"Well, sir, I thought I'd better ring up the Commandant at Garrison H.Q., which I did, and—"

"Oh, my hat!" groaned Travers.

"And he wasn't there, sir, and they said he hadn't been there."

Travers's eyes opened wide, and in the same moment he was furious. The strictest of all camp rules was that when there were prisoners or when prisoners were expected, any officer who left the camp must leave his whereabouts with the Mess and telephone orderlies. And there was Stirrop breaking his own rules. Had any other person done the same thing there would have been more than a first-class row.

"So what did you do?" Travers asked. "It's ridiculous that there should have been an extra prisoner?"

"Well, sir. Ebbing said we'd better count again ourselves, and when we did, the count came right, so we left it at that."

"I see. And how did the mistake arise?"

"Well, sir, I don't know what you're going to think of me, but it didn't arise. I mean, I'm dead sure those first two counts were right. You can't make a mistake, sir, over sixty-three. The officers were right all along."

"Show me your room counts," Travers said.

Then there was a sudden hesitation.

"I didn't take any, sir, till the last time."

"You mean to say you didn't jot down the totals of each room! What'd you do? Try to carry totals in your head?"

"Yes, sir," said the highly perturbed Dowling. "Ebbing was doing it as well, so I thought that was enough check."

"You listen to me, young feller," said Travers grimly. "I know Sergeant Ebbing and his kind. In the future if any old sweat suggests dodging duty or taking short cuts, you put him in his place. Now you'd better get on with your dinner."

A few minutes later Travers made his way to his office, and sent out both telephone orderly and runner for a half hour's breather. An idea had come into his mind.

In a camp, when walking unexpectedly into this room and that, one cannot avoid overhearing tail-ends of conversation. Travers knew that the Dance-Stirrop affair was still in progress, and he had heard mentioned a certain expensive road-house about seven miles from the camp. It seemed to him now that it might be as well to know just where Stirrop was spending the evening. To have the information in his possession might put him in a very strong position in the course of some future scrap, particularly if it concerned the breaking of the rule which Stirrop was then breaking himself.

So he put through some telephone calls. The first was to the Royal, asking for Captain Tester. Tester was there and was brought to the 'phone, whereupon Travers quietly hung up. Next came the home of Bertha Dance. Mrs. Dance said Bertha was out, but she'll give the message when she came in, and if she was late, would it do in the morning. Travers apologised and said he had just found the very paper he was looking for, and so Miss Dance needn't be bothered. Next came the road-house, where Major Stirrop was asked for. It was five minutes before he was brought to the phone, and as soon as the voice was verified, Travers gently hung up.

And he was chuckling. He could imagine his going back to Bertha—for Travers had no doubt she was there—and positively exploding.

"Would you believe it! . . . Some damn-fool rings me up and then when I get there, the line's dead. Etc., etc., etc. . . . And how'd the hell did the fellow know I was here?"

Next morning Stirrop was actually in Mess when Travers came in to breakfast.

"Morning, sir. Have a good dinner?"

"Not too good," Stirrop said, after a moment's hesitation. "If I was those people at Garrison I'm damned if I'd pay what they do. Too much money. That's the trouble with them."

"How's the Brigadier these days?"

Stirrop shot a look of which Travers was quite aware.

"As a matter of fact, I just had a word with him and no more. I think he was dining out."

Travers left it at that. No point whatever in arousing suspicions, though he rather hoped that when Stirrop read through Garrison Orders which had come through overnight, he would observe that the Brigadier had been away on leave since Friday!

There was no use in looking for Dowling. When an Orderly Officer has had a twenty-four hour spell and doesn't come off it till eight o'clock, he grabs a quick breakfast then and turns into bed for the rest of the morning. But when Travers arrived at the office, there was Dowling waiting at the door.

Travers smiled.

"Well, young feller, what's the latest?"

Dowling kept a very straight face.

"It happened again this morning, sir. The first count showed seventy-four, and when we did it the second time, it was all right."

Travers grunted.

"This is getting beyond a joke. I think I'd better have a word with Ebbing, then we may have to see the Commandant."

# CHAPTER VII
## SOMEONE SCORES AN OUTER

WHY WAS IT that Travers should have given any credence whatever to that extraordinary story related by Dowling? On the face of it the whole thing was too preposterous to be given a moment's thought. If the camp was so secure that no prisoner could possibly escape, then how could an additional prisoner get inside? And who in heaven's name should want to get inside? And Lading wasn't up to monkey tricks either. He had no extra prisoner up his sleeve, and even if he had, there was no method of smuggling him in. The camp itself had no secret entrances. To think of underground tunnels in a building constructed within the memory of some of the oldest inhabitants was more than fantastic.

The fact is that two things made Travers think Dowling's story at least worthy of serious investigation. One was the very earnestness with which that serious-minded young officer had expressed his own belief, and the other reason was Travers himself; that last a case of wishful thinking, to use the overworked phrase. For years Travers had been associated with Scotland Yard, where his life was the unravelling of mysteries. Moreover, a mystery would gnaw at him like an aching tooth, and until the mystery was solved, the tooth continued to ache. But the war changed the whole current of his life. For months his existence had been the routine and humdrum, enlivened only by irritations and new worries. No wonder, then, that when Dowling came along with a really first-class puzzle, Travers leapt at it.

There was one thing for which Travers had been famous at the Yard, that given a problem he would in the wink of an eye find a feasible solution. He was, in fact, a notorious theorist. His late colleague, Superintendent George ("General") Wharton was to remark later on to a critic, that much as he had himself laughed at Travers's theorising, he was nevertheless all for it. Travers, said George, had the Nelson touch. He laid his ship alongside, and be damned to any hammering. "Whereas you other fellows," said George, "are like those ruddy Italian admirals. You lie doggo and hope for something to happen, and you wonder why it doesn't—till it happens to yourselves."

But in the case of Dowling's supposed experiences, Travers had no immediate theory. What he did have was a kind of basis on which, with just a little more evidence, he would be able to build one. That basis was in itself none too solid, emanating as it did of the vague idea that the principal reason for Lading's mission was contact with people outside the camp. An extra prisoner could only have come in from outside. As to how he had got in—well, sufficient unto the mystery was the fact that it looked like one.


Before taking Dowling along to see the Commandant, Travers was careful to caution him as to what he said, and he rehearsed the evidence.

"I considered you'd been slack," he said, "and I told you so. If you tell the Commandant your story as you told it to me, I won't guarantee your being in his camp much longer. For your own sake you'd better leave the Commandant to find out for himself—as I did—where you went wrong."

Stirrop heard Dowling's story with only a few interruptions but the impatience grew towards the end. Then he exploded.

"Good God, man, what the hell yarn's this! It's damn-silly." And then he cast a baleful eye on his Adjutant. "Either you're right or Captain Travers is wrong. Were there seventy-three prisoners?"

"The escort officer brought seventy-three," Travers said. "I counted them myself, and he received my receipt for seventy-three bodies. They were twice counted afterwards and found correct."

"'There you are, then!" He waved a contemptuous hand towards Dowling, and at the same moment thought of something. "You don't believe it yourself, do you?"

Dowling blinked for a moment, then said that he did. He would be prepared to state before any Court of Inquiry that there had been seventy-four prisoners in the rooms on three specific occasions.

That was the confession Stirrop had been waiting for. Once more he cast a suspicious eye up at his Adjutant.

"Then why wasn't I at once informed about it?"

He lay back in his chair, pausing for a reply. It came.

"You were informed, sir," Travers said quietly. "You were rung at Garrison and you weren't there. That was at twenty minutes to nine last night, and they said you hadn't been there."

"What!" Before Travers's steady look, his eye fell. "Who said so? The fellow must have been a bloody fool." Then the hand was waved once more. "Still, that's not the point. You don't believe this cock and bull yarn, do you?"

"Why shouldn't I, sir?" Travers asked him. "After what Mr. Dowling has said, if I didn't think his story worth investigation, I might just as well—to put it frankly—call him a liar."

"Never heard such bloody silly nonsense in my life." The hand was waved with even more contempt. "I'll take my own count at midday, then we shall see."

"May I ask you something, sir?" said Dowling.

"What is it?"

"Well, sir, if there is anything fishy, it would be far more likely to take place at the night count. It was dark at both the other times."

Stirrop scowled, then with some taciturnity agreed.

"Very well, then; I'll take the night count. Let Mr. Pewter know."

Dowling saluted and disappeared. Stirrop's last rumbles died away.

"I'd rather not be disturbed this morning unless there's anything urgent." he told Travers. "I'd better get on with that infernal Army Form. What was the name of it?"

"B.199A."

"Lot of damn-nonsense. . . . Where *is* the bloody thing? . . . Now who the hell's been and moved that? . . . Damn it. I had it here a second ago. Would you believe it!"

"Is this it, sir?" asked Travers, retrieving it from under an issue of Midland Command Orders.

Travers fairly shuddered as the bitter wind met him outside, and he was glad to get back to the warmth of his own room. Ramble came in almost at once.

"Captain Friedemann wants to make a complaint to the Commandant, sir. He says everybody's cold."

"Cold be damned!" said Travers indignantly. "They've got their official issue of blankets, and they're sleeping in a heated building. What about the troops? Wouldn't they be glad to change places?"

"I quite agree, sir," Ramble said, "and so does Mafferty. The blanket issue is laid down, and we've issued, and that's for an unheated building."

"Tell Friedemann he can't see the Commandant," Travers said. "He's busy and doesn't want to be disturbed. And, by the way, he's taking the last count himself to-night. For your own sake, you and I had better have a rehearsal. I'll come up to your room."

Ramble had heard about the extra prisoner, and he was only too ready.

"What you'd better do is this," Travers told him. "First make dead sure who's in hospital. Say there are five—that leaves sixty-eight. The ten officers you can't go wrong with—that leaves fifty-eight, Make sure how those fifty-eight ought to be distributed in each room, and the very first room you come to where there's an extra man, stop at once and put the whole room under guard."

"That's it, sir," Ramble said, and then frowned. "If only the Commandant will agree."

Travers grunted. "If he's only half as much method as I give him credit for, he can't go to work any other way."

Winter looked up as Travers came through.

"What's all the excitement this morning?"

Travers told him about Dowling's strange experiences.

"If the Commandant hears that he'll properly twist Dowling's tail for him," Winter said. "What on earth was the young fool up to?" Then he smiled. "I say, you're not pulling my leg?"

"I certainly am not," Travers said.

"But surely you don't credit it yourself?"

Travers shrugged his shoulders.

"Why, the whole thing's lunacy," went on Winter.

"I know," Travers told him blandly. "If there weren't a little lunacy in the world it'd be a dull place. Haven't you ever behaved like a lunatic?"

It was Winter's turn to do the shoulder shrugging. Truth to tell, there had been times when he had half-suspected the eccentric Travers of something which, if not actual lunacy, was as near to it as made no odds.

"By the way," said Travers, "the Commandant is now closeted with his B.199A. I thought I'd let you know. Once he's finished it, he'll be pestering the life out of us for our own."

"I'll have a go at mine to-night," Winter said. "To-morrow night you and I might get down to those cards.'

Pewter came in to ask about the midday count.

"Take it yourself instead of the night one," Travers told him. "And you'd better see Mr. Ramble and give him my compliments and say will he accompany you round and work out what he and I were talking over. He'll know what you mean."

Wednesday was a heavy day for returns and Travers settled down to work in the office. At a quarter-past twelve Pewter came specially to report. The count had been absolutely correct.

In Mess that lunch-time the mystery, or the absence of it, was the main topic. Travers feared the Commandant would change his mind about taking the night count, but he needn't have worried. Stirrop was only too anxious to be in the limelight at least to the extent of being the one who rang down the final curtain. Then there would really be something to report to Garrison.

"I took the count myself, sir. A regular cock and bull story, sir. Nothing in it at all."

At eighteen-fifteen hours that night there was in the camp a certain subdued excitement. Winter was busy over his B.199A, but Travers, who was working overtime, thought it would be as well to go across to the building and be handy in case he should be wanted.

It was the custom for all the lights but one in the hall to be turned out as soon as the prisoners had moved out of their rooms, and the side doors were locked against them. Travers stood there in the gloom, listening to the sound of the feet of Stirrop and Ramble as they went along the corridors. Soon he pricked his ears. Stirrop's voice came quick and angry. Travers cocked an attentive ear and heard a quick patter of steps, and he knew that must be Stirrop, already in a rage and strutting off to another room. Then the feet died away. Now the count of one side had ended add the two would be going round the back corridor to begin the other side.

The steps were heard again. Slowly they came nearer, and then at last the count was completed, but at once there was a roar from Stirrop.

"I tell you it's damn' ridiculous! You've got the figures wrong."

"You were doing the count, sir," came Ramble's quiet reminder.

"Dammit, man, don't argue. Come on. Let's do it again, and this time make sure you really *have* looked the door."

"I was sure I locked 'em last time, sir."

But Stirrop was already making a furious way across the hall, with Ramble at his heels. Travers stayed put and unseen. Stirrop passed through the other side door, ready to begin the count again. Once more there were the footsteps, the closing of doors, the gradual receding, the sounds again, and the last room. Then came a triumphant voice.

"I knew you were wrong. There we are. The count's right!"

It was at that very moment that there was the roar of a shot. It echoed in the corridor, and startled Travers out of his wits. There was a bellow from Stirrop, the side door opened and he appeared, like a man seeking sudden cover.

"What the hell was that?"

"A shot, sir," said Ramble, none too calmly. "And pardon me, sir, look at your British warm."

It was ten seconds perhaps since the echoing roar of that shot had startled Travers, and he was not even aware that he had moved till he found himself near the two at the door. Then Ramble was darting out to the corridor, and there was a buzz of talk coming from the prisoners' rooms.

"What happened, sir?"

"Happened?" said Stirrop, a bit white about the gills. "Happened? Look at this. Some bastard tried to shoot me!"

A clean hole was drilled through the shoulder of his British warm within six inches of his neck. Travers was horrified.

"Who on earth could have done it! It couldn't have been an outside sentry letting off a round. Which way did the shot come from, sir?"

Ramble came quickly through the door.

"Nobody out there, sir. All the rooms locked tight."

Stirrop came to himself, with half a dozen orders at once.

"Get hold of Byron and have every spare man turned out. We'll search every room. Have sentries posted at the head of the stairs and send someone to fetch my revolver."

The main door opened and Mafferty came in. Winter was at his heels. That halted the proceedings for they had to be told. Stirrop resumed his orders. Travers ventured to make a suggestion.

"Don't you think it would be better, sir, if you didn't search the rooms? If any of those fellows have a gun, you bet your life it's where we shan't find it now, so wouldn't it be better to have a surprise search?"

Stirrop had never been so moderate or amenable. It was is if that sudden shot and his narrow escape had sobered and scared at the same time. He agreed it would be better. He then admitted that he'd definitely counted seventy-four prisoners at the first attempt, and he was equally sure there's been only seventy-three at the second.

"It's preposterous," he said. "The doors were locked, so how could anybody get out? Where could they get a gun from?"

"May I say something, sir?" put in Winter, and then turned to Mafferty. "Were you in the store just now, Mafferty?"

"No, sir," Mafferty said. "I was coming from the Sergeants' Mess and heard the shot. That's why I came in, to see what it was."

"Well, I think someone was in the store," Winter said. "I heard something there as I came by the window."

"Good God, man, why the hell didn't you say so before! Come on!"

Off went Stirrop and the rest at his heels. The main store lay at the end of the corridor nearest the front door, and in a minute he was rattling its door as if to pull off the handle.

"Open it, Mafferty!"

Mafferty unlocked the door, switched on the lights, and the Commandant peered gingerly in. The whole party crowded after him and a search was made. Travers gave a holler and held up his hand to keep people back.

"Someone's been in, sir. Here's some snow."

It was at the far end of the room: a dirty patch as if a foot had skidded, and the tiniest bit of unmelted snow remained.

"Well, I'm damned," said Stirrop, and looked round flabbergasted. "Would you believe it! How the devil could anyone have got in here?"

Then he suddenly made a dive for the windows. But there had been no tampering there. The vicious covering of wire was intact, and each sill had dust that was undisturbed.

"It beats me," he said. "This is something I never thought I'd come up against. Mafferty, to-morrow morning have everything checked and see if anything's missing. You come with me, Captain Travers, and we'll arrange about that search. You'd better fetch Captain Byron."

"One thing ought to be done, sir," said Travers. "The bullet that missed you went somewhere. It might to be found so that we can find out its calibre."

"I'll see to that," Winter said.

"I'll lend you a hand, sir," Ramble told him.

Later that night Travers managed to have a word with Ramble. The bullet had not been found, but another search by daylight ought to produce it. Captain Winter had found a mark on the wall where it had evidently ricocheted off."

"About that extra prisoner," Travers said. "The Commandant's now of the opinion that there *has* been some dirty work. But tell me. Did you do the first count the way we worked out?"

Ramble shook his head annoyedly.

"He wouldn't listen to me, sir. When I began to suggest it he shut me up. You could have heard him at the far end of the building. He said he knew how to count."

"And did you spot the discrepancy yourself?"

"I think I did, sir," Ramble said. "That room where the second lot of passengers are. When we first went there, there were fourteen and there ought to have been thirteen. When we came out I made specially sure the door was locked again, and when we came back the second time there was only thirteen there."

"My hat!" said Travers. "Did you mention it to the Commandant?"

Ramble sniffed.

"Not me, sir. He'd told me he was doing that count—not me, so I left him to find out things for himself. I did intend mentioning it to you, sir."

But Travers was frowning away in thought.

"What on earth is going on, Ramble? Wait a minute, though. Somebody in that room has managed to make a key that unlocks the door. You didn't bolt it as you do at night?"

"I'm sorry to say I didn't, sir. I merely made sure the key had turned."

"Well, someone slipped out when you were along the other corridor, and he nipped into the store. How he got a key for that beats me, unless we've got a super-cracksman on the spot."

"You can do a lot with a bit of bent wire," remarked Ramble.

"I suppose you can. And what I think is that you or the Commandant must have left in the corridor some snow off your boots. This chap stepped on it so that some adhered. That's the only possible solution. He simply couldn't have been outside himself."

"Makes you feel all uncomfortable," Ramble said. "It's like something going on you can't get at the bottom of." He smiled dryly, "The funny thing is, sir, I was a yard behind the Commandant and about a foot to one side, or, whoever it was, might have got me. I felt the bullet whistle by."

"There's to be a surprise search at fifteen hours to-morrow," Travers told him. "I don't place many hopes on it, but there we are. I won't say I've persuaded him, but the Commandant's decided to keep the whole thing dark, and make no official report for the present."

And that was all for the night. Mafferty and Ramble did, however, add their own particular postscripts over a final glass of beer.

"Well, here's how!" said Ramble, raising his glass to Mafferty who was standing treat.

"Here's how!" echoed Mafferty, "and may the next shot be a hell of a sight straighter."

Ramble nodded grimly.

"And if we should find that ruddy gun, I wouldn't mind subscribing a quid for buying the bloke another."

# CHAPTER VIII
# ZERO HOUR

ON TRAVERS'S MIND when he awoke next morning was the same thought that had been there in those last minutes when he had waited for sleep—that at all costs he must see Lading. In spite of previous theories Travers had become convinced that Lading must somehow be concerned with that queer business of the extra prisoner, but even if he were not, these was something which he either knew already or could discover within a matter of hours.

When before her capture that German ship had slipped out of a neutral harbour, she had aboard her—in addition to some ten men only of the regular crew—a mixed collection of planters, Nazi agents and wandering Gestapo men, who were put down as crew but whom the British authorities had classed as passengers. Excluding Beckner, *alias* Lading, that made fifty-two so-called passengers in camp, and they were divided up into three rooms.

As to the principle that governed the placing of prisoners in rooms, each camp would doubtless have its own method, but at No. 54 Camp it had been thought best for smooth working that friends should be with friends. Winter would call out how many were to go to a room, whereupon that number would get together and make a kind of family party. If friends, or people of the same class, were in the same room, it made for companionship, which in turn made for easy discipline.

In Room 5, therefore, there were a body of prisoners who ostensibly had the same interests. Into their room the extra prisoner had come, and he had left that room with their knowledge and probable aid. Why not, then, put the whole room under arrest, isolate each man, interrogate and discipline with close confinement till someone squealed? To that the answer is this. The knowledge concerning Room 5 was at the moment shared only by Travers and Ramble, of whom Travers was the executive. And Travers knew it to be bad policy to let Room 5 guess what he knew, and worse policy to put the whole camp in a ferment by arresting a whole room. And again, the situation was an unusual one. Everything had to be proved beyond all doubt before an outside report could be made. Geneva, for once, had certainly given no rulings and laid down no procedure.

But Lading would have ways and means of finding out, and at all costs Travers had made up his mind to see him that morning. The only question was how.

Ramble reported that the early count had been correct, for he had accompanied Pewter and had conducted it on the principles which Travers had laid down. On the face of it, therefore, it looked as if that extra prisoner lay doggo somewhere during the day and for some inexplicable reason turned up for the count at night, and. try as he might, Travers could find no method in that particular form of madness. The risks run must be colossal, and if one could lie doggo at all, then why not do so all the time, and only mingle with the genuine prisoners when they were scattered in hall and rooms or at exercise, when it would have been impossible to detect an extra man.

"I'll you what you'd better do," he said to Ramble. "Get a squad of men from Captain Byron, say about a dozen. If you go to work quietly the prisoners won't have the faintest idea what's on. Open the trap-door to the attic and search there first. Then work your way down to the first floor, and then if everything's all right, post double sentries out of sight at the head of the stairs. The main search at fifteen hours will then be only for the ground floor."

He went in to breakfast to hear the extraordinary news that the Commandant was already going round the camp. Not only was that unusual, it was extremely disquieting, for one of the things of which Travers had been afraid was that a confirmed chatterer like Stirrop would fail to stand the strain of keeping things, as he had promised, most rigorously to himself. Still, it couldn't be helped. Travers had a hasty meal and then went at once to the office. Before he had been there ten minutes the 'phone went. It was the more than unusually testy voice of the Commandant asking him to come at once to his room.

"I've virtually put Captain Byron under arrest," was the sensational announcement. "The fellow was bloody rude to me, and I told him not to leave camp till I'd decided."

Travers gave a sigh of weariness. Byron had been restive for a long while, and yet he was the last person to have lost control to the extent implied by Stirrop.

"Just how was he rude, sir?"

"That doesn't matter," Stirrop said impatiently. "He was rude, I tell you—bloody rude. When I was a Company Officer if I'd said half what he said, they'd have had the tunic off me."

"Well, what do you propose to do, sir?"

What he was beginning to gather was that Stirrop had acted over-hastily, was aware of the fact, had a slight wind up, and was now wishing to bring his Adjutant in as condoning the fiction.

"I'm asking you what you'd do," countered Stirrop.

"Well, sir," said Travers after a moment's reflection, "I think it would be as well if you looked up any necessary paras in K.R., and then wrote down, while you remember it, everything that was said and took place. Even if you decide to take no further action, it still might be useful."

The fact that Stirrop, even ungraciously, agreed, was proof enough in Travers's eyes that a situation had arisen from which he would be only too glad to escape. Travers escaped too—back to the office. The mail was hastily dealt with and Miss Dance got to work. Then the 'phone went again.

"Send Miss Dance in to me, will you? I'd like her to type down what I've written."

Travers duly instructed Miss Dance, then rose to stretch his legs. His eye caught Miss Dance going by the window. Then she stopped. Squinting in the mirror of her bag she hastily added a touch here and there to lips and eyebrows, then took from the same bag a wristlet watch, fastened it, took a quick admiring look, and then hurried on towards the Commandant's office. Travers raised his eyebrow. A present, probably, only to be worn in the donor's company, and one that was to be kept well out of the sight of Captain Tester.

Before Travers could sit down again, the 'phone went once more. This time it was Byron.

"No, I won't see you here," Travers said. "I'll meet you straightaway at your store if there's nobody there. I can't spare more than five minutes."

A telephone orderly was called in and in three minutes Travers was with Byron, and listening to the authentic account of the morning's flare-up.

"It was like this, sir," Byron said. "The Commandant started questioning the sentry who was nearest to where that shot went off last night, and he was very rude to the man, because he couldn't answer questions which I'd have found it hard to answer myself. Then he sent for the sergeant of the guard, and in front of two of the men started calling him God knows what. I know the sergeant didn't know something he ought to have known, but that wasn't it. I just couldn't help myself. I said point-blank, 'Excuse me, sir, but I must protest about you speaking like that to an N.C.O. in front of men.'"

"And that's all there was to it?"

"Absolutely, sir. He said he had a good mind to put me under arrest, and I wasn't to leave the Camp. I've been thinking it over and decided to come to you."

"Well, I've yet to hear both sides," Travers told him. "My advice to you is to write down everything that happened, and be sure you can have it duly witnessed if needs be. And, of course, you must stay in camp."

Byron made a gesture of helplessness.

"Whatever happens, sir, I've got to go to my Colonel. Sometimes I've been driven nearly mad. I simply can't put up with it any longer. The situation's become intolerable."

"And what reception will you get from your Colonel?"

Byron shook his head. "I don't know. What I do know is that I'm not one of his darlings. That's why I was side-tracked here."

Once more Travers argued and persuaded, but Byron was obdurate. If nothing was done he'd do something about it himself. Asked just what, he merely nodded forebodingly. But at last

Travers induced him to promise to hold his hand till the morning.

"By that time," he said, "I can promise you that something will have happened. You're not the only person with a grievance, and as for that blether about bucking the War Office, it just can't be done. Now go and do as 1 advised you, and for the love of heaven, do have a little confidence in me."

Travers went back to the office with his mind made up. Something would have to be done, and that very day he himself would do it. It should be action through the proper channels, and if there were a fight he would go into it with tunic off and sleeves rolled up.

Winter was in his own office working at prisoners' accounts. Miss Dance was not yet back. Travers found a used foolscap envelope, smothered it with red sealing-wax, and then slipped across to the building. Captain Friedemann was in the hall and came straight across to him. He wanted an interview with the Commandant. That afternoon perhaps, Travers said. The Commandant was very busy. Then he made his own request.

"I want you to do something for me, Captain Friedemann. I've got a document here which has to be translated from French to German. It's only a matter of ten minutes or so, and it's urgent, and Captain Winter happens to be very busy. Can you find me someone who speaks and writes French really well?"

Captain Friedemann said he certainly could, and inside five minutes he was presenting Beckner.

"We'll work on that table in the corner," Travers said. "You might see that we're not disturbed."

The scheme had succeeded. Friedemann had imagined some secret document the contents of which Beckner would later divulge to himself. Also to work in full view of everybody in the hall was to bring no suspicion on Beckner.

A quarter of an hour later the ostensible translation was completed, and Travers had left a wonderfully surprised Lading, and had gained little information himself.

For Lading could throw no light whatever on the matter of the extra prisoner. At first he, too, had thought that Travers was pulling his leg, and somehow he had never been quite convinced. For all that he promised immediate action and the quick handing over of anything discovered. As for the shot, the prisoners had thought it was loosed off by some windy sentry.

"And yet I don't know," he said. "Friedemann's got something up his sleeve. I can feel it but I can't get near it. I've got a hunch I'm on the edge of something really big. Give me a couple of days and I think I'll get it. That's when I shall leave here for good, so don't be surprised if I pop into your room one night when you're asleep."

As for what he'd already achieved, it was considerable. Two of the officers were not officers at all, but Nazi agents, and their names were Scribbnitz and Stein.

"Get that through to M.I. for me," he said to Travers. "Also tell them to keep an eye on the Italian Consulate here."

"But we're not at war with Italy," said the guileless Travers.

"And you've never heard of the Axis," retorted Lading. "And one little thing you might keep an eye on, beginning to-morrow. There's a project for a tunnel starting at Room 12 and coming out in the park not far beyond your office, just clear of the wire. If it's really started, next time you see me I'll have this roll collar turned up round my ears."

And Lading ended with one strange remark which was to intrigue Travers very much.

"I'll probably be seeing you at three o'clock."

"Why?" asked Travers.

"Isn't there a search on?"

"Good God!" said the startled Travers. "How on earth did you know that?"

"That's one of the things I'm here to find out," said Lading, clean across the question.

Travers had a quick suspicion.

"Heard any criticism of the doctor?"

"Dulling?" Lading shook his head. "Not a word. He seems a harmless sort of cuss."

And that was the gist of the strange interview, which left Travers in most ways as much in the dark as ever. The matter of the search leakage having occurred through Dulling was, however, still in his mind, for the doctor had been informed before that morning's sick parade.

It was no wonder that the search was a failure. No sign was found of a gun or of anything else that was liable to confiscation, though straw palliasses were emptied, and bolsters, and every prisoner's small luggage gone through with a small-toothed comb. Nor was there anywhere a sign of the extra prisoner, and at the close of the proceedings Stirrop was in none too good a temper.

Travers left the building at the earliest moment and took refuge in his office. An hour later there was something which he wished to refer to Mafferty, and he rang through. Mafferty was not there, and the ration clerk said he had not come back since attending the search in the main building. Another half-hour and Ramble came in.

"Have you seen Quartermaster-Sergeant Mafferty, sir?"

"I haven't," Travers said. "As a matter of fact I wanted him myself." Then he noticed the look of worry on Ramble's face. "Anything wrong?"

I think there is, sir," Ramble said. "He's gone off."

Travers looked puzzled.

"I think he's out of camp, sir. Would you mind ringing Main Guard to ask if he went through?"

Travers rang. Mafferty *had* gone through, about an hour previously.

"Then it's what I thought, sir," Ramble said, and gave a sign for Travers to step outside, away from Miss Dance's listening ears.

It was the old story he had to tell. Stirrop had vented his temper on Mafferty and Mafferty had answered back. Stirrop had ordered him out of the store and back to his office, and had said he would send him back to his unit. Mafferty had given him a look, then had turned his back and stalked out. What he'd do would be to stay out till heaven knew when, as he had done before when he had been upset by the Commandant.

"Oh, my hat!" said Travers, and inwardly groaned. "Nothing but these damnable squabbles and upsets."

"You're right, sir," Ramble said. "Something's got to be done about it, and it's up to you, sir."

Travers's eye narrowed, then he nodded.

"Right away. As you say, it's up to me. Let the Commandant know that I've had to go down town, and say I'll be straight back."

In various dealings with Garrison, Travers had run across a certain Colonel Caithby who had struck him as a real good sort and a man to have at one's back. The Colonel happened to be in when Travers arrived.

"What can I do for you, Travers?" he asked genially.

"I'd like a confidential talk with you, sir, if you can spare the time."

"Oh," said Caithby thoughtfully. "Particularly private, is it?"

"Very private, sir."

"I see. Well, perhaps we'd better go along to my room at the house."

They had begun tea before he invited Travers to open the ball. The opening was sensational enough.

"I've really come to you, sir, to save my own sanity and that of my warrant-officers. If something isn't done, we're going to crack up, or else be under arrest."

The Colonel never turned a hair. Travers went over the irregularities and gross injustices of the camp and it was a quarter of an hour before he had finished. Caithby had put in no more than a couple of questions but his comment at the end was very much to the point.

"You've surprised me," he said. "I had no idea that things were as they are. But they've got to stop. I know Major Stirrop, but that doesn't affect the situation. The kind of thing you've described mustn't be allowed to go on. What you'd better do is make a formal request through me for an interview with the Brigadier, then necessary action can be taken."

"I'd rather not, sir," Travers said. "It may prejudice my case, but all I wanted at this stage was to let someone like you, sir, know how things stood. What I'll do now, sir, is tackle this business once more in my own way, and then if there's no alteration, I'll make the official complaint."

"You're the one to know best," he said. "Still, I'm glad you came to me."

"I'm more than glad, sir," Travers said. 'I've been hoarding things up for months, and now my mind's easy. And I'm more than grateful to you, sir."

"Not at all," the Colonel told him. "But if I may suggest it, you wouldn't like a transfer?"

Travers shook his head. "That would be running away, sir. And it might make things even worse for my successor."

"Perhaps you're right," he said. "Let me know what happens, and I hope your news will be better."

As he made his way back to the camp, life for Travers had completely changed with that easing of his mind, and he had never felt more kindly disposed towards the Army, and even its brass hats. But as he drew near the camp again, the elation gradually went, and there was much of the old depression as he made his way through the main gate.

Before he went to his office he hunted up Ramble and heard that nothing had been seen of Mafferty.

"I know what he's like, sir," Ramble said. "He'll be wandering about like someone off his head."

"Be a good fellow and slip along to the Green Man later on and see if he's there."

"I certainly will, sir," Ramble said. "But it isn't drink he takes to when he's put out like this. He's too blind mad even to drink."

"It's a bad business," Travers said. "Still, I've some good news for you. There's going to be an alteration in this camp. Keep it under your cap, but I shouldn't be surprised if something even happens to-night. By the way, what happened when

Mafferty checked stores? That's one of the things I wanted to see him about."

"Not a thing missing," Ramble said. "Everything correct with the ledgers."

But when Travers hinted that something might happen that very night, what he had in mind was to approach the Commandant with a demand for immediate reform; in other words, to strike while the iron was hot. People at Headquarters had the habit of forgetting things; besides, Garrison Staff was a floating population, and if Colonel Caithby was transferred elsewhere—which at any moment he might be—then the chance of a lifetime would be lost.

Then, thinking things over, Travers knew that Stirrop must say something about Mafferty, which would make an excellent opening. But when Travers went into the Mess, Stirrop was not there, and he was not in his room or his office. The orderly thought he was doing some sort of inspection of the camp with Captain Winter.

Winter and Travers had arranged to have an early dinner that night and then to settle down to completion of the prisoners' cards. Travers arrived first, and he had just begun his meal when Winter came in, but he made no mention of where he had been with the Commandant. Then just as the two were going out, the Commandant arrived, and as he went through the door Travers heard Winter say: "I'll see you later then, sir."

When Winter caught Travers up, he explained.

"The old man wants to see me at a quarter to nine. I rather fancy he's springing some mine or other. You don't happen to know what it is?"

"He hasn't said a word to me," Travers told him. "Perhaps he wants to see your B.199A."

"Then he can wait," Winter said bluntly. "If he thinks I've got twenty pairs of hands, he's ruddy well mistaken."

Then a certain anxiety seemed to creep into his voice.

"But why that extraordinary hour? Why didn't he see me just now or wait till the morning?"

Travers was prompt with a theory.

"He may be wanting to get certain information. I don't mean information that's going to make trouble for you. After all, it's probably something perfectly innocent he wants to see you about."

"I don't know," Winter said. "I don't like it. And why's he dining in Mess? He doesn't do that once a month."

It was a dark night with lowering clouds, and there was a lessening of the intense cold. Travers thought a thaw was coming; Winter was prepared to bet there would more snow. But Winter's office was cheerful enough.

And here it should be explained that the making out of Index Cards for Alien Internees was a mightily important matter that could not be trusted to subordinates. Either the overworked Winter would have to do the whole lot, or someone with the authority of Travers must volunteer to help. Already seventy-three cards were completed except for the Commandant's final signature, and now three copies of each were to be made: one for Home Office, one for War Office, and one for the camp to which the prisoners would ultimately be sent, and every card would need to be scrupulously accurate.

"Here you are," said Winter, handing over about half of the completed cards, and sufficient unused ones. "You make three copies of each of these and I'll get on with the remainder. Whoever finishes first can help the other."

"Not enough cards, are there?" asked Travers.

Winter frowned. "They might last out. If they don't, I'll fetch some more from my room."

"Good enough," said Travers. "I don't think I'll work in here, by the way. We'll only get yarning and disturb each other. Also I might just as well let those two fellows off duty for an hour or so and see to the 'phone myself. Not that anyone's likely to 'phone."

So Travers settled down by himself, stoked the fire, and his pipe, and rattled off a score of cards. Then the heat of the room made him somewhat drowsy, and he happened at that moment to recall that highly successful interview of the afternoon, he began humming to himself, which effort also served to keep him from nodding over his work. Fifty more cards were done, the pipe was stoked again, and he saw by his watch that it was just half-past eight. With luck the whole job would be finished in another half-hour.

A few more cards, and that interview of the afternoon was remembered again. Then Travers smiled once more to himself, laid the work aside for a moment and unlocked his private drawer. Out came a sheet of paper, which, he was saying to himself, would no longer be wanted.

It was a queer sort of document—nothing less than a highly condensed synopsis of a work to be entitled *The Case of the Murdered Major*. Its composing had cheered many an hour and had often soothed to sleep, but there it was with that perfect alibi all worked out in detail, and how the fake incendiary bomb could be placed, and why murder could never be suspected.

Travers nodded with a certain complacence, and was about to make a burnt-offering of an old friend, when there was a slam that startled him. Damn that fellow Winter! thought Travers, and then a glance at his watch showed why there had been the slam and the scurry. It was a quarter to nine.

Travers went through to see how Winter had progressed with his cards. The light was off but he switched it on. Winter seemed almost to have finished, and Travers picked up the last card to admire how neatly the work had been done.

"Damnation!"

The ink was wet and he had smeared the card. Now a new one would have to be made out, and just as he was thinking that, the door opened and Winter came in.

"The Commandant isn't in his room!"

"He said he'd be?"

"Most emphatically he said so."

"Well, it's his funeral," Travers said. "After all, I can prove that you reported. What's he expect you to do? Stand out there in the cold?"

Winter hesitated for a moment, then took out his overcoat.

"Well, then, I may as well finish these few cards. I say! Who smudged this one?"

"Sorry, I did. I'll make another one out," Travers told him. "I was just having a look—"

He broke off. A padding of quick feet could be heard. His own office door opened, and he looked through to see who it was. It was Dowling, puffing away and face red from the run.

"The Commandant, sir, I've just found him!"

"Found him?"

"Yes, sir. He's dead, sir! Right on the far corner, sir, lying in the snow."

# PART III
# WHO KILLED COCK ROBIN?

# CHAPTER IX
## DEATH IN THE SNOW

Travers picked up the receiver, but knew the line was dead as soon as it touched his ear. He replaced it, picked it up again and tried dialling, but nothing happened.

"This cursed line's always going wrong," he told Dowling annnoyedly. "What're we to do now? Unless you do it, Winter. Find Ramble, and if you can't, then send a runner yourself down to Dulling. Or better still, tell him to stop at the Green Man and 'phone from there."

"But what's happened?" Winter said. "Did I hear something about the Commandant?"

"He's dead," Travers told him tersely. "Dowling just found him lying dead in the snow. Now for the love of heaven get a move on, and have Dulling here at the double."

Winter grabbed his greatcoat and hurried out, eyes still goggling.

"I'll come with you," Travers told Dowling. "If anyone rings up he'll find the line dead, and that's all there is to it."

He locked the communicating door and the office, and waved Dowling on.

"Now tell me again what happened."

Dowling said he'd arranged to meet Stamp at the main door at twenty-twenty-five hours to take the count, but had had to go to main guard first, he was late when he started back but he did notice a black something in the snow just beyond the inner wire and about twenty foot from the gravelled drive. He did the count and came out again at the main door, and as he came out on the drive, Stamp noticed the black something and the two went to investigate. Almost at once they knew it for a man, but wondered how a drunk could have got through the wire gates. Stamp flashed his torch, and there lay Major Stirrop, stone dead.

"Any sign of a wound or anything?" Travers asked.

"Not that I could see, sir. It looked to me as if he'd had a heart attack."

Stamp's torch guided them to the spot, then it flashed down on the body. Travers got down and felt over the heart. There was no beat and the cheek was icily cold. But there was something strange somewhere, and as he got to his feet again he knew what it was.

"Where's his cap?"

"Perhaps he didn't have one, sir," said Stamp.

"Don't be a fool," Travers snapped at him. "Out here, and wearing a British warm, and a scarf—and no cap? Lend me that torch of yours."

He flashed it round and there lay the cap, a good ten feet from the body and nearer the building on the deeper snow.

"How on earth did it get there, sir?" Dowling asked.

"Thai's what I'd like to know," Travers said. "The wind couldn't have blown it there, because there isn't any wind."

He flashed the torch again. There was something else that was very strange. Beyond the body was a deep depression, as if Stirrop had fallen there first and then rolled over to where he now lay. And yet there were no footprints in the snow!

For a moment or two he stood there in thought, and then gradually he began to feel something of panic. What was the correct procedure? Should the police be informed, or H.Q., or both? Or should nothing be done till the doctor had made some sort of report? But something had to be done, and quickly, and he pulled himself together.

"Stamp, leave me your torch, but nip along and fetch four men and a table-top. Don't say what for. And tell Captain Byron I want him."

Once more he stood thinking. In civil life he would have known every trick of procedure, now he feared to take even an obvious step for fear some ancient brass bat should call it in question. Then a shrug of the shoulders and he had made up his mind.

"Dowling, I'm going to leave all this to you. If Mr. Ramble comes, let him see Major Stirrop taken to his room and put on his bed. You and I will now move him clear. We don't want everyone trampling down the snow."

There was another deep impression where the body had been.

"That's what I wanted to see," Travers said. "You'll get a wrapper from stores and cover these two impressions up, so that a fall of snow doesn't affect them. Then ask Captain Byron to keep the spot under observation all night. A stick guard will do. The cap's on no account to be touched. You got all that?"

Dowling duly repeated it. Travers thought of something else.

"Don't let anyone go near where the body was. I don't want any more footprints than what you and I have made."

He flashed the torch round again, slowly, and letting it linger here and there. Then he handed it over to Dowling and made his way through the wire gates. A moment's indecision and he went by the swept path towards the Mess. Behind him he could now hear voices and looking back he saw the flash of torches. Ramble's voice could be heard, and Byron's.

He went past the Mess to his own room. A couple of walking-sticks stood in the corner, and he found some string and lashed them together to make a five-foot rod. There was a swagger stick too, and he added it to make the rod longer. Then he made his way round towards his office and let himself through the wire gates at the east corner. A procession was moving from where the body had been towards the Mess hutments, and as soon as it was clear, he made his way quickly to where Stirrop had been found.

Now he had his own torch, and he flashed it again to make sure where his own footprints had been when he had straddled the body to move it with Dowling clear of the snow. Setting his feet carefully he stretched out with his long arms towards the cap. The curved handle of the stick just reached it, and in a couple of seconds the cap was in his hands.

Now he crouched down on the gravel and, opening his British warm to shield the light of the torch from observation, he had a good look at the cap. What he could see, even by that over-concentrated light, made him snap his eyes. There was no blood, just as there was no blood on those impressions which the body had left in the snow. But the cap was discoloured by something yellow and a feel of it showed that it was sand. Then with his long fingers he felt between the lining and the top, and now he was utterly puzzled. There seemed to be sand inside the lining of the cap itself.

A moment or two and he was making his way towards his office. That there was something more than fishy about the death of Stirrop had been plain from the moment he had caught sight of that cap, and now he knew in his heart of hearts that it was no question of anything but murder. Take the body, for instance. It had been just off the gravelled drive and yet there was never a footprint between it and that drive. The snow lay heaped as it had been when the drive was first cleared. In other words, Stirrop had been killed elsewhere, and his body laid where it had been found. What the second impression meant he had no idea, but whoever had laid the body down had remembered the cap, but had not dared to go near the body again, and therefore had thrown the cap to the body. Unfortunately for him the throw had been hurried and the cap landed ten feet from where it should have dropped.

At the wire gate Travers halted, and his fingers went fumblingly to his glasses. There was one other thing. The body had been found in the shadow, where the dim light that shone down from the wire surround could never reach it. It was by chance that Dowling had seen it. And yet it had been placed so that it must be found. If Dowling had not found it, then it must have been seen by the N.C.O. of the guard who came that way with the nine o'clock reliefs.

In his own room Travers made straight for the safe, and locked that cap up. A second or two and Winter came in.

"Sorry to be so long, but I fixed that job up. Found a man with a motor-bike and sent him along. The doc. ought to be here at any minute."

"You're a good fellow," Travers told him. "What's beating me still is if I ought to ring Garrison and let them know. Or should I wait and hear what the doctor says. And there's the question of his wife. What about her?"

"'Phone all right?"

"Lord!" said Travers, "I'd forgotten the 'phone."

But when he picked up the receiver, the 'phone was alive again. Even then he seemed to be wondering what to do.

"What do you think it was?" Winter said. "A heart attack?"

"Ask me another. I didn't know he had a heart."

Winter frowned. "The whole thing happened so quickly that I still don't know if I'm on my head or my heels. And what's been worrying me is what on earth he was doing out there in the snow when he was supposed to be seeing me! The whole thing doesn't make sense."

"I know. It is queer, hut this camp's been a damn-queer place. Go outside there and stand in the dark where the body was, and then you'll feel it. The whole place has been sort of shot through with loathing of Stirrop. It got to be like a weight pressing on people's minds—not your own, perhaps, but there were plenty of others." He got to his feet. "Perhaps I'd better go and meet Dulling. Wait a minute, though. There ought to be someone here. Be a good fellow and get those two orderlies back."

Winter went towards the communicating door.

"Wait a minute," Travers said. "You'd better have the key. I locked—"

But Winter's hand had already gone out and the door was open.

"That's a queer business," Travers said. "I'm damn-sure I locked that door when I locked my own."

Winter switched on the light and gave a look round.

"Nobody's been in here." he said. "Wait a minute, though. What the devil's that? Who's been spilling water?"

On the floor well inside the outer door was quite a small pool of dirty water.

"Someone *has* been in," Travers said. "Someone came in with snow caked on his boots and stood behind the door. It couldn't have been the orderlies coming back and into this room because they couldn't get into mine. They wouldn't stand behind the door."

"Good God!" said Winter. "I've got some stuff here that's regular dynamite. If the Commandant ever found—" He broke off, shaking his head. "For a moment I was talking as if he was still alive."

The telephone went and Travers nipped back. It was Main Guard reporting that the doctor had come through. Then by sheer chance the two orderlies turned up.

"You see if anything's missing from here," Travers said to Winter. "Or better still, first get hold of Colonel Caithby at Garrison and make a report as from me. If I'm wanted I shall be somewhere round the Mess."

The doctor had had his car to park, and he had been in Stirrop's room only a very few moments before Travers arrived. Who should be with him but Tester, wearing that fur-collared coat and looking as unconcerned about being in a prohibited area as if the said area was his own home. Ramble sprang to attention as Travers came in.

"This is a bad business," began Dulling heavily. "You could have knocked me over with a feather. Did I understand he was found out in the snow?"

"Yes," Travers said laconically. "Excuse my butting in, as a layman, but can you more or less determine the cause of death—say in a few minutes or so?"

Dulling made a wry face. "I can try."

Travers nodded. "Good man. Get to it. And you might as well light this oil-stove. It's none too warm in here."

Tester's voice came suitably hushed at his ear.

"I say, I'm awfully sorry about this. Perfectly dreadful affair."

"Yes," said Travers. "Can you spare me a minute? You too, Mr. Ramble?"

He led the way to the deserted Mess. A bleak-looking orderly appeared but was waved away.

"How is it you are here, Captain Tester?"

"Well,"—he smiled sheepishly—"I happened to be with the doctor in his car. We agreed he'll have to take me home, so I came in with him."

"But I thought I'd explained the regulations to you? When either prisoners or internees are in camp, nobody's allowed in except on lawful business or with special sanction."

"Yes, but my dear fellow, I have a pass. And Major Stirrop"—he broke off with a little titter that somehow made Travers's hackles rise—"the late Major Stirrop, I should say, told me it didn't matter."

"I see," said Travers slowly. "Well, I don't want to be officious, but at the moment I'm Commandant of this Camp, and I'm seeing regulations are carried out. Mr. Ramble, you'll accompany Captain Tester at once to Main Guard and see him through the gate."

"Very good, sir."

"But, my dear fellow, have a heart. How on earth am I to get home? And what harm am I possibly doing? It isn't as if I'm a pukka civilian."

"I don't give a damn what you are," Travers told him curtly. "I'm dealing with regulations as laid down. You of all people ought to recognise the fact."

"Sorry." He shook an apologetic head, then looked up with a smile. "No bones broken?"

Travers's smile was grim. "Not at present. By the way I'll tell the doctor you've decided to walk home. You thought the exercise would do you good."

Before Travers could leave, Winter came in, and he was scowling.

"Wasn't that Tester? What on earth is he doing here?"

"Come for a joy-ride," Travers said. "He's evidently a pal of the doc's. You've no particular use for him, have you?"

"Lounge lizards are not in my line," Winter said. "But what I came to report was that Colonel Caithby's coming at once. Yes, and that there's nothing missing from my room as far as I can judge. Things have been disturbed, though. Anything else I can do?"

"I don't know that there is," Travers said.

"Then I'll go back and finish those cursed cards. No use turning in. I know I'd never damn-well sleep. No more news of any sort?"

"Nothing at all," Travers said. "But what I would do if I were you, is have a good stiff tot. You're looking a bit under the weather."

"I'll finish those cards first," Winter told him, "and have a nip of some sort before I turn in."

The body had been stripped and Dulling was at work when Travers went in. The doctor looked round at once, and was about to speak when Travers got his word in first.

"Pardon a personal question, doc., but how did young Tester come to be in your car to-night?"

"As a matter of fact," the doctor said, "I was almost at the gate here when I saw him on the side of the road, going towards Shoreleigh. I almost ran over him, in fact. I said, 'If you like to wait for me I'll give you a lift.'"

"You knew he shouldn't have come inside the camp?"

"I didn't. Besides, I knew he had a pass."

Travers explained. The doctor apologised profusely. Always, he said, he seemed to be putting his foot in it.

"Well, he's decided to walk home after all," Travers said. "A friend of yours, is he?"

"Well, I know him. My wife and I met him at Mrs. Martelli's. You know—wife of the Italian consul. She's English. Went to the same school as my wife."

"Really?" said Travers politely. "Curious how many of these foreigners marry English girls. But about—that. Found anything out?"

"That's just what I was going to mention," Dulling said. "Do you think I might have another opinion? The S.M.O., if you could get hold of him for me."

Outside, Travers saw the lights of an incoming car, and guessed it was Colonel Caithby. A Mess Orderly was sent with an urgent chit to Winter to ring the Senior Medical Officer, and Travers went towards the car.

Travers always thought Colonel Caithby the most picturesque figure he had ever seen. "The Artist's Delight" was his private nickname, for nothing more colourful had ever gone on two legs. His frame was lean, his shoulders slightly stooping, his nose hawk-like and predatory. Against the deep tan of his face his brushed-up moustache was like snow, and the whole blended amazingly with the worn khaki, the red tabs, the triple row of ribbons, and the gleam of the belt and buttons. If ever a man looked a soldier, it was Caithby.

"Evening, Travers," he said quietly. "Bad news—eh?"

Travers told him the gist of what had happened, with everything that mattered kept back.

"What was it? His heart?"

"I wouldn't like to express an opinion, sir," hedged Travers. "Would you care to see where he was found?"

"By all means," the Colonel said. "Through these gates, is it? Oh, yes, I remember."

The stick guard was sent to a distance, and Travers removed the sacking wrapper.

"That was a most ingenious precaution," the Colonel said. "I used to be a police-wallah myself. And this is where he lay. Bit off the beaten track, isn't it? Whose footprints are those? And what's that second depression?"

Travers did more explaining, but what he could not explain was where Stirrop's own footprints were and why he should have arrived at that spot at all.

"Unless he was carried here, sir," he said tentatively.

"What's that? Carried here?"

He grunted to himself and began flashing the torch that Travers had handed him. Travers let out the least bit more—about the hat. The Colonel stood for a full minute before he spoke.

"Let's work back a bit. I take it he'd have come out of the building and not round it. Mind if I use the torch?"

The two went back to that monstrosity of an entrance, Caithby flashing the torch on the snow, but there was never the mark of a foot.

"If I may point it out, sir, we've been in the deep shadow all the time," Travers said.

"I'd noticed that," Caithby said. "But where's the nearest sentry?"

"Along the east side there," Travers said. "We can see him if we go along that path to the wire."

"And all the front of the building is not under any observation?"

"No, sir," Travers admitted. "I won't say that it doesn't look risky, but it isn't, really. It's virtually impossible to get out of the building, and the sentries at the sides do get a diagonal view of the front wire, though they can't see the actual front of the building itself."

"Well, security's your funeral," he was told. "But it's curious. Let's suppose someone did put the body there. In the first place, the body, as you say, wasn't dead, because the two depressions show that he rolled over. Still, leaving that out, someone put the body there, as I said. Then that someone knew the sentries couldn't see. Therefore, if there was any fishy work, it was done by someone inside the camp.'

Travers could feel those quizzical eyes peering at him interrogatively in the dark.

"Well, sir," he said, "don't think me rude, but we could have arrived at that in any case. If there's been dirty work, it must have been done by someone inside for the plain reason that this camp's a watertight compartment. As far as human beings are concerned, it hasn't got an outside."

"Good!" chuckled the Colonel. "Fools rush in where adjutants know how to tread." Then the chuckle went. "Do you think we might have a look at the body?"

The lights of yet another car could be seen. It was the S.M.O., and the three went towards the Mess together. Inside Stamp's room the doctor was waiting anxiously.

"Why exactly did you want a second opinion?" the Colonel asked him.

The doctor said there was the question of a post-mortem, for one thing, and, for another, there was the matter of the slight issue of blood from the mouth and nose and ears. The S.M.O. pricked up his ears at that and had a good look at the corpse. There was some whispering between him and Dulling, and confirmatory nods. The S.M.O. made the announcement.

"It looks like a fracture of the base of the skull, sir."

The Colonel raised his eyebrows.

"Any contusions?"

"Nothing that I can see," the S.M.O. said. "Of course, sir, he needn't have been struck by anything. A man can fracture his skull by falling from too great a height and lighting on his feet. The spinal column's jarred clean up against the skull."

"Of course. I'd not thought of that. And what do you propose?"

"We must have a P.M. Any objections to getting him away?"

Travers said he would ring for an ambulance. A slight hesitation and he ventured to ask the Colonel if he would he so good as to come across to the office too.

"It's getting rather late," the Colonel said when they were outside. "Was there anything in particular you wanted?"

"Only to show you the cap, sir."

"Any blood on it?"

"Not that I noticed, sir."

The Colonel nodded. He would be along in the morning, he said. If the P.M report came through it was to be 'phoned to him at once.

"One thing I ought to do," he said, "and I'd like your consent. Things have got to a certain extent out of your and my hands. The Brigadier ought to be told of that visit of yours this afternoon. Don't you agree?"

Travers agreed. Then before he left, the Colonel said it was a matter for Headquarters to communicate with Mrs. Stirrop. The funeral arrangements he would let Travers know about later. As for what both he and Travers suspected, nothing whatever must be said.

So an orderly was sent with yet another chit for Winter, and Travers went back to Stirrop's room.

"If you don't mind," he said, "I'd better go through the contents of the pockets and make a list, then everything can go in the ambulance."

While the two were making yet another examination, he began jotting down his list which the S.M.O. would sign. Even the pocket-book held nothing of interest, hut there was a folded sheet of paper in the tunic breast-pocket which made him frown. Stirrop had evidently been making notes, but to what they referred Travers could not even hazard a guess:

> Ring W.O. and see if Harry Cross still B.C. . . . . Get 'phone num . . . (Garrison?) *Weinholst*, and what about beard? Mention Trav.? Two birds one stone. After to-night.

There were doodling marks scrawled round those curious words as if Stirrop had written them with much thought. The paper was clean and the folds not too tight, so apparently the notes had been written that same day. As for what Travers could deduce, B.C. was Border Command and Trav. was himself.

That first interpretation was why the paper found its way into Travers's own pocket. Only one other thing of consequence was to happen that night. He sent for Ramble and saw him in the open, out of all earshot.

"Mafferty back?"

"Yes, sir," Ramble said. "He hadn't been near the Green Man, but when I got back I looked in his room and he was curled up in his bunk."

"What time was that?"

"Just before half-past eight, sir. He'd come through the gate at just before eight."

"Have you spoken to him?"

"No, sir. If he was asleep, all the better, I thought."

Travers nodded. "Perhaps you're right. But when he wakes in the morning, you tell him what's happened. See how he takes it."

"Yes, sir." He fidgeted for a moment, then shook his head. "But he had nothing to do with it, sir."

"To do with what?"

"Well, sir, killing the Commandant."

"Who said he'd been killed?"

Ramble fidgeted again, then said it was all over the camp.

"Another case of wishful thinking," Travers told him. "Whatever the camp says, you say nothing. You and I—and Mafferty—may have an awful lot of that to do in the next few days."

"A lot of what, sir?"

"Saying nothing," repeated Travers, and left it at that.

# CHAPTER X
## TRAVERS ON THE CARPET

SNIFFY CAME IN much earlier with tea the following morning, and announced that Dr. Dulling would like to see Captain Travers.

"Come in!" hollered Travers, and reached for his glasses.

"Sorry to disturb you," Dulling said, "but I had to come this way to see a patient, so I thought I'd drop in with that P.M. report."

"More snow, then," Travers said, noticing the white on overcoat and hat.

"Wicked weather," Dulling said. "And now about this report. The S.M.O. sent it straight through to Headquarters, by the way, so you needn't worry about that." He gave a queer, interrogatory look. "It's an uncommon report. I don't know what you'll think of it."

Now if Dulling had been George Wharton, Travers would have said: "I'll tell you what I'll do, George. I'll write down what I think on this sheet of paper and give it you, then you shall tell me. And I'll bet you a new hat we don't vary very much." But Dulling was not George Wharton, and this was not civilian life, and Travers had never been less inclined to give away what he knew.

"It was a fracture at the base of the skull all right," Dulling said, "and it wasn't caused by dropping on his feet from too great a height. He was struck on the head with tremendous force. There weren't any abrasions, so it must have been something that expanded."

"Like the old-fashioned dollop of sand in the corner of a nice little sack."

"That's it. Good old sandbagging like we used to read about when we were boys."

Sniffy came in with a cup of hot tea for him, and the stove was lighted. Travers said he might as well sit down.

"I'm not stopping,'" Dulling said hurriedly. "As soon as I've drunk this tea I'm off."

"If you should happen to see Ramble when you go out, you might ask him to come to me," Travers said. "It isn't all that important, so don't send a message or anything."

Then, having brought in so tactfully the mention of Ramble, he could proceed.

"By the way, Ramble was tremendously bucked when you told him those German words and phrases the other day. He fancies himself no end."

Dulling coloured to the very roots of his hair.

"You don't think it was indiscreet of me?"

"Why should it have been?"

"Well, after what I told you. I mean, about our family history. But, you see, it was like this. I knew I'd have to be about a great deal among the prisoners, at sick parades, and so on, so I bought one of those little books—*How to Speak German*—and swotted up what I thought might be useful."

"And a very sensible thing to do," commented Travers.

But when the doctor had gone he was not so sure. The excuse had been an admirable one, but there were other things to consider. And on the spur of the moment he made a couple of entries in his private notebook:

*Re* D. Find out—

*(a)* What is the condition of his practice.

*(b)* How he came to get this job.

Everybody was in Mess, except Dowling, which was a rare enough happening. There was a relief in the atmosphere, tempered with a diplomatic gravity, for while people's tongues were loosed, voices were suitably hushed.

"Are you going to make an announcement in camp this morning?" Winter asked. "If so, will you want me?"

"I think I'll drift across after sick parade," Travers said. "Friedemann can act as interpreter."

"What about a new Commandant? Will they be sending one down or will you carry on?"

"Thy servant is as a dead dog," said Travers. "I mean, in the eyes of the War House. But you bet your life they'll do whatever's the most awkward."

"The War House always runs true to form," Byron said. "Any news, by the way? I thought I saw Dulling."

Travers thought it discreet to say at least something. Stirrop, he let out, had been the victim of an extremely nasty accident, though whether that accident was of his own causing or someone else's design was not to be discussed.

Long before his usual time he was in his office. Stirrop's cap was transferred to an attaché case, then he switched the 'phone through to the Commandant's office and went there to ring up the War House in privacy. The case was locked up in the Commandant's safe.

He was lucky in his telephoning. Not only did he get W.O. in a very few minutes, but he was put through to his own department where, more amazing still, was someone who knew what he was talking about. Travers, helped by the immunity of distance, and taking a firm line, said that of course he could carry on. As he pointed out, he knew every working of the camp, and new blood would only be a hindrance. No, he did not even want an adjutant at the moment. If he might be permitted to ring up again in a day or two, then perhaps the situation might be reviewed. In the meanwhile he could give an assurance that everything was, and would be, well in hand.

Travers replaced the receiver with an enormous satisfaction. Unless some other meddling department threw a spanner into the works, the camp would have rest for many days. Then, as a reminder that rest was a very relative term, the 'phone went. It was Miss Dance, asking if she should open the correspondence. Travers told her he would be along at once.

She greeted him in a monstrously little voice. Her eyes were red too, but Travers made no comment on the sadness of things. Miss Dance, but for the smell, would have been fully capable of seeking the melancholy aid of an onion.

"Work will go on just as usual," Travers told her. "I shall work here, but if there are any interviews I shall have them in the Commandant's office."

"But isn't it dreadful, though?"

"Yes," Travers said. "And when did you first hear of it?"

"Just before I came," she told him. "That's why I was so upset."

"And who told you?"

She flushed slightly. "Well, it was Captain Tester—really."

Travers wondered what the "really" implied, but thought best to leave it at that.

Ramble had the seventy-three prisoners lined up in the hall when Travers arrived. Captain Friedemann gave his usual obsequious bow from the waist up, and said he would be happy to translate.

The ranks broke into quite a babble of conversation when the news was heard, and Ramble had to give one of his best *Achtungs!* Then one of the so-called passengers approached Friedemann and made a short speech, and there was more interchanging of bows.

"What's he say?" asked Travers.

"He says that everybody is very sorry," Friedemann said.

"Tell him his condolences will be conveyed to the proper quarter," said Travers dryly.

The new order of things was explained. Friedemann said that as Captain Travers was now Commandant, could he have that interview he had been promised? All in good time, Travers told him suavely.

What in fact he would have liked to do was to lure Friedemann into one of those stiff bows, and then to administer a running kick at his pants. For when Travers had caught sight of Beckner, a pullover collar had been ostentatiously rolled up round the ears. In other words, the tunnelling had been begun. Somewhere floor-boards had already been removed, and day and night shifts would be working at the hole which its optimistic diggers imagined would emerge outside the encircling wire.

No sooner was Travers back in the office than Mafferty was asking to see him. The interview took place in the Commandant's office, and in one way it was rather amusing, with Mafferty standing stiffly to attention, and his tone as rigid as the ends of his waxed moustache.

"I've come to apologise, sir."

"What for?"

"Losing my temper with the Commandant, sir. And being out of camp contrary to orders."

"You expect in be charged?"

"Yes, sir. I committed the offences, sir, and I'm prepared to take the consequences."

"Don't be a B.F.," said Travers bluntly. He got to his feet, then wheeled round, cigarette case in hand. "Have a cigarette. And sit down in that chair."

"Now then, Mafferty, you and I are going to have a talk," he said. "Tell me exactly what you did when you left camp yesterday."

Mafferty took a long time getting it out. There were some things, he said, he didn't even remember, he had been so blind with rage. What he presumably had done was to head straight for open country, and when he really came to himself he was at the Piebald Stag at Mantlebury. It was almost dark then and he went in and had some tea. There was no fire in the room and he had been deadly cold, so the landlord laced the tea with rum and he had another stiff tot before starting back to camp. There he arrived at round about eight o'clock and he went straight to his quarters. The air and the rum had made him sleepy, and he lay on the bed just as he was with a couple of blankets over him.

"We'll forget it," Travers said, hoping to heaven the easy optimism would be justified. "Only one thing I have to say, and it's in the strictest confidence. Major Stirrop didn't die by accident. He died because someone caught him a terrific crack on the back of the skull in the dark."

"I wouldn't have done that, sir," Mafferty said, jumping to it. "If I'd hit him, sir, it'd have been on the point of his jaw."

"Forget that too," Travers said. "The less said about hitting, the better. But what you've got to remember is that in the very near future someone's going to ask a whole lot of official questions about your last night's movements. That someone won't know you as well as I do. He'll have heard about what happened yesterday and he'll have your record in front of him."

Mafferty licked his lips.

"Yes, sir, I see that, sir."

Travers got to his feet again.

"Now you know as much as I do. If I thought you'd told me a lie, I'd throw you to the lions. As it is, all I'll say is this. Get on with your job and keep your mouth shut." He held out his hand and for the first time allowed himself to smile. "One other little word—which is that I'm on your side."

Then the 'phone bell went again.

"Call for you. Captain Travers. I'm putting you through."

It was Colonel Caithby speaking from Garrison.

"That you, Captain Travers? The Brigadier would like to see you as soon as you can manage it."

"Very good, sir," Travers told him. "I'll be there inside ten minutes."

There are few dyed-in-the-wool infantrymen who feel at home at any Headquarters. Travers felt particularly uncomfortable that morning, and for no special reason, unless it were old prejudice. As he waited outside the brigadier's room listening to the very faint murmur of voices from inside, one or two elegant young officers came by with casual glances that seemed to show how great a gulf there still yawned between such as himself and the very elect. The mere fact of waiting was none too soothing to the nerves, and it seemed an age before Colonel Caithby came out with a smile and a nod.

"Sorry to have kept you waiting. The Brigadier will see you now."

The two went in. Travers had met the Brigadier at least twice before, though only as a satellite of Major Stirrop, but he had remarked the taciturn directness and the steely grey eyes. As they met those of Travers that morning, they seemed more gimlet-like than ever. And to Travers's guardee salute and brisk "Good morning, sir," he merely gave a nod and, "Stand easy, Captain Travers." Then he was into the heart of things straightaway.

"You have seen the doctors' report on your Commandant? What do you make of it?"

Travers's fingers moved upwards towards his glasses, then fell.

"Do you want me to say everything I think, sir?"

"Of course."

Travers began at the discovery of the body, his observations and precautions, and what Colonel Caithby and himself had further deduced. Then, feeling rather like a commercial traveller with samples, he produced the cap. The brigadier and Caithby had a good look at it.

"To be perfectly frank, Major Stirrop was murdered," the Brigadier said, his voice as cold and impersonal as if he had remarked that the bottom button of Travers's tunic was unfastened—which it was.

"I'm afraid that is so, sir."

"Have you any ideas, or suspicions?"

Travers shook his head. "It's rather too early for that, sir."

"Too early?" His eyes narrowed. "That's one way of looking at it. But you have no idea whatever as to who might have done it?"

Then he leaned forward in his chair, eyes glancing up from under his thick white eyebrows.

"Yourself, for instance. You didn't do it?"

"No, sir."

"Can you prove that you didn't?"

"Yes, sir. Major Stirrop was killed at about a quarter past eight. From before eight o'clock until a quarter to nine I was in my office at work. Captain Winter was in the adjoining room and could prove it."

"You went both in the same room or in constant contact?"

"No, sir, but we were doing parts of the same job. Captain Winter must have heard me every now and again. Besides, if I may point the fact out, sir, it would have taken at least a quarter of an hour to kill Major Stirrop and dispose of his body."

"I see." He leaned still farther forward. "The reason why I put that direct question was that yesterday you had an interview with Colonel Caithby, in which were made certain disclosures about your camp. I've no reason to disbelieve what you said. I think you'd have been a fool to report what you couldn't substantiate. But when you turned down Colonel Caithby's advice to make an official complaint to me, you gave as your reason that you preferred at the moment to handle Major Stirrop *in your own way*—or words to that effect."

He sat back in his chair as if to watch the effect of his own bombshell. Travers gave explanations, but what he was saying he hardly knew. Those steely eyes were holding his own till he was as if mesmerised, with his own voice coming from some enormous distance. Then the Brigadier was saying that murder was a serious thing and ordinary policy must be overridden—at least Travers thought afterwards that that was what he had said. For in the next moment the whole of Travers went endways. A sheet of paper was being held towards him and he was being asked to account for it.

He blinked, polished his glasses, then had a look. His staring eyes met those of the Brigadier again. The sheet of paper was headed *The Case of the Murdered Major*, but what was beneath the heading was at the moment nothing but a blur.

"This was taken from my office last night, sir."

"Indeed? It reached here this morning, presumably with your office correspondence, and it was addressed to Captain G.S."

"May I see the envelope, sir?"

"I'm sorry, but the envelope was destroyed. What I'm interested in is your explanation of that paper itself and what's written on it."

"I'm afraid you'll find the explanation rather feeble, sir."

"Leave me to be the judge of that."

"Exactly, sir." He smiled feebly, then began what he knew was sounding even more feeble. It included Scotland Yard, and George Wharton, and a rather scarifying description of the last few months in the camp.

"I see," said the brigadier. "Colonel Caithby and I were wondering why you handled the matter so well from the start, and he seemed to recall your name in connection with Scotland Yard. This morning we rang them."

"Thank you, sir," said Travers, even more fatuously.

"The point now is this," said the Brigadier, disregarding the gratitude. "None of us want the local police to go into the matter. It would make too much talk. I am prepared to regard your camp as what it is—a Prohibited Area—if I can justify the situation."

Colonel Caithby put in a quiet word.

"The Brigadier would like to hear your suggestions."

"Well, sir," Travers said, "the matter is primarily one for the Home Office and the War Office together. If you yourself were to get into touch with both departments, sir, you might get someone sent down. If I may so, sir, I think Superintendent Wharton would be the ideal man."

"Got that, Caithby?" the Brigadier said, and pushed back his chair.

The interview, Travers supposed, was at an end. Feeling more like a commercial traveller than ever, he began replacing the cap.

"Your name was on that sheet of paper," the Brigadier was suddenly saying. "I knew a Gunner—a Ludovic Travers; I was at school with him, in fact. Any relation of yours?"

"My father, I expect, sir."

"Really?" said the Brigadier, in a tone that was almost human. "Is he still alive?"

Travers again explained. The Brigadier gave a nod that might have been anything from consolation to dismissal. Travers gave as good a salute as the attaché case would allow, and departed.

Colonel Caithby accompanied him downstairs.

"You'd better go back in my car," he said, and, at the door: "The brigadier's bark is worse than his bite. I expect you gathered that. Good-bye. I'll keep you informed of events."

As Travers was being carried back towards the camp, he was feeling like a convict reprieved. Then as his fingers went fumblingly towards his glasses, he smiled sardonically. He, of all people, saved by the old school tie. But for that, and a clean bill of health from the Yard, he might have been in the local clink. And then as he neared the camp, the smile went. What he had remembered was the sending of that paper, the typing of his name on it, and the motive that must have laid behind it all. If the million to one chance came off, and George Wharton did come to Shoreleigh, there would be things to relate that would make the old General's eyes pop out like marbles. Which reminded him. Someone else must be told the state of affairs. By hook or crook he must get hold of Lading.

Wherever Travers directed his gaze during the rest of that morning, he saw a something that gave him a kind of cold shiver—those steely grey eyes that held his own. Every time he recalled his own gaucheries, he would wince. Army discipline had always been a fearful and eccentric thing, but in the old days one had been resilient and took what came. Now, in one's years of maturity and with the knowledge that one knew one's job better than the beak before whom one happened to be hauled, there was also the wonder whether it was the beak who might make an ass of both the law and himself.

And, but for a series of happy coincidences—the old school tie, for example, and having had a father, and Colonel Caithby— there might have been something of disaster if circumstantial evidence had alone been taken into account.

"Looking at the matter fairly and squarely," said Travers to himself, "it wouldn't have been a bad break for whoever killed Stirrop if I'd been put out of action for a few days. Which was just what the murderer had in mind when he sent that blasted paper to H.Q. With me out of the way there'd be opportunity to remove various pieces of evidence. And, wait a minute. One or two other little things, I'm beginning to see."

At once he was jotting down ideas as they came, and highly promising they were. Above all, he was glad he had told the Brigadier nothing whatever about Lading, or the queer business of the extra prisoner. In the former he had in any case been bound by secrecy, and the latter was still no fact beyond possibility of doubt.

He settled again to that tray piled with arrears of work. Once or twice he looked through into Winter's room, but he was not there. It was nearly midday when he came in.

'I had a brainwave," he said. "I thought to myself, it'll be a hundred to one that some brass hat or other will be round the camp at any moment, and you know what they always want to see—P.A.D. stuff."

"My hat, yes!" said Travers. "What's this for, and what're you doing about that, and why haven't you got something else."

"Lucky I did go round," Winter said. "Those blasted troops must have scrounged some of the buckets. A couple of stirrup pumps were missing and other stuff had been shifted about. Mafferty's going round now, having a check."

"You're a good fellow," Travers told him, thinking with horror of what might have happened if some officious brass hat had come prowling around. And in the same moment he was realising that he had not been quite fair to Winter—the last person to have been kept in the dark.

Five minutes later a pow-wow was begun in the Commandant's room. Ramble and Mafferty were there, with Winter, but Travers had seen no reason for including Byron.

"We four have got to run this camp now," he said. "It may mean extra work, but we don't mind that, and we haven't got to be too particular about doing the other fellow's job. But what I really wanted to see you all for was to keep you informed and to ask for your help."

He began at the actual method by which Stirrop had been killed. Winter interchanged glances with Ramble.

"You're really sure he was sandbagged?"

"Absolutely certain," Travers said.

"Then I'll tell you something that Ramble and I both noticed this morning. The sand in the buckets had been interfered with. One or two of them definitely hadn't as much in them as they should have had."

"Let's get this clear," Travers said. "We're to assume it was one of the P.W. who contrived somehow to kill the Commandant. That fits in to this extent—it shows why there were no footprints outside. On the other hand, it doesn't explain how on earth the body could have been taken outside and deposited where it was found. Still, leaving that out for the moment, we assume a P.W. decided to kill him by hitting him on the skull with a few pounds of sand in the end of a bag. In order not to raise suspicions, the sand was taken from several buckets. Is that what you're getting at, Winter?"

Winter said it was. P.W. had access to all the fire-points on the ground floor, practically all of which were in the corridors.

They talked that over without getting much further, then Travers came to that vital matter of the man who had entered Winter's room and for some reason or other had stood behind the door. Two things proved that he had been there: the melted snow on the floor, and the stolen document—as Travers described it—from the Adjutant's office.

"I've lost something too," Winter said. "This morning I wanted a list of P.W. divided into categories—you know, Nazi, not-so-Nazi, and all that sort of thing. It wasn't where I'd left it. In fact, I'm sure it isn't in the room at all."

They discussed the usefulness of that and once more arrived nowhere. Then Travers divulged that someone would almost certainly be coming down from the Home Office. Everybody must expect to be questioned, himself included, and there must be no standing on dignity.

Lunch hour had already gone and the conference was dismissed. Travers called Winter back and gave him in the strictest confidence the astounding news of Lading's presence in the camp. Never had he seen a man more surprised, and pleased. Everybody got on well with Lading.

"Wouldn't he have been the very one to have tackled this business?" Winter said. "If he shaved off that beard and got back into uniform, nobody inside would dream of suspecting him."

"I think he's doing better work inside, and so does he, apparently," Travers said. "And about that tunnel, you agree it's best to do nothing till it's well on the way? Lading will keep us informed."

Winter agreed. Travers added a final word.

"What we've both got to do is to be damnably careful how we make contact with him. One careless step and we may land him in the soup. The best policy, in my opinion, is to ignore him. He's a cunning devil, is Lading, he'll get in touch with us if he wants to."

Winter gave a reminiscent smile.

"I'd like to see him in the Mess again, wouldn't you? A tankard of beer, and yarning away. Devil of a chap to yarn."

"All in good time, young feller," said Travers confidently. "All in good time."

But what Travers was thinking when he had gone was of a most peculiar thing. Stirrop had been instantaneously killed. What, then, was that other depression that lay in the snow beyond where the body had been? Could the body have been put in the one place and then moved the few inches into another? And why? Looking at it all ways, Travers knew it made no sense.

## CHAPTER XI
## ENTER A SLEUTH

JUST AFTER FIVE o'clock that evening a telephone call came from Headquarters, Colonel Caithby speaking.

"That you, Captain Travers? I thought you might like to know that Superintendent Wharton is coming down this evening. The Brigadier will see him first, and he should be with you at about eight."

"Very good, sir," said Travers, and no sooner had he replaced the receiver than he knew he should have thanked the Colonel for his good offices that morning, but Travers had been too surprised for clear thinking. Wharton had been put down as a million to one chance, and now he was actually on his way. Three more hours and he would be in the camp.

So Travers took out his notebook, reached for more paper, and began jotting down the things that would have to be told if George were to have an immediate and comprehensive view of the case. More than once in his scribbling he would look up or pause to stoke his pipe with the look of a man who has had good news.

George Wharton—the old General, as the Yard affectionately knew him—was the most likeable personality Ludovic Travers had ever known, and the opinion was not that of a few chance meetings, but the outcome of co-operation in work that often frayed the nerves. Whenever he thought of him, Travers always smiled, for George had always about him something of the forlorn and whimsical, with his harassed pater-familias air of which the vast overhanging moustache was a kind of symbol. And there were his little tricks of showmanship: the asking of leading questions to give triumphant answers, the snorts and grunts to register contempt, and the bland assumptions of ignorance when wishful to conceal.

But no mere mountebank can rise to be Superintendent at the Yard. At his work, Wharton was a bulldog, possessed of enormous patience and tenacity, and with a memory that went incredibly far back. Cross-examination was his speciality, and there his little tricks were his asset, for no man looked more like a patient vendor of vacuum cleaners and less like the tough, go-getting detective of novel and screen. Wharton could wheedle and cajole, he could laugh with them that laughed and mourn with them that mourned, and he could give a sudden look or make a sudden remark that would send as sudden a shiver down the spine of his listener. Of two things only had he been known to boast: that his *métier* should have been the stage, and that he could smell a liar a mile off. Travers could vouch for the truth of both assertions.

Travers, like a nephew waiting a favourite uncle, was all agog that night. His own dinner had been put off and there he was, well before twenty hours, waiting in the comparative cold of the guard hut. At every car that approached he stuck out his head like an amiable secretary bird, and then at long last a car slowed down and he heard George's voice. In Travers's inward eye was at once the dark overcoat, the bowler hat, and that huge walrus moustache.

Travers flashed a torch on himself for the sentry's benefit and made for the car at once. But he was too late. Wharton was on the roadside with his bag, and the car had moved off to reverse.

"Well, well, well," said Wharton, as Travers flashed the torch again. "Here you are, then. All dolled up like a real soldier."

"That's right, George," Travers said, and grasped his hand. "Let's have a look at you."

"Don't flash that damn' thing in my eyes," began Wharton, but he was too late.

"My God!" said Travers. "You're beautiful. Grey coat, grey soft hat. What's happened? Come into money?"

"Just had to see some of the big-wigs," George said modestly. "This is my Sunday rig-out, when there're any Sundays." Then he gave his prodigious grunt. "What're we doing? Staying here all night?"

A waiting guard carried his bag the short distance to the Mess, Travers trying as well as he could in the dark to explain something of the lay-out. Byron and Winter were still in the Mess and were introduced, but what they saw was quite another George Wharton—a burly, dignified, and yet urbane represent-ative of the law.

A short drink and George was taken to Stirrop's room, where Timms had the stove lighted.

"Regular palaces you have here," George said. "No wonder this war's costing seven millions a day."

Travers watched him have what he called a sluice down.

"How'd you get on with the Brigadier, George?"

"Knowledgeable sort of chap," Wharton said. "I liked the other one better. A Colonel Somebody-or-other. Told me you'd been trying your hand out. 'In that case, sir,' I said, 'I might as well go back to town.' He laughed."

"No wonder,'" said Travers dryly. "But to be serious, George, did he give you the outlines of everything?"

"Only this," Wharton said, and rehearsed twice as much as Travers had hoped for. "No suspects, I gathered. Everything nice and blank, ready for me to sign on the dotted line."

Travers hauled him off for dinner. No sooner was it over than he insisted on being taken at once to where the body had been found. The wrapping was removed and he spent a good few minutes with a torch, while Travers shivered in the bitter wind. Then he asked if he might see that office Travers had spoken about, and he was taken to the Commandant's office, which was to be his own.

"Not a bad little spot," he said, and proceeded to light the oil-stove. "And now what about you earning your money for a change? You tell me what happened and what you really think about it—not what you told that Brigadier."

It was nearly eleven o'clock when Travers at last left that office. Wharton had heard all about Lading, the queer case of the extra prisoner, and, in fact, all that Travers could dig up about the case.

"I won't go into your suspects," he mercifully declared. "What I'm going to do is get this camp into my bones. No work till I've met everybody and seen everything."

He took off his antiquated spectacles, replaced them in their even more antiquated case, and then his voice was so honeyed that Travers knew something was in the wind.

"What time did you say the next count was?"

"Seven in the morning," Travers told him.

"Right," he said. "I think I'll be there. Give me a knock at half-past six."

"Knock be damned," said Travers. "What do you think you've got a batman for?"

So in the cold half-light of the following morning four people prepared to take the early count.

"Carry on just as usual, Mr. Pewter," Travers said. "Superintendent Wharton and I will come inside with you, and that's all. Everything's to be done as if we weren't here."

The party moved off. As Sergeant Ebbing unlocked the first door, there was no need to call the room to attention, for each man was standing at the end of his palliasse. Ebbing closed the door and stood by it. Pewter counted.

"Thirteen?"

"Correct, sir," said Ebbing, and out the party went to the passage, and so to the next room. In the officers' room, Friedemann once more made his request for an interview, and Travers instructed that he was to be brought to the Commandant's office at ten. So the count was uneventfully completed, and it was correct. The rooms were unlocked again and the prisoners were free to circulate.

"Anywhere handy here where we can talk," Wharton wanted to know.

The party moved into the store. Wharton asked if it were not a bit risky having so much valuable stuff where prisoners went by the very door.

"Not so risky as you'd think," Travers said. "Only three people have keys: myself, the Quartermaster-Sergeant, and the storeman. Also, since that discovery I told you about on the night of the shot, we've had another lock fitted—this Yale."

Wharton gave a grunt which probably implied that the stable door had as usual been locked after the horse had gone. Then he had a good look at the two locks, and another grunt implied that given two inches of wire and two minutes, and he'd make short work of either.

"One thing other I'd like to clear up," he said. "Sometimes you talk about 'prisoners' and sometimes it's 'internees.' What are these people you've got here?"

Travers explained. These were actual prisoners of war, taken in action. Internees were people interned: enemy aliens, for example. The term 'prisoners' was just a slack way of talking, and it meant any enemy occupants of the camp.

"I've got it," Wharton said. "And now, if all you gentlemen will help, I'll get this count business settled. Mr. Pewter, would you be prepared to swear that there was an extra prisoner on certain occasions when you took the count?"

"Yes, sir. I'm certain there was, sir."

"And you, Sergeant?"

"Yes, sir."

"That sounds good enough," said Wharton genially. "And I take it, like two people who don't like being beaten by anything, you've tried to worry out how it happened. What're your ideas?"

Pewter was only too ready to talk. What he'd arrived at was this, and he drew a rough plan for Wharton's benefit. Let there be four rooms along each corridor, with what might be called an open corridor as a connecting link at the north end. Remember, too, that during the hours of darkness, the corridors were not brightly lighted. Assume, too, that soon after arrival some prisoner had obtained or made a key to his room which, since all the locks were identical, would be a key to each room.

*A* has been counted, the door locked again, and the O.O. and O.S. go *inside* the next room. Then the same with *C*, but, since they are *inside C*, they do not see what happens in the corridor

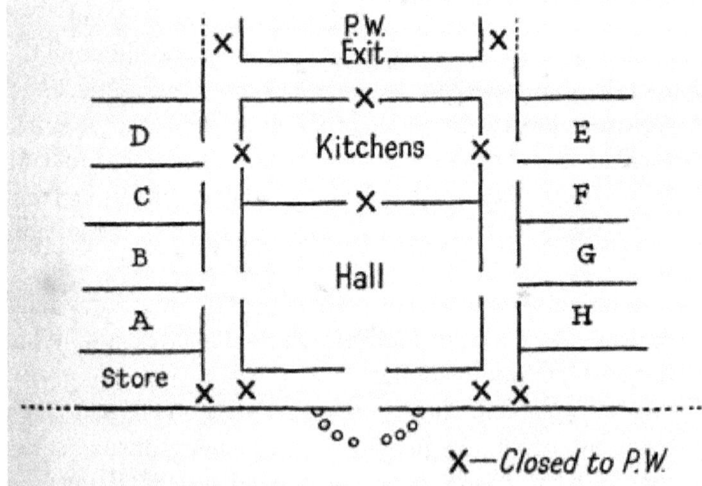

—that the prisoner slips past the door *C*, or it might have been *B*, and lets himself into *D*, or any uncounted room. There he is counted again, and hence the milk in the coconut.

"Yet, but don't you know how many should be in each room?" asked Wharton.

Travers explained about the hospital, though that did not excuse the undoubted absence of method there had been over the count. Also, it seemed an easy job to count a mere seventy-three prisoners in very few rooms. Dowling had got the count wrong and then had made it come right, so he had on this first occasion assumed that he himself had been wrong. On the second occasion he had been of another opinion, and then action had been taken to ensure that there could be no mistake. But it had been the late Commandant who had taken that count, and as he had preferred to trust his own memory, he had ignored the foolproof method, and the count had been wrong. After his second, and correct, count, he had been fired at and had narrowly escaped being killed.

"That's all clear," Wharton said. "Ever since the proper precautions have been taken there's been no extra prisoner. And there can't be any jiggery-pokery in the hospital because an orderly sleeps there. And now about the night of the shot. This prisoner with the key didn't slip into another room so as to make the count go wrong. He slipped in here."

"No, sir, not at first," Pewter said. "He went into another room first and was counted twice. Then he slipped back to his own room for the second count, and as soon as his room was counted, he took a shot at the Commandant—"

"Wait a moment," said Wharton, consulting the plan. "The Commandant was shot at when he was outside *H*, and presumably whoever shot him did so from round the corner of the open corridor near *E*. Then why did the prisoner not slip back at once to his own room? Why should he come in here?"

"He certainly did come in here," said Travers.

"Yes, but why? What was the natural procedure for you people after the shot? Why, to call out the guard and have every room searched. Catch that prisoner here, and he'd be done for."

"As I see it, it's like this," Travers said. "He did come in here, for we saw the unmelted snow off his boots. I told you about that last night. Then we went back to his room. That's what happened, even if it doesn't make sense. Don't ask me why, or how he got a key to this room, because I don't know."

"How do you know he went back to his room? There wasn't a third count taken?"

"He wasn't to know there wouldn't be," Travers said. "He simply had to be back in his room."

"I see. And nothing's missing from here."

"That's quite right," Travers said. "We can find no earthly reason why he should have slipped in here at all."

"And about this melted snow. You think it came off the Commandant's boots, or the Sergeant-Major's, and the prisoner picked it up on his own boots. But if the prisoner is clever enough to have a key to here, and the rooms, why shouldn't he have one to take him outside by the back door?"

He gave a look of complacent inquiry.

"The doors closed well before dusk," Travers said. "After that it's under the direct observation of a sentry."

Wharton grunted.

"Well, we'll leave that for a bit. Now one question to you, Mr. Pewter. Just why do you think all this extra prisoner business was done? Nobody's escaped from the camp?"

"My idea is this, sir," Pewter told him promptly. "I think it was a rag on the part of one of the officers. Two or three of them are just twerps, sir; you can see that by the sneering way they look at you. I think one of them did it to show how clever he was."

That was all. Wharton did say he would like a word with Ebbing if he wouldn't mind waiting outside.

"I didn't like to hurt that young officer's feelings," he said to Travers, "but he was talking pure tripe. Answer me this, if you can."

"All right, George, but don't glare at me."

Wharton grunted. "Answer me this. What's the best use of keys in a place like this? To get out—isn't that so?"

"I thought I was to do the answering," Travers said mildly. "But you're right. And you're going on to ask why a prisoner should give himself away by using for a rag what would be a vital thing if he wanted to escape."

"Oh?" glared Wharton. "Then answer me this. Was the shot all part of the rag? Nearly got him, didn't it? And suppose it had really got him. What advantage would that confer on the prisoner who did the shooting?" He made a noise that sounded like the most profound and contemptuous disgust. "Ask the sergeant to come back for a minute."

In came Ebbing, looking none too happy. He was a huge lump of a man, concerning whom Byron once remarked that if he were boiled down he would make the nucleus of a brewery.

"You're a re-enlisted man?" Wharton fired at him.

"Yes, sir," said Ebbing nervously.

"Patriotism, or safety?"

Ebbing's mouth gaped. He obviously didn't get it.

"Last May," Wharton said waggishly, "you were a witness at the Old Bailey in a certain arson case—and I've heard better witnesses. So had the judge."

Ebbing licked his lips.

"Well, got any fresh ideas about this extra prisoner business?" asked Wharton amiably. "Anything you didn't like to say in front of the officer?"

Ebbing licked his lips again, then said he hadn't.

"Right," said Wharton, and look a step forward. "I'm holding nothing against you, neither is Captain Travers, while you do your job here. You got that?"

Ebbing said he had. Another lick of the lips, some sort of a salute, and he departed.

"Nothing like having a memory," Wharton announced complacently. "When I was on Intelligence in the last war I walked into a little café at Rouen and sat down right against a bloke I'd wanted for months. When I said, 'How's the printing trade these days, Charlie?' you ought to have seen his face. It was a picture. So it was when I stood him a drink. Which reminds me. When do I get any breakfast?"

Travers led the way out, and towards the Mess. "And what after breakfast?" he asked.

"Oh, I don't know," Wharton said in that non-committal tone which meant he had something already up his sleeve. "I think I'll just mooch round and see what there is to see. Nothing like knowing your way about."

Travers went on to the office and found him a set of keys that would admit him anywhere, and wrote an official pass to admit and pass out at all hours.

After breakfast Travers left the old General reading the *Telegraph*, and got to work on the morning's mail. Miss Dance arrived only five minutes late, and once she was at work too, he settled down to something he had promised Wharton—a list of suspects with comments. Between 'phone calls and callers he got his rough notes down, and then typed them himself, well out of the way of Miss Dance's inquisitive peerings:

> DULLING.—If Stirrop had known family history, D. would almost certainly have been dismissed. S. always harping on spies and aliens, and mouthing against "the old Bosche." If D. lost the job, he lost £1 a day. £365 not bad for a job done between surgeries and visits. Suggest find out: (*a*) D's financial position, (*b*) How he got the job.
>
> BYRON.—Loathed S. Had been publicly insulted by him at various times, and virtually put under arrest. Expressed himself to me as at the end of his tether, and proposing to take the law into his own hands. Had also the welfare and treatment of own officers to consider. S. often gave them very bad time.
>
> DOWLING and PEWTER—*See* Byron.
>
> TESTER.—A queer fish. Near camp that night and brazenly entered with D. Why? Lied about it to me. Jealous of S. Had threatened to sock his jaw.
>
> MAFFERTY.—Worst grievance of all. No alibi. Under influence of drink at 20.15. Brainiest man in camp.

N.B.—Cases stated are *against*, not for. Additional suspects:

Extra Prisoner.—???

Ebbing.—? Had been unmercifully rated by S.

Then Travers began to wonder about Ramble, He certainly had grievances, and was the kind of one to stick at nothing. As he lay back in his chair, eyes closed, Travers could hear Ramble at reminiscences of the last war—all of them obviously true and unadorned. "I simply let him have it clean in the guts, sir." "One of our chaps threw a bomb and I threw another, and blew the bastard's head clean off."

"Yes," thought Travers, "Ramble wouldn't worry about a little thing like a crack on the skull. And yet somehow it isn't quite in keeping. A bullet in the belly some dark night—yes. But not creeping up behind with a sandbag. And Ramble was the one person who could never be suspected of having fired that shot in the corridor."

So Travers decided to leave Ramble out. He was even sorry he had put down Mafferty, and yet it was better to let Wharton know all rather than cast suspicion by trying to conceal.

The 'phone bell went. Wharton, using his more unctuous tone, was asking if he might see Miss Dance. There was a letter to dictate for one thing. Then might he see Ramble and Mafferty.

Miss Dance went off in a flutter and came back beaming. Wharton had a way with women. Most thought him "an old darling," and Bertha Dance was no exception, except that she considered him "rather a duck." In the interval Travers had seen Friedemann and had conveyed to that gentleman in no uncertain terms that the camp was entirely under new management.

Wharton was not in to lunch, and the Mess orderly said he had left a message that he might not be back before dark.

"He was wandering round the hutments about an hour ago," Dowling said. "I asked one of the men who it was and he said he thought it was a new manager for the N.A.A.F.I."

Travers laughed. "I must tell him that."

"I like him," Byron said. "I ran across him and we had a bit of a yarn together. Then he went on inside the building, by the way. Didn't seem to give a cuss about being alone with the prisoners."

"Did you see the snowballing this morning, sir?" asked Dowling.

"What snowballing was that?"

"The old Hun. Having a regular romp in the yard. I didn't know he could be so frivolous."

"The Hun has his moments," Travers said.

Later that afternoon he mentioned that snowballing to Winter. Winter wasn't up to the game, so Travers explained.

"It's to do with that tunnel. They've got to dispose of the earth somewhere. You know the usual method, to carry it out of the room in their pockets and scatter it outside. They can't do that because it would be seen on the snow, so they've been faking a game of snowballs and hiding the earth under the snow."

"I say, that's ingenious," Winter said. "And funny. Doing all those comic tricks and thinking we don't know. It's a pity we can't get them red-handed at it."

"All in good time," smiled Travers. "Let 'em go on sweating blood for a bit, and then when we're ready, we'll pounce. Or when Lading's ready."

"I saw him this morning," Winter said. "Gave him a chance to make a sign, but the crafty devil never batted an eyelid."

Travers, feeling quite another man as things now stood, felt also a new appreciation of Winter, and he gave him a rough idea of what had happened at that interview with the Brigadier. Travers had told the yarn as rather a joke. Winter was most indignant.

"If I'd been there I'd have told him your alibi was all right," he said. "I think it was damn' cheek. And there'd be a row if you reported it."

"I don't know," Travers said. "It's just as well to have been given a clean bill of health. Besides, when we get down to brass tacks, you couldn't prove I was in my room all the time."

"I could go very near it," Winter said, and smiled to himself. "At about eight o'clock you did something I'd never heard you do before. I nearly hollered through to ask if you'd come into money."

"What was I doing?"

"You were humming 'Roll out the barrel.'"

"Good Lord, so I was!"

"Then at about a quarter past you changed the tune. It was, 'There'll always be an England.'"

Travers laughed. "Patriotic sort of cove. Anything else?"

Winter shook his head.

"I don't know that there was. Wait a minute, though. I remember glancing at the time to see how far off a quarter to nine it was, and I heard you stoke up the fire."

"That's right," beamed Travers. "You and I'll tell that to the Brigadier if he does any more funny business."

Winter said he must get back to work. The cards had gone and the prisoners' accounts were all in order. All he had to do was make out for W.O. another list like the one that had been stolen.

"That was a remarkable business," Travers said frowningly. "What use could it be to anybody?"

"To the prisoners themselves, the very devil of a lot of use." pointed out Winter. "It had the names of the four secret anti-Nazis on it. If our local Gestapo has got hold of it, those four are in for the hell of a time."

"We'll see to that," Travers said grimly. "All the same, it's remarkably strange. Whichever way you turn in this case you run up against prisoners. That extra prisoner business, and now this, and what's more, I think Stirrop was killed inside the building. And we know he was shot at by a prisoner."

"It's got me beat," Winter said. "Still, perhaps the Superintendent will get hold of something that we haven't seen. By the way, now things are a bit slacker, I thought I'd go down town after tea."

"My dear fellow, do," Travers said promptly. "You've been sticking to things too closely as it is."

Just before six o'clock Colonel Caithby rang Travers to say there were certain items connected with Stirrop's funeral arrangements he would like to discuss. Winter was still in the Mess and said Travers might have his car. He was going down town with Byron.

It was seven o'clock when Travers got back, and who should be waiting at the office but Winter.

"I changed my mind about going down town," he said. "The most extraordinary thing has happened."

# CHAPTER XII
# EXIT LADING

THE FACT THAT Byron was going down town in his car had made Winter alter his arrangements. Winter did have a job of work to do in Shoreleigh, but he promptly arranged to meet Byron for dinner, and then to do a cinema and come back to camp together. But Byron could not start out till later than Winter had intended, so he decided to write a hasty letter or two in his room and catch the last post with them in Shoreleigh.

It was while Winter was writing that he heard the tap on the door. Thinking it was Sniffy, he called a "Come in," and went on with his writing. Then a voice said quietly, "Hallo, Winter. What's happened to Travers?"

It was Lading, still in his prisoner's clothes, and carrying a handbag which he set down just inside the door.

"Good God!" said Winter, startled out of his life. "How the devil did you get here?"

Lading reached out and switched off the light. The oil-stove made a certain glow in the room.

"Just used those keys Travers gave me," Lading said.

"But how the devil did you get through the gates without a sentry seeing you!"

"Ways and means," Lading told him laconically.

"And how did you know Travers had told me about you?"

"He'd have to after what happened to Stirrop," Lading said. "Besides, there was the way you looked at me this morning. You can take these keys, by the way. I shan't be needing them again."

"What're you going to do, then?"

"First of all, have a shave. Cold water'll do. You keep *cave* at the door. Is this black-out effective?"

Winter said it was, but he had a look from outside to make sure. Lading unlocked his bag and got out shaving tackle. The beard was scissored, then removed, and then Lading was careful to sweep up every hair. Winter put them in a foolscap envelope, and said he'd stuff them down the Mess stove.

"When's Travers likely to be back?" Lading wanted to know.

"Couldn't say," Winter told him. "If you like to hide under that bed or something, I'll ring him at H.Q. and make out he's urgently wanted."

"Can't wait," Lading said, shaking his head. "What I'd like you to do now is to fetch me a suit of battle-dress. You've got some in your store, haven't you?"

"But I haven't got a key," Winter told him. "Tell you what I'll do. I'll try and get hold of the Quartermaster-Sergeant and borrow his on some pretext or other."

Lading shook his head again.

"Too damn' risky. Besides, I've got to be in Shoreleigh soon after seven. You've got a car, haven't you?"

Winter explained, then had a brainwave.

"If you're game, I'll tell you what you can do. I'm supposed to be going down town in five minutes' time with Byron—you remember him? The guard officer. He'll draw up his car outside the Mess and I'll make an excuse to send him somewhere for a minute and you can slip in at the back. He'll never dream of looking behind. When he gets down town, you can slip out at some of the traffic lights, I'll say I've been detained here and I'm coming down to meet him later in my own car when Travers brings it back."

"Sounds good to me," Lading said. "But you'd better lend me a waterproof of sorts and a civilian hat."

Winter handed over his own at once.

"Anything else you want?"

"I could do with three inches of whisky," Lading told him.

"Nip under that bed, then," Winter said, "and I'll slip round to the Mess. I'm afraid you'll have to gulp it."

Lading had his drink while Winter listened at the door for the sound of Byron's car.

"Any urgent message for Travers?" Winter asked.

"Not much," Lading said. "I've finished inside, and next time he sees me, whenever that is, I'll be coming through the front gate. Just tell him I've made some useful contacts which I'm going to try out. Oh, and that tunnel's off. There's an idea that someone's blown the gaff"—he gave a wink at that—"which may be one reason why I skipped."

Winter held up a warning hand and switched off the light.

"Watch out from here," he whispered. "I'll be standing by the car and the near side door will be open. When you see me look up at the sky, nip along like a streak."

Everything went according to plan. Winter threw an old rug into the back. Byron came out and was told about the new arrangements, but Winter added that as he had something to do at Main Guard he might as well ride that far.

At the gate the car drew up. Byron gave the usual holler and the voice was recognised. The gates were opened, Winter slipped out, and off the car shot towards the town.

That was the astounding news that Travers heard when he got back that evening.

"And he didn't tell you where to get hold of him?" he asked Winter.

"He didn't give even an inkling of what he was going to do," Winter told him. "I gathered he'd be turning up here in due course. Mind you, he hadn't much time to say a thing. You wouldn't believe how queer it all was. And all over in about ten minutes. You ought to have seen him hack that beard off!" Then he gave a look of comical dismay as he felt his pocket. "My God, I've forgotten to burn the hair!"

"Drop it in the stove when you go in," Travers said. "But it's most exasperating about Lading. The one thing I wanted to do was contrive a meeting between him and Wharton."

"I wouldn't worry," Winter said. "He's the cleverest devil unhung—and the most erratic. For all we know he might turn up to-night. Which reminds me. You'll have to square the night count."

"My hat, yes!" said Travers, and smiled. "You're a damn-good feller at times. Always hauling me out of holes before I fall in 'em. And now you slip off or you'll be late down town."

"I think I will." He turned at the door, a look of amusement on his face. "Do you know, wherever we are to-night I'll be expecting him to turn up. You know how he used to pop up from nowhere, with his, 'Hallo, the gang!'"

"Yes, he's a great chap," said Travers. "Hope to heaven Byron doesn't take it into his head to look in the back of the car."

Winter chuckled. "If he did, you bet Lading'd swing clear somehow. And, my hat, wouldn't he give the old Bosche a time if ever he was a prisoner in Germany!" Out he went, still chuckling, then gave a last look back. "Don't forget squaring the count."

"And don't forget to burn that envelope," countered Travers. "And, hi! Was Superintendent Wharton in the Mess?"

"Who's taking my name in vain?" said the familiar voice, and Wharton himself walked in. "What's the excitement? And what's the idea of being in here?"

Travers took him to his own room and told just what had happened. Wharton was quite indifferent.

"If he's half as clever as you make out, he's told you all he knows you ought to know," was his comment. "And if he tells you, it's the same as telling me."

Then he gave a grunt of profound disapproval. "There weren't such goings on in Intelligence in my day. What *is* this? A camp or a penny-dreadful? Hiding in backs of cars and all that damn-rubbish."

"You're just peevish," Travers told him. "Been gadding about too much down town. Got traveller's headache probably. And where exactly have you been?"

A certain unction at once crept into Wharton's tone

"Oh, just having a look round. Getting my bearings, so to speak. I did have a word or two with a couple of our men from the Special Branch."

Travers stared. "What're they doing here?"

"Didn't you pass on a message from that—what's his name? Lading—about the Italian consulate here? Well, what do you think we did. Shaved off our beards and hid in the backs of cars?" He snorted. "Got a couple of men down and had the place under observation inside four hours. That's what we did."

"Good for you," Travers told him.

"They give you a good lunch at the Royal," went on Wharton complacently.

Travers stared again. "Never knew you go in for lunches at four-and-a-kick a time. Cup of tea and a doughnut's more your line."

"The Government pays," Wharton told him amusedly. "Also I wanted to clap eyes on a man called Tester whom you mentioned last night."

He peered up, looking for applause. Travers laughed.

"Always catching me out, George. A whetstone for your wits, as the Bard has it. And now get the city grime off your face and meet me in the Mess. I've a quick job of work in the office."

What he did was to ring guard company orderly-room, and leave an urgent message. The Orderly Officer and Orderly Provost to be informed at once that a prisoner, Beckner by name, had left camp under Commandant's supervision and the count would therefore be only seventy-two. A chit was sent to Ramble by a runner, and a message was left on Mafferty's table to the effect that there would be one less prisoners' rations as from that date.

As he walked across to the Mess, Travers wondered if he had done right. Two courses had been open to him in that matter of Lading's departure. He might have announced the escape of a prisoner. That would have meant disciplinary action against the rest, as the confining in their rooms and a general search. There would have been a lot of talk among the troops, and something would have leaked out to the Press, and then W.O. enquiries would have come down, and the whole business would have been a living up to and remembering a whole series of lies and subterfuges. So the second course seemed far better. If Byron discovered that no prisoner had passed out through the main gate, and began asking awkward questions, he could be told tactfully to mind his own affairs. As for the prisoners, they could be left guessing. In a game of bluff of that sort, he could always win. Besides, if Lading was not going back inside, what did it matter what Friedemann and his gang either thought or suspected?

Travers saw Wharton approaching and slipped into his hand that list of suspects and comments.

"Put that in your pocket, George."

"What is it?" asked Wharton jocularly. "A tip?"

"Maybe," said Travers. "But not the kind you're thinking of."

There was a special darts' competition in the N.A.A.F.I. hut that night, with Dowling and Pewter both performing, so Wharton and Travers had the Mess to themselves. The Mess orderly on duty even asked if he would be wanted any more. Travers had drinks brought in, and sent him off.

It was cosy in that little room, with a blazing fire and comfortable chairs. Travers, after dinner, had *The Times* crossword expectantly on his lap, and it was Wharton who began talking about the case.

"I got some quite good prints of that Captain Tester," he said. "Sent them off to the Yard with the others."

"You're a quick mover," said Travers admiringly. "But what others?"

Wharton glanced round and lowered his voice.

"Byron's, the other two officers', Mafferty's and Ebbing's."

"Good Lord!" said the horrified Travers. "You sending officers' fingerprints to the Yard!"

"Why not?" asked Wharton unconcernedly. "You're not ham-stringing me with any of that old school tie bunkum. These are queer times, aren't they?" He gave a snort. "I remember in the last war, just before Messines—" He broke off. "Still, we needn't worry about that now. Where'd I put that paper you gave me?"

He found it, adjusted those antiquated spectacles, peered at Travers over their tops like a suspicious gnome, then began to read. The first grunt arrived.

"I saw the doctor this morning. Quiet little chap. And how do you expect me to find out how he got his job?"

"As Lading was always saying, there're ways and means."

Wharton grinned again and resumed his reading. Strange to say there were no more comments beyond the inevitable question why Travers had not put the case *for* his list.

"That's soon done," Travers said. "As a matter of fact, I've given you most of my objections already." He thought for a moment. "Dulling, we'll leave *sub judice*, as it were. I can't say anything on behalf of Tester except that you could have access to his record at W.O. You ought to know enough about the three guard officers if you've got so pally as to be able to purloin their fingerprints. Ebbing you know more about than I do, except that I wouldn't trust him farther than I can throw a battleship. Mafferty's the danger. He stands out yards. He's a genius at his job, which means he's got brains, but I just happen to think he wouldn't have killed Stirrop in quite that way. If he did kill him, I'd swear in any court of law that he had more than abundant provocation."

"Nevertheless he's got something on his mind," Wharton said doggedly. "I couldn't have been more genial but he wouldn't meet me half-way."

"Don't misunderstand me, George. Mafferty doesn't speak the same language as you and I. He's dyed-in- the-wool Service, and his life's governed by it. As for having something on his mind, you might have if you guessed you were under suspicion of murder."

Then he changed the subject, not wishing to seem too partisan.

"Here's a paper I'd like you to look at, George. I don't know if I mentioned it, but it was the private writing among Stirrop's possessions that intrigued me. Tell me what you make of it. But first of all I should say that he must have written it on the day he was killed. You'll gather that for yourself."

Wharton adjusted his specs. again and began reading aloud.

> Ring W.O. . . . See if Harry Cross still B.C. . . . Get 'phone num . . . (Garrison?) *Weinholst* but what about beard. Mention Trav. . . . Two birds one stone. After to-night.

Wharton frowned away, then read it to himself a second time. Then he waved an impatient hand.

"Don't tell me Let me find out for myself. I'm not such a fool about the Army as you'd think."

"Ring War Office—that's easy. See if Harry Cross—why call him by his Christian name?"

"That shows he's some old Army pal of Stirrop's," Travers said. "Someone who either soldiered with him or was out in Burma with him."

Wharton grunted. "That's it, is it? Harry Cross still at B.C. . . ."

"Border Command," put in Travers. "In other words, some brass hat pal of Stirrop's at Border Command, Beauchester."

"H'm!" went on Wharton. "Get his phone number. Obviously in order to talk to him. Doesn't say what about. Then what's this *Garrison?* in brackets?"

"Local headquarters, where you saw the Brigadier."

"What's that got to do with what went before?"

"Ask me another," Travers said. "The only thing I can think of is that he needn't have rung W.O. to get the 'phone number of Border Command. Local Garrison H.Q. would be bound to have it."

"Well, it's working out," Wharton said complacently. "Now there's this German name—Weinholst, underlined. Any prisoner of that name in camp?"

Travers shook his head. "No, but that isn't to say one of them hasn't a different name from the one we've got on his card."

"Several of the prisoners have beards," Wharton said reminiscently. "We might do worse than follow that up."

But he didn't indicate how, as Travers somewhat cynically thought. He went on with his reading instead.

"Mention Travers. That's you. Who to? And why?"

"Heavens knows," Travers said. "All I do know is that he'd have been mighty glad to see me out of his camp, and—*de mortuis* be damned—he'd have done any dirty trick to achieve that object." He gave a Whartonian grunt. "Such as mentioning my imperfections to Command behind my back."

"Then who are the two birds to be killed with one stone? You're one. Who's the other?"

"As I see it, there weren't two birds," said Travers, quick as ever with a theory. "The two birds to be killed with one stone were that when he rang up Cross he could also put in some quiet word against me."

"Really as bad as that, was he?"

Travers made a gesture of impatience.

"I thought I'd knocked that into your head, George. He was what young Pewter would elegantly call a twerp of the first water."

Wharton gave a shrug of his shoulders.

"Well, that middle part about Weinholst doesn't make sense to me. There's no continuity. Why drag him in when you're the main topic?"

"Stirrop's brains—those he had—were woolly. They went off at tangents. He always was a muddled thinker. These notes are merely an example."

"Well, I'll take your word for it," said Wharton. "Then what's this about after to-night?"

"I don't know," Travers admitted. "I can guess, but that wouldn't be much good. At a quarter to nine that night, he was having a mysterious interview with Winter. I told you he talked about people to others and I think he was going to try to get some—what he might think—damning evidence about me from Winter, ready to hand out the next day to Border Command. Hoped they'd refer back to Midland Command. As you know, that interview didn't take place."

That was that. Wharton asked if he might keep the paper, then tried another tack.

"Just go over quickly what happened to yourself that night. Start at when you went to your office after dinner."

Travers went over it all again, with emphasis on that perfect alibi with which Winter had provided him. It was not till he arrived at the discovery behind Winter's door that he was interrupted.

"Just a minute. This melted snow behind the door. Could that have blown in when Winter went out to the Commandant's office?"

"Oh, no," Travers said. "Winter had forgotten the time and when he saw it was a quarter to, he must have fairly shot out. The door slammed to behind him. There wasn't a second for snow to have blown in."

"And while he was gone? Couldn't someone else have heard the slam and slipped in then?"

"That's the idea," said Travers, and his fingers went to his glasses. Then he shook his head.

"It wouldn't take a minute to get to that office from his own. Say two minutes if he waited to see if Stirrop would turn up. And I can tell you this. When he sprinted out he was in the middle of writing a card. The ink was still wet when he got back again."

"That's good enough for me," Wharton said. "We assume the man came in while you were both out. And now that list that was stolen from Winter's room. What's the exact use of it?"

Travers would much rather have told Wharton the use of the paper that had been stolen from his own room, and then, while he was explaining about the camp victimisation of non-Nazis, Byron and Winter turned up.

"Good Lord!" said Travers. "I ought to have been in bed half an hour ago."

"Don't go yet," Byron said. "Have a drink instead."

"You all have one with me," Wharton said. "What's it to be?"

The drinks were poured and glasses raised. Travers scribbled a Mess chit for Wharton to sign, and the four gathered round the fire.

"Damn-fine dinner they give you at the Golden Ball," Winter said. "We tried it to-night."

"The pictures any good?" asked Wharton.

"A lovely one," Byron said. "Best spy picture I've seen. That chap Veidt is frightfully good. Not much in your line, sir."

"I don't know," Wharton said "Mr.—I beg his pardon—Captain Travers and all of you seem to think I'm a back number. The Army hasn't moved all that far since my day."

"Oh, yes it has, George," said Travers feelingly.

Wharton bridled up.

"How has it?"

Travers suddenly smiled. "Well, you've just stood us all a drink. Isn't that so?"

"Yes," said Wharton blankly.

"Well, what you did was contrary to regulations. Implicit Army Orders are that there's to be no standing of drinks in any Mess."

There was a laugh. Wharton laughed last.

"Good. Then you can give me back that chit I signed."

He was pleased with himself at that.

"Still, talking of spies, there was a time when I'd have thought those yarns all bunkum. Now I'll spin you a real yarn, and every word of it's true. It was when I was attached to the 154th French Infantry Brigade near Messines in '16. I began that tale to Captain Travers earlier to-night, but somehow we got off it. Well, there was a certain officer joined our little headquarters a couple of days before the attack. A very charming fellow he was . . ."

Travers stirred himself to realise he had dozed off. For how long he couldn't tell, but he was in time for the dénouement.

"Now whoever would have supposed that fellow was a Hun? Even the Froggies took him as read. And every word I've told you is dead true."

"Extraordinary!" Winter said.

"I don't know," put in Byron. "A week or so ago we had a letter from my brother who's in France, with the Royal Sussex. He was saying . . ."

Travers had managed to get to his feet, and was beaming a sleepy good-night.

"I think I'll leave you coves to it. Someone's got to be up in the morning, and I reckon it'll be me."

# CHAPTER XIII
## SABBATH WELL SPENT

You may or may not remember that it was stated that to Ludovic Travers all days in No. 54 Prisoner of War Camp were alike, so that he often lost track of the week, except perhaps on Fridays, which were pay-days for troops.

Perhaps at the time you said to yourself something like this. "There's something I can't quite swallow. Perhaps an adjutant is a busier man than he was in my time, but I can't exactly believe he's as busy as all that." Now ask yourself an honest question. But for the heading of this chapter, would you have known that when Travers woke the following morning, it was Sunday?

Travers himself didn't realise it for a moment or two. It was just a difference in the camp sounds, and, somewhere a long way off, a tolling bell, that warned him what day it was. Then his thoughts ran on something like this. *I must read up the last batch of Army Council Instructions. Wonder what Torquemada will be like in the* Observer? *I ought to check those P.W. accounts. Was it twelve or twelve-thirty I said I'd ring Bernice? Must have been twelve-thirty on account of taking the count. Must tell B. about Wharton. Wonder what time he got to bed last night?, etc., etc., etc.*

On his way to the Mess, he looked in on Wharton. Timms, who had been assigned to him as batman, was just coming out, and there the old General was, sitting up in bed and sipping away at a cup of hot tea.

"What time did you get to bed?" Travers asked him. "You didn't keep those people up all night?"

"They cleared off soon after you went," Wharton said. "I turned in soon after three."

"Three! What on earth were you doing?"

"I woke that telephone orderly in your office, had the 'phone put through to my place and then rang up a few people."

"The devil you did!" said Travers. "Not private calls?"

"The Government pays," said Wharton philosophically. "But as a matter of fact I kept to business. Which reminds me. Intelligence are ringing you up at nine sharp this morning. Don't ask me what for. Sunday, isn't it?"

"By the calendar," Travers told him laconically.

"Any difference does it make here?"

"Some of the troops may go to church. Miss Dance has a holiday. Now I'm acting-Commandant I can treat myself to a holiday this afternoon if I want one. What about my standing you a lunch in town?"

"Can't be done," Wharton said, putting the empty cup on the side-table, and wiping his moustache with vast sweeps of a handkerchief. "As a matter of fact, Ramble said the Sergeants' Mess would be highly honoured if I'd have dinner there to-day. I take it your lunch is their dinner."

Travers had to laugh. "That's your version, George. I'll bet a fiver you wheedled and wangled the whole damn' thing."

Wharton chuckled.

"One way of killing a cat is choking it with cream. Besides, I have to be friendly, don't I? How can I get to know the place if I don't meet people?"

"You needn't apologise," Travers told him. "All I suggest is you don't let them catch you collecting fingerprints. I suppose, by the way you've added Timms's to the collection."

"No," said Wharton blandly. "Timms is a very useful man. He's told me quite a lot."

"Such as?'

"Well, he and the Mess orderlies between them have provided me with Stirrop's movements that night. Like to see?"

His notebook was actually under his pillow.

"I keep it there," he said. "Might wake up in the night and think of something. Here it is. Bottom half of this page."

07.55 Rang Mess Orderly. Ordered stiff rum, hot.
08.00 Drank rum. Swore because too hot.
08.05 Left mess. Timms in room. Found scarf for S. S. changed to thicker boots.

08.12 S. looked impatiently at watch. Cleared Timms out.
08.15 Mess O. thought saw S. going towards building.

"Convey anything to you?" Wharton asked.

"Not much," Travers said. "It's confirmatory rather than anything else."

"You don't think he went across to the building to have a private look at the prisoner he suspected of being Weinholst?"

Travers's fingers went to his glasses.

"I have an idea. It wouldn't be time for the count and the prisoners would be in the hall. *After to-night*, that's what he wrote."

Then he began blinking away as he polished his glasses.

"That makes a complication. Last night I thought of what he meant about killing two birds with one stone. This would make *three* birds. Wait a minute and I'll explain.

"It's like this, really. I ought to have told you that, besides having a down on me, Stirrop was also fed up with Winter."

"Why?"

"Well, the more I look into things, I realise we weren't Stirrop's kind. I'll wager that when he got rid of us two, he was going to wangle two of his pals into our jobs. He actually told me on the day he was killed, that Winter wouldn't be much longer in the camp. I haven't the slightest doubt that he told Winter the same thing about me. That's why I now think that Winter and I were the two birds he was going to kill. Weinholst would have been a third bird." He was shrugging his shoulders as he replaced his glasses. "Still, as I told you, he was incapable of thinking consecutively for more than two seconds at a time. When he wrote *two* birds, he might have been taking the third for granted."

Travers took a peep into next door where Winter was shaving.

"I didn't get a chance to ask you last night. Everything O.K. about Lading?"

"Must have been," Winter said. "Byron didn't say a thing. But I didn't half have the wind up. You know that rug I chucked in behind for Lading to get under? That was the one Byron puts over his radiator in cold weather."

Travers smiled. "I'll bet Lading hopped out at one of the traffic lights."

"You bet he did," Winter said feelingly. "And then there was something else. When he went to his car to come home, Byron flashed his torch behind to put the rug back, then he said, 'What clumsy devil's been in here with snow all over his feet?' I said I thought it was me when I got in the back by mistake."

"All's well that ends well," Travers said, and then peeped in again. "Intelligence are ringing me at nine. I'll let you know what it's all about."

"Good Lord! I nearly forgot something myself." Winter said. "The telephone people rang yesterday and said you'd complained again about the 'phone. They're coming to fix it."

It was well after nine when that call came through. A Major Carterson was speaking.

"Superintendent Wharton gave me to understand that a prisoner named Beckner has left your camp. We rather expected him here. You have no more news?"

"None at all, sir."

"I see. And one other thing. When you rang us the other day you said you were speaking on behalf of Beckner, and you gave certain information about two prisoners, Scribbnitz and Stein. Can you send those two up here?"

"Yes, sir. When?"

"Straightaway. We'll take 'em over at Liverpool Street."

"Very good, sir. Is that all?"

"That's all, thank you. Good-bye."

Travers cursed under his breath. Just the sort of thing that would happen on a Sunday. Two minutes later he was looking into Winter's office and finding him there.

"Take a short holiday?"

He explained. Two prisoners would have to have an officer escort. Pewter was on duty, and one could hardly call on Dowling. Byron might like to go, but why not Winter himself? With luck the eleven-fifteen could be caught, and Winter could have a night in town and come back at his leisure in the morning. Winter thought it over, then said he'd love it.

"You'd better get across and warn the two prisoners then," Travers said. "I'll lend a hand with documents and accounts and so on."

There was transport to fix up, an armed escort, the R.T.O. to ring, rations to arrange and railway vouchers to write. It was a quarter to eleven when the party left, and Travers had a breather. Word came through that the train had been caught, and then Liverpool Street had to he warned. Travers stoked his pipe, settled at last to his A.C.I.'s and then saw that in two minutes he was due for midday Commandant's count. Then there was kitchen inspection and Staff Quarters, and another morning had gone. Of Wharton there had been never a sign.

Alter lunch Pewter dozed for a few minutes in an easy chair across in the far corner of the Mess. Then he woke, wondered if he had been snoring, and disappeared. Travers, with the room to himself, seized both *Observer* and *Sunday Times*, and prepared for a lazy afternoon. An hour went over the beginnings of Torquemada and then Wharton appeared.

"Going to sleep it off?" Travers suggested craftily.

"When I go out to lunch I behave myself," Wharton said, good-humouredly. "Nice lot of fellows in that Mess. Did me well, too." He peered from under his shaggy old eyebrows. "Like to see something interesting?"

"Not particularly," Travers told him. "Depends on what it is."

"Well, you just step across to your office," Wharton said. "I might interest you."

On the way he began asking questions. Was he right in saying that on the night Stirrop was killed, the 'phone had gone phut? And was it the only 'phone? In other words, were the others only extensions from which people could ring only to Travers's office. And was the 'phone often going wrong?

Travers said yes to them all, and he gave the 'phone a bad name. Not only did it go wrong but always when it was most needed. That one night was not an exception. The telephone people had tinkered with it, but never really got at the seat of the trouble. They were coming again, probably in the morning.

"Well, have a look at this," Wharton said.

The main entry wire came from a wall bracket outside the window of Ramble's upstair room, which lay above Winter's. Some sort of rough repair seemed to have been done at some time.

"Two ends have been joined," Travers said.

"That isn't the point," said Wharton triumphantly. "We're not so much concerned with the join. The interesting point is the break. Come up and have a look."

Then Travers saw that the wire had been cut clean, and afterwards stranded together again. Crude work, as Wharton pointed out, but effective.

"And done that night," he said. "And repaired the same night, too."

"Yes, but why?"

"Well, once the wire was cut, every line was dead. If Major Stirrop wanted to 'phone anybody, then he couldn't. After he was dead, the line was repaired in two shakes, and apparently it didn't matter then who 'phoned who."

"But who on earth could have done it?" Travers said. "Surely only the man who stood behind Winter's door." Then he suddenly stared. "Good Lord! While Winter and I were talking down here, he must have hidden up here!"

Wharton shrugged his shoulders.

"Maybe," he said. "What I want to connect up is just why it was important to whoever killed Stirrop that Stirrop shouldn't be able to receive a message or send one. Find me an answer to that."

"It's got me beat," admitted Travers, for once at a loss for even a wild theory.

"And one other thing," went on Wharton. "The bullet that nearly killed Stirrop was never found. I saw the mark where it hit the wall and if it ricochetted, which it must have done, then it could only have fallen, a bit squashed, against another wall. Then why wasn't it found?"

"I always thought one of the prisoners found it," Travers said. "They had the run of the corridor the next morning after count."

"You think that extra prisoner fired it, and afterwards picked it up?"

"Well, if you pin me down—yes. But I didn't think you were any too keen on the idea of there having been an extra prisoner at all."

"Why on earth should you think that?" asked Wharton with virtuous indignation. Then he nodded confidentially and his chin approached Travers's ear.

"Like to have a bet? Just a new hat?"

Travers smiled sardonically.

"When you bet, George, you take care you're bookie, and owner and trainer and jockey, and the whole bag of tricks. What chance does an outsider like me stand?"

Wharton snorted contemptuously.

"What you mean is, you're afraid to risk it."

"Have it your own way," Travers told him. "A bet it is, but I'll shout the odds. Bet you a new hat that there *was* an extra prisoner."

"I'm not betting," said Wharton, with a haste that was only too informing. He changed the subject abruptly. "Bit chilly up here, isn't it? I think I'll get back to my office."

Travers suddenly remembered that B.199A, which he had somehow never had the time to fill in. A quick hour before tea might complete the job. So he took the twin forms from his safe and planned to get really down to things. A couple of minutes and he was drawing at an empty pipe and puzzling his wits over Wharton.

For Wharton, even at his most secretive, had become for Travers as easy to read as a map with contours plainly marked. Wharton had been anxious to bet a new hat that there had been an extra prisoner, and Wharton bet only on certainties. From somewhere he had obtained new information, and Travers was trying hard to fathom what that information was.

And there was another point. Travers had been prepared to bet, but only out of cussedness and to spike Wharton's guns.

When he had stuck by Dowling and had told Stirrop point-blank that he did believe in the existence of an extra prisoner, he had been relying not so much on the earnestness of Dowling's evidence as on a hunch arising out of the immediate attraction of the mystery to his own mind. But whenever he came down to earth and sheer hard facts, that existence of an extra prisoner seemed utterly fantastic. The building had been searched with a small-toothed comb, and methodically from attics to coal-cellars. It was all, thought Travers, like some macabre essay on the theme, "He being dead yet liveth." There was no prisoner in fact, yet his deeds as it were, answered for him, as witness his ghostly presence in the count, and the far from ghostly shot that had been fired at Stirrop.

Travers's thought ran on to a wondering where Wharton had obtained that new evidence that had convinced him of the very real existence of the palpably non-existent. Wharton, he knew, could never keep a secret long, and therefore it seemed safe to judge that the information had only just readied him. *From the Sergeants' Mess?* Was that it? Was that why he had wangled an invitation to Sunday lunch?

At that moment footsteps were heard outside. There was a tap at the door and Mafferty came in.

"Superintendent Wharton in his office, sir?"

"I think so," Travers said.

Then before he could put a question, there was a "Thank you, sir," and Mafferty had gone. Travers frowned, then nodded to himself. Just as well, perhaps, not to have questioned Mafferty as to how that lunch had gone. A shrewd word or two in the morning might be less dangerous.

He settled to his B.199A again, and almost at once was away on a new line of thought. Stirrop's record had been only just begun, and Travers had burnt it with other papers that had seemed of no consequence. If W.O. ever asked for it, the answer was simple—that the officer concerned had died before completion. As for the little Stirrop had filled in, it seemed that Burma had been his first foreign station, and from there he had come home in 1917. There the record ended, though it was enough to explain why, after the war he had gone to Burma again. Side-tracked, perhaps, by someone who'd assessed his brains, or else found a cushy job by some dear old pal like the unknown Harry Cross.

Voices were heard outside, and there was Wharton and Mafferty making their way towards the building: Wharton guffawing hugely and Mafferty also apparently on the best of terms with himself. Mischief was afoot, thought Travers, and promptly got into his British warm again. Just inside the hall he caught the two up. Wharton looked neither self-conscious nor annoyed.

"Where are you two off to?" Travers asked unconcernedly.

"Just having another look round that store," Wharton said.

"Then I'm coming too," said Travers with heavy humour. "We've missed things out of that store before."

Wharton had a good look at the floor and windows. Then, like an ordinary interested person, he had a look at what was on the shelves, and began fingering this and that. The safety razors were examined, and he had a real look at a suit of battle-dress.

"I wouldn't mind one of those pullovers," he said. "Any chance of scrounging one?"

Mafferty laughed.

"Not nowadays, sir. If I lost one of them, there'd be a Board of Inquiry."

Wharton waved a hand round.

"But you issue them to prisoners? And these trousers?"

"Ah, that's in order, sir. They sign a receipt which covers us."

"It's a hard world, George," Travers said consolingly. "But I'll buy you a pullover for next Christmas."

"Right," said Wharton. "I'll hold you to that. What are all these pails?"

"Those are latrine buckets, sir," Mafferty said. "These are pails."

"Why have some got yellow paint on?"

"They're P.A.D. pails, sir. They're for replacements of various fire-points all over the camp. The yellow paint acts as a gas detector."

"Which reminds me," said Travers. "Didn't Captain Winter find some buckets missing when you and he checked up the other day? What about replacing them? And how do you square the ledgers?"

"You wait, sir," Mafferty said. "I know how many are missing. When this present guard marches out, I'll wangle the deficiency on them."

"That's how it's done, is it?" said Wharton. "Then they tell me it isn't the same old Army. And where are these fire-points by the way? I'd like to see one."

"You must have passed them in the corridors," Travers said. "Here's one here, outside the door."

Mafferty locked the store again, and Wharton began wandering round. Travers recalled to his memory how Winter had discovered deficiencies of sand in some buckets, which might have accounted for the sand in the weapon that had killed Stirrop, if the job had been an inside one. Wharton merely nodded and went wandering on. Up the first stairway he went, and as far as the top attics, and then slowly and solemnly down again.

"What's that door?" he suddenly asked.

"Leads out to the top of the entrance porch," Travers said. "It's a kind of semi-circular veranda."

"Major Stirrop thought it would make a good machine-gun post," put in Mafferty, with much comfort in the word 'thought.' "You got the key, sir?"

Then he gave a gasp. As he tried the handle, the door opened.

"That's queer," Travers said. "Who on earth should have been up here?" Then he smiled. "But Ramble, of course. He opened the door when he searched the building, and forgot to shut it."

"Those are his footprints, are they?" asked Wharton.

"I expect so," Travers said, and smiled. "That comic porch always amuses me. Damn-great pillars enough to support St. Paul's and all they actually hold up is this priceless veranda place. The snow's rather like icing on a Christmas cake, don't you think?"

"I thought it was rather a handsome effect," Wharton said, and made his way through the snow to the low railing that made a futile sort of surround. A good look round, and he was back again, kicking the snow off his boots.

"A grand view of all this part of the camp." He nudged Travers roguishly in the ribs. "Next summer you'll be having a deck chair up here and taking your afternoon nap."

It was that nudge in the ribs that Travers remembered that night when he lay as usual to the borderline of sleep. Wharton was never jocular without cause. What new thing had he discovered up on that comic veranda? And why was he so friendly with Mafferty? And why had Mafferty lost all his nervousness and suddenly become a wholly new person of smiles and quips and jokes.

"Yes," said Travers to himself, almost in the moment of sleep, "it's up to me to protect Mafferty. All this gambolling about and taking Wharton's fleece for genuine sheep's wool. If George is trying any of his tricks, I'll take the law into my own hands and pull him up with a jerk."

## CHAPTER XIV
## WHARTON IS MYSTERIOUS

Travers woke, automatically reached for his glasses, blinked as he put them on, and then began an orientation of Ludovic Travers in time and space.

"What the devil day is it? Yesterday was Sunday. Wonder where Wharton went to in town last night? Monday. My hat! and end of pay period. All those cursed accounts for Regimental Paymaster. Wish I could get a rubber stamp so I didn't have to sign my name about two hundred perishing times. Dammit, and it's the funeral. Wonder if Garrison have arranged transport? And I must see Ramble. Which reminds me. Did we or did we not get those blasted 157's away on Saturday?"

There was more to it, but enough to show that Travers had travelled far from that rather scholarly if easy going Londoner of pre-war clays, to whom a damn was an event and who could wince at the pain of an ill-turned phrase. Bernice had more than once said—with a reproof which he hoped was wholly humorous—that the change was not altogether for the better, and Travers himself, trying to think back a mere six months, would feel as if he was peering into some dim and forgotten distance.

Sniffy come in with the tea and a message.

"Mr. Wharton would like to see you, sir, when you can spare a minute. Timms just told me."

Travers cursed Wharton, the funeral, Regimental Paymaster, and his razor. A sense of proportion came with each garment he put on, and he was almost his normal self when he looked in on Wharton. The old General was sitting up in the bed like a benevolent walrus, except that the cup of tea was balanced on his hand and not on his nose.

"What are you so pleased about?" Wharton demanded.

"Just things in general," Travers said, and sketched the day that lay ahead.

Wharton grunted. "A little work never hurt anybody. And I'm not going to make any for you. All I want is a few answers. What was that Captain Lading wearing when he left here?"

"The clothes he was issued with as a prisoner," Travers said. "Pullover, trousers, army-grey socks, and underwear. Why?"

"I just wondered," Wharton said. "And why did he ask for a suit of battle-dress?"

"Shoreleigh's full of troops," Travers told him. "Battle-dress would make him absolutely inconspicuous."

"Did he have a key to the store?"

"No. He didn't have any reason to ask for one. Also, if he'd have been able to pick the locks he'd have helped himself to battle-dress."

"And all the prisoners' baggage is kept in that room I saw yesterday afternoon?"

"All the heavy luggage."

"How did Lading get his bag out of it? Did he have a key?"

"He didn't need a key," Travers said. "He had only light hand luggage which he was allowed to keep with him in his room."

Wharton seemed rather disappointed, then he brightened up again when Travers pointed out that with himself twenty miles away that afternoon, he would be left to his own devices.

"Who'll be in charge of the camp?" he wanted to know.

"Winter, when he gets back," Travers said. "Miss Dance will have to answer any questions till then."

During breakfast Travers kept thinking about that curious look which Wharton had given. Undoubtedly, for all his attempts at concealment, Wharton was delighted at being more or less alone for a few hours. Then Travers was once more wondering what scheme it was that Wharton had on his mind, and why that visit of the previous afternoon to the store should have prompted questions about Lading. And what had Lading to do with Wharton in any case? He had been in the camp before Wharton arrived, and now his job was over and he had gone, how could Wharton possibly be concerned? He had never met Lading, and all he knew about him was what he had been told.

A quick word with Byron and Travers was hurrying to the office. The guard were finding a funeral party of twenty and it turned out that transport was already arranged. Miss Dance arrived and was sent down town to buy a Staff wreath, and then he saw Ramble. The R.S.M. announced in as melancholy a voice as he could muster, that his batman was already poshing up his best rig-out for the occasion. He also expressed himself as having no qualms about being general master of the mournful ceremonies.

Travers remembered something. Ramble had better lock that door to the veranda which he had probably forgotten to shut after the search. Ramble stared.

"I never opened it, sir. It was locked, and I knew nobody could be hiding out there."

"Well, it's open now," said Travers, equally startled. "And there're footprints where somebody's been. Not very clear ones because that last snow covered them, but they're footprints all right."

He gave Ramble the key and then hurried in to Wharton, who appeared to have just looked in at his office and was now leaving. Wharton tried hard to be suitably impressed but failed to try hard enough.

"But it's damnably important, George," insisted Travers. "Two things stand out as clear as day."

"I know," said Wharton. "One of them's that the extra prisoner was hidden up there while Ramble did his search. And what's the other?"

"Well, that that P.M. report may have been wrong. If we have any suspicions of Dulling, why not go the whole hog? Dulling may have faked that report. I know the S.M.O. was in it too, but one man can easily influence another when there's necessity for it. What I'm getting at is that we don't know any more about Stirrop's movements that night than that he was seen going over to the building, then he vanished as it were. But why shouldn't he have gone up to that veranda for some reason? He might have had to jump for it to save himself from some attack, and his fracture of the base of the skull was due to too heavy a fall on his feet."

"And what about the blow on the head?"

"There weren't any actual abrasions on the skull," Travers pointed out. "He may have had a crack on the skull when he was attacked, just before he jumped."

"And what about that double impression? If Stirrop was killed at once, what made them? Somebody laid his body down in two places and there weren't any footprints. What about all that if he'd died of a high jump?"

"Perhaps he wasn't dead at once," Travers said. "Perhaps he staggered along the drive and then fell and rolled over."

"Well, it's a theory," Wharton said, and then, piously, "Theories are useful things. I may look into it a little bit more. Where's that key?"

Travers said he had just given it to Ramble.

Wharton hurried off in the direction of the front entrance.

It was five o'clock that afternoon when the motor-coach came back. Travers still had in his nostrils the heavy scent of lilies, and in his ears the sound of his own uttered consolations which he hoped had not seemed forced and pretentious. But he had enjoyed that half-day out of camp, and a sight of the countryside, even if it was deep in snow. And he had enjoyed quite a long chat with Ramble.

They had talked mostly about the last war, and then Travers had contrived to bring in the matter of Wharton and the Sunday lunch, but without finding the slightest clue as to what the General's scheme had been. The only thing that Travers did learn was this.

Ramble went across to the building to lock the veranda door with the key Travers gave him and Wharton arrived just as he was doing it. Captain Travers, he said, had told him to take the job over and the key. But Ramble did have a look at the footprints that Travers had mentioned.

"Those are all mine," Wharton said, and Travers could imagine his gesture of guileful dismissal. "I had a look here when we were going round yesterday."

"You must have been up twice, then, sir." Ramble pointed out. "Some of those footprints have had snow on them."

Wharton winked shamelessly.

"Haven't you ever heard of putting snow on *afterwards* to make it look as if they were there before?"

Then as Travers duly noted, having got Ramble into an impossible tangle, he locked the door, pocketed the key and changed the subject of conversation. And Travers knew too that there would be no point in questioning Wharton or trying to drive him into some argumentative corner from which he could not escape. Wharton would either wriggle out, or barefacedly deny. And, after all, the case was his. For the first time in his Yard career, Travers was working with Wharton not as a colleague and collaborator, and his methods would have to be his own.

As he went by on his way to his room, Travers peeped in the Mess. There Wharton sat, cup of tea in hand, while the three guard officers listened goggle-eyed to some yarn he was spinning. Undoubtedly Wharton was going down very well, and Travers was glad to find him so popular, if somewhat critical of his methods. For he very definitely was popular. Ramble spoke of him with awe and affection, and wherever he went in the camp he met with smiles. And he was known everywhere. The N.A.A.F.I. hut had seen him throw a skilful dart, and he had had more than one extra cup of tea in the men's cookhouse. Miss Dance, after a few minutes in his office, would come back to the comparative austerity of Travers's room all giggles and smiles. Timms had reported, according to Sniffy, that he wouldn't mind if Wharton stayed on for the duration.

"Come and have some tea," Wharton said, as if the place were his own.

"In a minute or two," Travers told him. "I'm just going along for a polish. Captain Winter back?"

"Just after you left," Wharton said.

"And nothing's been happening? No brass hats?"

"Not a soul," Byron said. "You know we've been very lucky recently, sir, about inspections. The main gate sentries always love 'em though."

He explained for Wharton's benefit. Nobody was allowed to enter camp without a pass. Along would come some visiting or inspecting brass hat, to be promptly held up by the sentry. There would be indignation or worse, the sentry would hold his ground—as ordered—then the sergeant of the guard would be called and the position explained. Then the brass hat would be hugely delighted that a sentry could carry out orders even at the risk of reprimand, and the sentry would be congratulated and almost promised a medal, and everybody—brass hat included— would be beaming.

Travers left in the middle of that explanation and went straight to the office. Miss Dance had gone, but Winter was working away at accounts.

"I thought I'd better work here as you were away," he said.

"The very best place," Travers said. "Have a good time in town?"

"Pretty good," Winter said, and smiled. "No trouble with those two birds either."

"Splendid. Nothing's been happening this afternoon, so they tell me."

"Not a thing. I've just been sitting near the 'phone doing odd jobs all the afternoon. The man called about the 'phone, by the way."

"What was wrong?"

Winter smiled. "Between ourselves I don't think he found a lot. You know how these fellows are. They talk a lot of technical stuff and try to impress you. He tried to make out it was something inside the old box of tricks."

The box of tricks was the cabinet of contraptions with a front all knobs and levers. Press this and depress that, and you might put yourself through to the extension you wanted, or be warned to take an incoming call. On the other hand, you might not.

"He tackled that did he?" asked Travers amusedly.

"Had its inside all spread over the table," Winter said, stretching his legs. "Now I'll fix up a telephone orderly for you, and then get a spot of tea."

He gave Travers a quiet, appraising look.

"Why don't you go down town to-night and ease off a bit? The whole gang's going, Wharton included. I'd much rather you went instead of me."

"Sorry, can't be done," Travers said. "But you're a good feller all the same. Now cut along and get some tea. I'll see to that telephone orderly."

Once more he began wondering just what Wharton's idea was. Off down town with the two guard officers and Winter—and why? What confidences was he trying to wheedle out of them? Once on the trail, Wharton knew no morals and had no scruples, and, as Travers had often reluctantly admitted, he was always right. If Wharton had dealt with Hitler, there would have been no appeasement: his way would have been to flatter the *Führer*, outlie Goebbels, and even, if necessary, wear more medals than Göring. And yet somehow Travers didn't like the idea of Wharton's hob-nobbing with all and sundry in the camp. That night probably somebody would drop an unguarded word, not necessarily about himself but incriminating someone else, and to obtain that word, Wharton was going out with the young bloods to kick up his ancient heels.

Something in those thoughts made Travers remember Mafferty and he rang through. The box of tricks was working well, for Mafferty answered at once.

"Sorry to have left you in the lurch like this," Travers said, "but I'll be along after tea. Anything for me to do?"

"About a couple of hundred papers to sign," Mafferty said, and with his newly acquired good-humour, "And don't forget to check your accounts, sir, and the copy of Company Account."

"You go and get yourself some tea," Travers told him. "Then bring your stuff down here. Twice as quick as running up and down those cursed stairs."

It was dark by the time Travers had finished tea, and as he came out of the Mess, Wharton called to him. Travers was the least bit on his dignity, but Wharton appeared to notice nothing. He was even inclined to be communicative, which made Travers still more suspicious.

"I thought you'd like to know the doctor's O.K.," he said. "He's making money out of his practice and he got this job in a normal way. From what I can gather, when the W.O. got out the scheme for a camp here, they consulted the local authorities and mentioned a doctor. The authorities consulted the local doctors and Dulling was willing to take the job. One or two officers turned the offer down."

"What about his wife and the Italian consulate?" Travers asked.

"Now you're getting to something a bit outside my line," Wharton said. "The Special Branch are on that. What I do know is that both the Martellis are in the thick of everything: whist drives, bridge drives, dances—anything to raise money for war charities."

He gave Travers a roguish nudge in the ribs. "That means a lot of organisation. All sorts of people calling. Regular hive of industry. Very nice to have all sorts of officers to entertain and hear all the latest. Tester's there quite a lot, they tell me."

"So I believe," said Travers. "And what about you, George? Any nearer getting your man?"

"Man?" said Wharton mysteriously. "Why man?"

"Now you're being deliberately obscure," Travers told him. "The only possible woman is Bertha Dance, and I can't see her murdering Stirrop on a snowy night."

"Come, come, come," said Wharton placatingly. "You don't get the idea. Why should it be one man only? That's what I was getting at."

He edged nearer and his voice lowered.

"Remember telling me what this place was like? Everybody on edge and loathing the Commandant, and going through the hell of a time? And thinking how different things would be once he was out of the way? You thought the same or you would not have contrived that alibi of yours which someone sent to the Brigadier. Very well, then. Suppose two fellows A and B. A's the master mind and gets B in to help. B doesn't know just what he's in for, and then when Stirrop gets murdered, he has to keep his mouth shut to save his own skin. Well, isn't there something in that?"

"There certainly is," said Travers.

"And one other little thing. You made a list of suspects and you ought to know. But didn't you leave one out? What about that bull-necked swine of a Friedemann?"

Travers's fingers went to his glasses, and then there was a quick tap at the door and Winter came in, greatcoat collar up to his ears.

"Where're we going?" Wharton asked genially, eyes on the fur gloves. "With Scott to the Antarctic?"

"You get your coat on and come along," Winter told him. "We're all lined up and waiting."

He whispered in Travers's ear.

"Wish I could get out of it. We're going to the Royal. That nancy-boy Tester's going to be there."

For two hours Travers worked steadily on with Mafferty, till his fingers were cramped and he was sick of the sight of his own signature. Then Mafferty gave an approving nod and said that would be all. There were one or two things he could finish in the morning and still have plenty of time to catch the first post.

Travers stretched his long legs, gave his glasses a polish and wondered what there would be for dinner, and he had more than a suspicion that he was in for rissoles. And Wharton now probably filled to the eyebrows with a five-courser at the Royal. An intriguing idea, that, about two people being concerned in Stirrop's murder, and B, who had opened his mouth too far perhaps, now afraid to give away the murderer A. Too complicated, though, to work out with a tired brain.

And then Travers moistened his lips as he thought of something else. When Wharton gave away information it was for one or two reasons: to obtain something more important in exchange, or to conceal real evidence behind the smoke-screen of his own verbosity. Then why had he volunteered that theory about two men having been concerned, and at the very moment when he was going out with Byron and Dowling? Dowling could never have murdered Stirrop—*or could he?* That pretended visit to Main Guard just before the count that night, could it have been the creating of some crude alibi to explain away the time when he was doing Stirrop in? Or had Byron been mainly concerned, and had Dowling, as Orderly Officer, been used to lure Stirrop into the very position and circumstances in which Byron wanted him?

Travers worried his wits over that, and knew his brain too tired. Besides, as he could assure himself, neither Byron nor Dowling was the sort to commit murder. And then again he did not know. A furtive, sullen, treacherous sort of place the camp had been in Stirrop's time, and furtiveness breeds furtiveness. And never had a man sounded more desperate than Byron had sounded when he had admitted that Stirrop had at last driven him beyond his tether.

As for Friedemann, Travers though Wharton's inclusion of him in the list of suspects as very far-fetched. It was as nebulous as that question of the extra prisoner, even though one could believe anything of a fawning, shifty-looking swine like Friedemann to be civil to whom was to make one's gorge rise. And so Travers gave a kind of lung-clearing sigh, reached for his British warm, and thought once more about dinner.

Outside it was inkily dark, with low clouds that threatened still more snow. Then as he shone his torch on the slippery path, he suddenly halted as he heard voices. Two of those sentries talking again, and he was making up his mind to twist Byron's tail.

Then he changed his mind, he would stroll quietly across and catch the two red-handed, and would blast hell out of them. Over and over again that order had been read on parade, and it was time for drastic action. But as he neared the dimly lighted wire, he saw the far sentry approaching, and knew his opportunity had gone.

But he stood where he was. The sentry came to the end of his beat, halted, gave a smart about-turn, and moved off again. Travers smiled grimly. Was it genuine smartness or was he trying to keep his feet warm? Probably a bit of both, and with that grudging tribute he moved off too. Then he halted again in his tracks, breath held.

Someone was almost through the wire gates and making for the main building. A faint light from overhead caught him for a second, and no more, and yet Travers was certain that the somebody was Wharton! Yes, Wharton it was—and as suddenly gone. Wharton, who should have been in town. Who had gone to town, and, if it came to that, who must still be in town!

Travers moved on towards the Mess, and he found himself walking softly as if he himself were also some furtive kind of conspirator. The time by the Mess clock was a quarter to nine.

# CHAPTER XV
# APPROACH OF A CLIMAX

NEXT MORNING Travers went straight to the Mess without dropping in on Wharton. Dowling was finishing breakfast.

"You changed duties with Pewter yesterday, did you?" Travers asked.

"Yes, sir, I did," Dowling said. "He wasn't keen on going down town last night."

"Have a good time?"

"Oh, fine. Early dinner at the Royal, and roped Tester in. Then we went on to the second house at the Palladion. Topping show. One comic who was genuinely funny, and a really great troupe of acrobats. Superintendent Wharton had hard luck. He was called out soon after it started. Someone at H.Q. wanted him, but he got back in time for the comic."

"Well, enjoy yourselves while the going's good," counselled Travers. "The count all right?"

"Yes, sir. Seventy, the same as last night."

Travers went out to the office almost at once and ran into Winter, who admitted he'd also had a good time.

"Heard anything about Lading?" he asked.

"Devil a word," Travers said. "Still, Intelligence won't consider it's their duty to let us know at once."

"Wonder what he's up to?" Winter said frowningly. "He didn't ask me for a railway warrant, so presumably he's still in the town."

"If he was in civilian clothes, he wouldn't dare try and use a warrant," Travers thought. "He's a queer bird, though. Lord knows what he's up to."

The mail was opened and sorted. Miss Dance arrived, and Travers noted that she was now wearing openly and regularly that wrist-watch which he had thought a present from Stirrop. A quarter of an hour later, who should look through the communicating door but Wharton.

"Can you come in a minute?"

"I've just been talking over something with Captain Winter here," he explained. "I've got the idea that another tunnel's being constructed. Would it be out of the question to examine all the doors?"

"I don't think so," Travers said, "if you consider it necessary. I can ring D.C.R.E. to send three or four men, and we can shift the prisoners to the first floor and keep them there all day. What do you say, Winter?"

"It ought to be easy enough," Winter said. "When's the move to take place?"

"Now," Wharton said. "I'd like it all over by dinner-time."

"Then if you'll see Ramble and take charge at the building, I'll do the rest," Travers said. "If Friedemann asks any questions, jump on him with both feet."

Winter nodded meaningly.

"I will, and from an enormous altitude as they say in the classics."

Wharton came through to Travers's room and waited there while the D.C.R.E. was being rung up. Everything was fine, Travers reported. Four men with the necessary tools would be along at ten hours.

"Can you come along to my room a minute?" Wharton asked mysteriously. "There's something urgent I want to talk over."

On the way out he paused for an avuncular word with Miss Dance, and left her with the usual titters.

"Nice girl, that," he remarked to Travers. "Knows her job too. Come along in for a minute. I won't keep you longer."

He adjusted the wick of the oil-stove and made a few comments, then at last he was ready.

"I think I'm on to something really important."

"Really?" said Travers.

"Yes. At seven o'clock tonight I'm having a highly confidential meeting with someone in town. Tell me, how does one get to a place called Natal Square?"

"You go right past it on the way down in the tram," Travers said. "Get off at the second traffic lights and turn sharp left. It's about a hundred yards on."

"There's a pub there called the Crown and Anchor," Wharton said, "and my rendezvous is in the private bar. I thought I'd let you know in case I'm at all late."

He was already getting to his feel.

"I'll let them know in the Mess," Travers said, "and I'll wait up if you're not too late. Have a good time last night, by the way?"

"First-class," Wharton said. "One of the real old music-hall shows. You were in bed when we got home."

"I'm an early bird these days," smiled Travers. "Ever hear anything about those finger-prints?"

"Nothing any good," Wharton said, locking the door carefully behind them. "And now I think I'll get across to the building for a front seat in the stalls."

It was easy work making that move of the prisoners. The upstairs rooms were always ready for reception, so that all a man had to do was to take his personal belongings, and be transferred with his room *en bloc*. Then the doors on the landings of the twin stairways were locked, and there was everything as it was before. Latrine buckets were handy, so that no man could make an excuse to go outside, and for once each individual room would be its own recreation-room.

By a quarter past ten the move was completed and the R.E. men got to work. Bedding had been placed to one side, and now the floor-boards were prised up and the joists exposed. The job was far easier than might have been expected, for the boards had luckily been laid north and south, and since a tunnel would run east or west, it was plain that it must have been begun on the side of a room nearest an outer wall, in order to save excavation. It was easy too for the engineers to tell whether boards had been tampered with at all, and so less trouble was taken with a room whose floor had obviously never been disturbed since the day it was laid.

"Whoever laid these floors made a rotten bad job of it," the Sapper sergeant told Travers and Wharton. "It's a wonder the place hasn't had dry-rot."

For years, it appeared, the correct and only safe method had been to set the joists in concrete and to proof both joists and setting with tar. But the floors in that old hospital had the original earth immediately below the joists, so that all that had saved the floors from dry-rot were the air bricks which allowed some small circulation. If bricks had got choked, which one or two of them were, air could never have circulated and a fetid damp would have attacked the joists.

The first excitement came at that room where Lading had reported the beginnings of a tunnel, for it was plain from the start that here the boards had been removed. The corner of the room, under the six-foot length of a prisoner's bed-boards and palliasse, had been chosen for the entrance. But, to the vast disappointment of all concerned, no entrance remained. When its excavators had somehow got word that everything was known, they had decided to fill it in.

And there a problem met them. The earth already taken out had been spread round the other joints till they were packed. The sergeant proved that by showing where the earth had marked the joists. But quite a lot of the tunnel must also have been completed, for not only had all that earth been put back in the hole, but more earth had been excavated round the joists. And even then the hole had not been quite filled, for there remained the deficiency caused by the earth which prisoners had transferred from the room in their pockets and disposed of in the exercise yards.

Still, there it was. The tunnel had been abandoned, and filled in sufficiently for the floor not to sound too hollow to an inquiring tread. And after that there was no other excitement at all, but only one false alarm. In the last room but one, boards had definitely been prised up and a site tested, but for some reason the attempt at escape had been either postponed or abandoned too.

"Well, that's good enough for me," Wharton told Travers and Winter. "I told you I had an idea another tunnel was in the wind and I was right."

"How did you know?" Winter asked.

"Ah!" said Wharton, with a roguish wag of the head, "that would be telling."

Travers was fetched by a runner, as being wanted urgently on the 'phone. It was Intelligence, with a brief, important instruction. Major Carterson had left for Shoreleigh, and would be there at thirteen-thirty hours. Could he be met, and if necessary accommodated for the night? And about the prisoner Beckner. Was there any more information? There wasn't. Well, Major Carterson would be going into the matter on arrival.

It was lucky for Travers and all concerned that he mentioned no word to a soul until a few minutes later he ran into Wharton. Wharton pursed out his lips beneath the huge moustache, frowned heavily, then led Travers mysteriously aside.

"Now look here. For once I want you to do just as I say. A whole lot may depend on it. First, unless it's absolutely necessary, I don't want you to let that Major Carterson enter the camp. I don't want him even to be mentioned. That's even more important."

""What am I to do then? Meet him at the station?"

"That's it," Wharton said. "And take me with you. Work it like that. Join me in the Mess in a quarter of an hour's time and ask Byron to lend you his car for an urgent job. I'll ask if you're going down town. You'll say you are—some of the way—and I'll scrounge a lift."

Travers went back to his office to spend that quarter of an hour with profit, and there a remarkably strange thing happened. If he had been less busy that morning he must have noticed something peculiar about Bertha Dance. More than once she had gone through all the preliminaries of making a confession, but the absorption of Travers in something else had been a deterrent. But during his last absence she had evidently screwed her courage to the desperate sticking point.

"Captain Travers," she said, "I wanted to ask your advice about something." She gave an incipient titter. "It's something personal—really."

"Always pleased to oblige," said Travers flippantly.

"It's about. . . . Well, what would you do when anyone's jealous?"

"Depends on the person, and the extent of the jealousy," he told her warily. His fingers went to his glasses. "Would it make it easier if I suggested that you wanted to ask my advice about you and Captain Tester?"

"Well, yes," she said, and tittered slightly again. "He was ever so jealous. Of Major Stirrop, it was, and I kept telling him there was nothing in it. I know I went out once or twice with him, but it was only friendliness and he wouldn't see it—Captain Tester wouldn't, I mean."

The nervousness had gone and she was away at full swing.

"When I had to come to the camp on the night he was—I mean, on the night Major Stirrop died, he was watching me and he—"

"Just a minute. Just a minute!" interrupted Travers. "Just why did you come to the camp, and why haven't I heard about it?"

"Because I didn't really come," she said patiently. "You see, it was like this. I'd left my bag in the drawer by mistake, and I didn't remember it till I was nearly home. Then I wanted something out of it, so I came right back to the camp and got them to ring from the guard. I thought the runner would bring the bag to me at the gate—see? Then I wouldn't have to come in. Only I couldn't make anyone hear. The 'phone must have gone wrong, and so I thought it didn't matter after all. Then when I got a little way back along the road, I saw Captain Tester, and I knew he'd been following me. I actually taxed him with it, and he couldn't deny it. We had a fine old row and I nearly gave him his ring back, and then I wouldn't let him come home with me, and when I left him he was walking back towards the camp."

Travers nodded judicially.

"Well, it appears to me that unless you're having an affair with somebody else, young lady, your jealousy troubles solved themselves when Major Stirrop died."

"Oh, but he never has forgiven me. Or I haven't forgiven him, rather. I hate to be pried on. So would anybody."

"At what time was it when you got to the camp?"

"About half-past eight, I think. You see, I didn't pay much attention to the time." She got to her feet and began collecting her things. "Don't let's talk about it any more. And thanks ever so much for being so helpful. Would you mind if I went early to-day?"

"If you mean now—why not?" smiled Travers.

A glance at his watch showed he had still five minutes in hand. At once he was ringing the guard orderly-room, and asking for their sergeant-major. Who was in charge of Main Guard on the night Major Stirrop died? Last Thursday night, to be precise.

A minute, and the sergeant's name was given.

"Is he available?" Travers asked. "If so, I want to see him. Not here—make that clear. Tell him to be waiting inside the guard hut at main gate in ten minutes' time."

The main scheme worked. Just before thirteen hours Travers was driving Byron's car through the main gate. Just beyond it, under cover of the wall, he called to the sentry to send that sergeant of the guard.

"You were on duty the night Major Stirrop died?" Travers asked him.

"Yes, sir."

"Then listen to me. Anything I say to you now is to be forgotten. If ever I learn that a word's got out about any question I ask you, you're for it. Have you got that?"

"Yes, sir."

"Then at what time on that Thursday night did Miss Dance come here and ask to use the 'phone to call up any office?"

The sergeant stared.

"She didn't come—not here, sir."

"You're dead sure? What about when you were absent on guard-mounting?"

"I wasn't, sir. Corporal Westley mounted both guards and I took over at midnight."

"You were in the hut from say, nineteen hours till twenty-one hours?"

"Yes, sir. Never left it. I was in the room where the 'phone is, sir, reading a book in front of the stove."

"Good enough," said Travers, and nodded approvingly. "That's all then, Sergeant, except to forget you've been talking to me."

"What was all that about?" asked Wharton as soon as Travers moved the car on. Travers told him. Wharton fairly beamed.

"What made you think her yarn was fishy?"

"The fact that she made me Aunt Daisy of *Flossie's Weekly*," said Travers. "That young woman's quite capable of handling all the intricacies of love. And I wondered if a woman would ever leave a bag behind, and not rumble it in the first minute.

Also, if Bertha got as far as the gate, after having walked a mile on a filthy night, why didn't she walk a couple of hundred yards farther when she found the 'phone out of order? And, above all, when she mentioned the name of Captain Tester, why didn't she do what she's always done—blush!"

"I get you," Wharton said. "The yarn was ready beforehand. But there's some truth in it. The 'phone was out of order at the time she states."

His hand went out.

"Slow down here, will you? Pull up against the kerb."

He got out and looked round, then got in again.

"Would you mind taking that road over there? I know a way that's a bit of a short cut."

"You seem to have learned a lot," Travers told him, and moved the car on again. "What's the idea? Want to avoid seeing somebody in town?"

"More or less," said Wharton, and then seemed highly amused at something. "Ten minutes ago I couldn't have said what I'm going to say now—which is this. Unless I'm vastly mistaken, by about ten o'clock to-morrow morning we're going to have the hell of a lot of fun."

Major Carterson was a man of middle age, quiet and unassuming, but it was soon clear that he knew his job. Travers was not to worry, he said, about night accommodation, because he hoped to return to town by the 16.15. He had not had lunch on the train, so the three adjourned to the Station Hotel and talked shop over a square meal.

He was worried about Lading, that was clear too, but he smiled at the way Winter had managed to smuggle him out of camp.

"He's got an absolute flair for this kind of work," Carterson said. "In some ways he's the most promising lad we ever had. Utterly reckless and yet never makes a mistake."

"Well, I'm perfectly convinced he'll turn up," Travers said. "And my own private idea is, he's still somewhere in this town."

Wharton said nothing, and Travers wondered why, for if there was one thing of which he was convinced, it was that the rendezvous that night at the Crown and Anchor was with Lading himself.

"I suppose it's silly to worry about him," Carterson agreed, "especially since we had to wash our hands of him, so to speak. He told you, didn't he, just what his job was?"

He went on to amplify. The Union Government knew that one particularly important agent had been smuggled into Southern Rhodesia, and that his job was to unify the whole Nazi movement in Southern Africa. It was suspected that he had two other highly placed Reich agents with him, and Intelligence were reasonably satisfied that Scribbnitz and Stein were those two. The other was probably in camp under a false name. Forged documents were easy enough to manufacture.

That man, Carterson said, was probably a prisoner named Hauffner—Karl Hauffner—as Intelligence had just heard through a Cape Town cable, and he wanted to take Hauffner back with him that afternoon, Friedemann too, just in case he could be induced to squeal.

That other business of sabotage in Shoreleigh had been suggested by Lading himself, which was probably why he was still in the town.

"My own idea is this," Carterson went on. "I think he wanted that tunnel to be completed. He may even have acted as *agent provocateur*, and started it. Then he'd have sent the tip outside to let the prisoners escape, and find out where they made contacts. Still, it's too late to worry about that now. I expect he found a short cut with the same ends in view, which is why he's still out on his own."

Travers rang the camp and asked Winter to make arrangements for transport and escort. There was the R.T.O. to see about a private compartment, and Liverpool Street to be warned at the other end. It was half an hour later when Travers got back to the hotel, and there were Wharton and Carterson still in the most earnest conversation. Wharton was reinforcing some argument with lifted linger and wagging head, and Carterson was frowning away and nodding.

"Well, everything's arranged," Travers reported. "Your two birds will be here well in time, Major. And now where do we go?"

"I don't think I ought to keep either of you," Carterson said. "I'll be watching at the station ready to take the two birds over."

"Then if you're sure, I'll push off," Travers said. "You ready, George?"

"I'm staying on," Wharton said. "No use going back now and coming all this way again later on. You get along home. Captain Byron may be wanting his car."

Travers had to laugh.

"Any other orders?"

"Just my little joke," Wharton said. "And if you really want to know, the Major and I were talking about a chap known as Weinholst. The Major thinks he once heard of him." He waved a cheery hand of dismissal. "See you later then. Don't sit up. I may be late."


But he was not late. That night the three guard officers were all in the Mess, with Winter tackling arrears in his office, but there was that rare event—a four at bridge. Pewter had to knock off while he took the count, and the game had hardly been started again when Wharton looked into the room. Then he came inside.

"The gamblers' den," he remarked facetiously.

"More like the gabblers' den," said Byron dryly. "There's more argument and inquests than anything else."

"Good. Very good," said Wharton, "What about a drink?"

"You have this with me," Byron said.

The accounts were settled, the cards laid by, and the five gathered round the fire. Winter came in and joined the circle. Wharton gave no sign to Travers of what had transpired that night, but he was as usual the life and soul of the party. It was well after ten o'clock when he remarked that he liked the company but not their hours.

Travers went with him. In the dark, Wharton's hand felt for Travers's sleeve, and Travers was gently drawn into his own room, and the light was not switched on. Wharton's voice came in a whisper.

"A good interview tonight. Tomorrow things ought to get going."

"You think you've found something?" Travers whispered back.

"I know it," Wharton said. "I've got all the pieces but one, and I may have that before to-morrow's out. You got a revolver here? If so, let me have it, and some ammunition."

Travers handed the gun over, and said it was fully loaded. Wharton peeped from the door, and then without another word was gone. Travers's fingers went instinctively to his glasses, then fell bewilderedly.

PART IV
WHARTON KNOWS

# CHAPTER XVI
# INTRUSION OF A BRASS HAT

TRAVERS HAD A bad night. It was a very long time before he
fell asleep at all, for he lay listening for the sound of Wharton's
gun. Whenever he woke up he was listening again, and once he
gently opened the door and looked out into the silence of the
camp. Then as he lay waiting for sleep again, he was trying to
make coherence out of the happenings of the last two days, and
wondering what lay behind Wharton's secretiveness and even
his overnight confidence, and wondering above all what the
coming day would have in store. Wharton had promised action
before eleven o'clock, but Travers could even add the fear that
in the morning Wharton might not be alive. Never before had he
known him use a gun.

When Sniffy came in with early tea, Travers was in a heavy
sleep, and it took him longer than ever to get his bearings.

"Is Superintendent Wharton about?" he said.

"I don't think he's up, sir," Sniffy said. "I heard him and
Timms talking as I went past."

No sooner was Travers dressed than he was along at Wharton's room. The old General was shaving, and before Travers's
lips could frame the first word, his finger was at his own lips,
and he was making frantic signals for silence. Then he began
the greetings.

"Hallo! What gets you up so early?"

"Guilty conscience," said Travers, taking the cue.

"The cold, more likely," said Wharton, getting on with the
last stages of shaving. "Never knew such cold.'

From the weather he switched to Travers's private affairs:
the last time he had seen Bernice in town, how that Travers was
surely well overdue for leave, news about old friends at the Yard,
and so to the progress of the war. When his tie was adjusted and
he had given a final brush to hair and moustache, he said he
had to slip across to the building, and he'd be seeing Travers at
breakfast.

"I might as well stroll across with you," Travers said, once more taking the cue.

"I didn't tell you before," Wharton said, when they were well out of earshot of the neighbourhood of the Mess, "but there's been a certain amount of eavesdropping going on round my windows and yours. I found where the snow had been trampled down at the back."

"You don't say so!"

"It cuts both ways," Wharton told him. "It's annoying I know, but on the other hand whoever it was may have heard something he was wanted to hear."

"Such as what?"

"Ah, now you're asking," said Wharton, closing up at once. Then he changed his mind and did a bit of explaining.

"I want you to be patient and just trust the old man for once, before this day's gone, all sorts of things ought to happen, or my name's Robinson."

"That's all right, George," Travers said. "This has been a queer sort of case for me—in it and not in it, so to speak. And I guess I'm about ready for a spot of leave."

"If Stirrop hadn't died, you'd have cracked up," Wharton told him, and not without concern. "I'll tell you now what I didn't tell you then. When I first clapped eyes on you down here, you gave me a regular shock."

"We'll get over it," Travers said. "But tell me just one thing, George. Was it Lading you met last night?"

Wharton pursed his lips.

"To tell the truth, it wasn't." Then he nodded. "But we'll be seeing him all right. Sooner perhaps than you think."

They went into the building, stayed for a minute or two, and came out. As they went through the gates, Wharton had a last instruction.

"Sometime this morning I shall send for Miss Dance. Don't ask me any questions, but as soon as she gets in my room, pick up your 'phone as if you were waiting for a number. If anybody comes in your room, wave them away. That's all, but cling on to that 'phone whatever happens."

Travers nodded. Wharton gave him a look, then added one more thing.

"Whenever you're with me to-day in the company of no matter who it is, look out for cues. Doesn't matter if what I say don't make sense. You play up to me, that's all I ask." He nodded to himself with something of the old complacency. "You trust the old gent., and I'll see you don't go far wrong."

Just after nine o'clock a spanner was thrown into the works. Colonel Caithby rang from H.Q.

"Good morning, Travers. I've got some news for you that you won't like. A Colonel Fraser, who's something to do with Prisoners of War, is coming down here, and I promised to bring him along to see your camp."

"That'll be no trouble, sir," Travers said. "What time, sir?"

"Oh. elevenish. He's an awful good chap and he won't give you any trouble. See you then. Goodbye."

"Oh, my hat!" groaned Travers, and wondered with horror if the receiver had been properly replaced. Just like those ruddy brass hats! Thinking all the world had nothing to do but spit and polish, and then conduct Cook's tours, while they asked fatuous questions and made their laboured jokes. Damn all brass hats! Not Caithby, for it wasn't his doing and he was a thundering good sort, but damn Colonel Fraser, or whatever his name was, to the nethermost depths of perdition.

"Have you had bad news?" Miss Dance was asking.

Travers caught her goggled eyes, and smiled sheepishly.

While she gathered in Winter and Ramble and Mafferty, he gave the news to Wharton in the Commandant's office.

"How long's he likely to stay?" Wharton wanted to know.

"You never know," Travers said. "Anything from half an hour to an hour and a half."

Wharton shrugged his shoulders.

"Bit of a nuisance, as you say." Then he gave what was meant to be a highly suggestive wink. "Bring him into the Mess for a drink. I like meeting these Army top-notchers."

The bad news was passed on to all concerned, and the whole camp was at once a hive of activity, short words and shorter tempers. Travers was due for a preliminary inspection before eleven hours, and meanwhile got on with the morning's routine. But his mind was far from his work. All the time he would find himself wondering just what was going to happen when Wharton sent for Bertha Dance.

Then the 'phone went.

"Can you spare Miss Dance for a minute?" came Wharton's voice.

"Superintendent Wharton would like to see you for a minute," said Travers, receiver still off.

Miss Dance smiled to herself, took a quick look at her make-up, found a notebook and pencil and went smirkingly out. Travers replaced the receiver, then lifted it again and prepared to listen. That he should hear anything at all was manifestly absurd, and what lay behind Wharton's mysterious instructions was utterly beyond him, but he listened all the same. Then his eyes suddenly goggled. Voices were coming through, and as clearly as if they were in that very room.

Two things have been mentioned about Wharton—that he never missed a chance to display his consummate showmanship, and that he had a way with women. The two combined were almost to be his undoing.

"Good morning, good morning. And how are we this morning?"

"Oh, about the same as usual," smiled Bertha. "Cold, isn't it."

"Cold as a lawyer's heart," said Wharton.

She giggled. "You do say the funniest things."

"Anything to brighten up life," Wharton told her. "And how are things with you these days? Dreaming about wedding-bells?"

"Nothing like that," she told him archly. "Nothing like being sure of everything before you settle down."

"Too true, too true," said Wharton piously. "That's what I used to tell my own daughter." He heaved a sigh. "Still, you and I mustn't sit gossiping here or we'll have Captain Travers after us."

"Oh, he's not so bad. A solemn old stick. Not like you."

"None of your flattery," Wharton told her roguishly. Then he heaved another sigh, "Come on now, and let's get to work. Just one letter to take down."

The pencil was nicely poised and she expressed herself as ready. Wharton solemnly lighted his pipe, leaned back in his chair and began dictating.

"Dear Captain Tester—"

She stared, wide-eyed. Wharton calmly resumed.

"I regret to say I shall be unable to do any more work for you. Superintendent Wharton has discovered what is going on and—"

Site was on her feet, face a fiery red.

"Hallo. What's up?" asked Wharton amiably.

"This letter. . . . Is it . . ."

"It is," beamed Wharton. "It's a letter from you to Captain Tester."

Her mouth gaped, then she let out a shriek. A second, and she had grabbed the notebook and was out of the door. Another long shriek rent the air. Ramble, coming through the wire gates, looked round startled and broke into the double. In the far distance a sentry was peering round the wire. Travers had dropped the receiver and was at the door. It opened with a swish, and he was nearly sent sideways.

"Mr. Wharton," she said, and paused for breath. "He had his arm round me. . . . He tried to kiss me!"

Wharton was in the room, motioning Ramble through. His voice was a cold menace.

"Sit down there, you! Mr. Ramble, keep your back against that communicating door and let no one through."

He turned his key in Travers's door and then came slowly across.

"You keep that mouth of yours shut, young lady, and listen to me. What you didn't know was that Captain Travers heard every word that passed in that room. Now you're going to answer a few questions."

She shook her head furiously.

"I won't say a word!"

"Captain Travers," said Wharton gently, "will you be so good as to ring the police and ask them to send someone straight away." He peered sideways at her. "Or would you rather talk to us? Nice and friendly-like."

Then he was nodding down approvingly.

"That's better. Just one simple question. When did you first meet Captain Tester?"

She gave a dab at her eyes.

"In October. I met him at a dance."

"That's all," Wharton said, and looked round as if for applause. "Now you'll go home and stay there. If you're wanted you'll be sent for, but you can take it from me you'll not be wanted here. Anything due to you will be sent on."

A minute, and she had gone, and there was no flaunt as she passed through the door. Wharton heaved a genuine sigh.

"That might have been a very awkward situation. It scared you, Mr. Ramble?"

"It did a bit, sir," Ramble said. "I couldn't think what the devil was happening."

Wharton look a look outside, then locked the door again.

"I'll tell you what's been happening. I had an idea before that some sort of eavesdropping had been going on, and when that man came from the Telephone Office on Sunday, I was just a little suspicious. I couldn't do anything about him because I wasn't sure, but we may lay hands on him later. What I did do was to lay a trap for the lady. Yesterday morning I told Captain Travers I had a rendezvous in town last night at a certain secret place. That place was kept under observation. Who should approach it last night, and prepare to listen at a window, but Captain Tester." He peered from under his shaggy eyebrows. "Wasn't that good enough proof?"

"I get you, sir. She was the only one who could have told him."

"That's right," Wharton said, "and this morning Captain Travers and I clinched the matter. That question I asked her proved another thing. Captain Tester, as he calls himself, managed to get acquainted with her *after* she got her job in the camp. She must have been used for quite a considerable time."

"Was it she who took those papers the night Stirrop was killed?" asked Travers.

Wharton shook his head.

"I'm not going to be too specific at the moment. I will point out that it was through her that Tester got his pass into the camp."

It was Travers's turn to heave a sigh.

"Well, I'm not too sorry she's gone. Now I'd better get hold of Labour Exchange, to see if they've got a shorthand-typist."

He was turning from the window, replacing the glasses which his long, lean fingers had been automatically polishing, and then he appeared suddenly to have gone mad, for he made a wild dash for the table where lay his cap and belt.

"Oh, my God! Those brass hats! Just coming through the gate!"

Wharton had never known him move so fast. Ramble disappeared too, like panting time toiling after him in vain.

Colonel Caithby was as usual a sight for sore eyes. He gave Travers a most charming smile as he introduced him to Fraser. And there was not much of the look of an interfering brass hat about Colonel Fraser. Travers had never before seen a brass hat wearing glasses, and he lacked that bristly white moustache which always gave a pukka air.

"What would you like to see first, sir?" Travers asked.

"The Confines of the camp, I think," he said, genially "Just a quick look at your methods of security."

The procession moved off, Travers with the two brass hats, then Winter, then Byron and the Orderly Officer; and Ramble, Mafferty and the guard Sergeant-Major bringing up the rear with the R.A.M.C. sergeant as a kind of after-thought behind. At the back entrance a move was made to the guard huts, and Fraser was glad to see there was a N.A.A.F.I. Then came the building.

"The prisoners are in their rooms, sir," Travers said. "Would you like to see them there?"

"Any place you can have them all together?" he said, and turned to Caithby. "I always like to see the old Hun in a mass. It gives you a better idea."

So Winter went on ahead with Ramble and when the main party arrived, the prisoners were lined up in the ball. Fraser had a good look at them, then got Winter to ask if there were any complaints. The situation was apparently too awe-inspiring and there were none.

Then their rooms were inspected, and Fraser expressed himself as very pleased.

"You're an excellent camp here," he said. "I might also call it a model camp. And what about discipline? Do those Bosche give you any trouble?"

"None at all," Travers said.

"They're a harmless lot of sheep," added Winter. "No real trouble at all, sir."

"Just like the old Bosche, eh? Truculent when he's on top and nauseatingly servile when he's down. What were those clothes they were wearing, by the way?"

Mafferty was beckoned forward to say his little piece. The Colonel glanced in the store, and then the whole party moved outside. The Colonel glanced up and around at that massive semi-circle of pillars, straight as candles and smooth with sham facings.

"A bit imposing all this, what?"

Caithby smiled.

"Those corner towers take my fancy," he said. "Like something straight from Switzerland."

"Well, I expect you were mighty glad to have the place," Fraser said to Travers. "I think that's about all, and thank you very much for showing me round."

"Not at all, sir," Travers said. "But won't you come across and have a look at the Mess, sir. It's only just over there."

"Thank you, yes," he said, with a look at Caithby. "You're in no hurry?"

Caithby wasn't, and the whole party was once more on the move. The other ranks saluted and dismissed themselves, and the officers slowed down outside the Mess door. Travers nodded back for the whole batch to come in.

Wharton was in an easy chair by the fire, and he got to his feet, peering over his antiquated spectacles. Perhaps, thought Travers, he had put them on for effect, for they somehow gave a scholarly look and added a dignity. Travers introduced him to Colonel Fraser, and added that the Superintendent was in Shoreleigh on a special job.

"No loss of the Mess silver, I hope," Fraser said.

"Not to my knowledge, sir," Wharton said. "What there'll be after I'm gone is quite another matter."

Fraser was pleased to chuckle, and in that pleasant atmosphere the sherries were drunk. A second was refused, and then he shook hands all round. With Wharton he had a word about the Yard and the old General actually contrived to stroll with him as far as the car. Then came the last salutes, the last smiles, and away the car went. Main gate closed on it, with a sentry riding frantically into the "Present!" and yet another inspection was over.

"A nice bloke, that," said Byron.

"Best inspection I've ever had," said Winter.

"It might have been worse," admitted Travers. "And now what about some lunch?"

"I could do with something," Wharton said, and almost plaintively. "This cold weather gives you an appetite."

"The way you tacked yourself on to those brass hats was positively shameless," Travers told him.

Wharton refused to be drawn. Travers, as he said, always had to have his little joke. And what had the brass hats to do until lunch anyway?

The meal was almost over when Wharton let fall his bomb.

First he cleared his throat, and when he spoke it was with an unusual and startling solemnity.

"I have an official announcement to make which I think concerns everybody here. It's confidential at the moment and I rely on you not to repeat it. Captain Tester was arrested this morning, and is now in the custody of the civil police."

There was a startled hush.

"Good God!" Byron was the first to speak.

Winter smiled cynically.

"I'd hate to say, 'I told you so,' but I never did like that fellow. There was something fishy about him from the start."

Wharton said nothing in the babble of talk. Travers said nothing either. For one thing the arrest of Tester, foreseen as it had been after the events of the morning, came to him as something of a damp squib; and for another thing, he was wondering what his cue was supposed to be.

"What was he arrested for?" he finally asked.

"For killing Major Stirrop," burst in young Pewter with assurance.

"Did he kill Stirrop?" Travers asked point-blank.

Wharton was getting to his feet and wiping his moustache with huge sweeps of the napkin.

"In all probability—yes," he said. "But one further word to all you gentlemen. Everything's strictly confidential. Any loose talking and I shall have no hesitation in taking very drastic action. I may say that I have the full backing of Colonel Caithby to whom I mentioned the matter this morning."

"But how could Tester have done the killing?" persisted Travers, who saw a carry-on look in Wharton's eye.

"Tester's now in town," Wharton said. "I think I can divulge that much, and he refuses to talk."

He paused for effect, and a smile of the utmost complacency was on his lips.

"But what he doesn't know is that I happen to have a means of making him talk. What that means is, I haven't confided to a soul, but you can take my word for it that after I've spoken to our friend Tester tomorrow morning, I'll know all I want to know."

"You're going to town?"

"By the first train in the morning," Wharton announced blandly. "There's one little spot of information I still want, and that I may not get till late to-night," he nodded to himself and then was shaking his crafty old head. "No hurry—that's always been my motto. This time to-morrow I'll know all there is to know about Tester—and his accomplices."

"Someone else was in it too?" Pewter was asking at once.

"Sorry," said Wharton, with an air of finality, "but I have no more information to give. If anybody here has anything of interest to tell me, they'll find me in my office."

And with that effective curtain Wharton majestically made his exit.


# CHAPTER XVII
# NIGHT OF HORROR


TRAVERS WAS BACK at his office early that afternoon. There were arrears of work to clear off, and no Bertha Dance to help. The afternoon mail came in and he had his own typing to do and returns to render. Then the Labour Exchange sent three likely people to be tested for the vacant post, and it took an hour before Travers could be sure he was suited. It was a middle-aged man, not likely to be called up for service, that he finally chose. No more flirtatious females or Whores of Babylon for Ludovic Travers.

It was about five o'clock that he had occasion to go up to Mafferty's room, and who should be there but Wharton. Travers had come through as usual without knocking, and there were the two with their heads together, but Mafferty looking uncommonly serious, even for him. Wharton looked the least bit confused, and, more ominous still, he tried no jocularities. Nor did he budge, and when Travers had got the ruling which Mafferty gave him, Wharton was still there and apparently about to resume whatever surreptitious scheming Travers's unexpected arrival had interrupted.

The post was not cleared and yet Travers found himself unable to concentrate on work. There was Mafferty to worry about and whether it was he whom Wharton was drawing into the toils. Was he one of those accomplices Wharton had mentioned? Impossible, surely, and yet, the more one came to look at sheer facts, the more impossible was everybody in the camp.

Was Wharton lying when he said that Tester had killed Stirrop? Travers did not know. He was not lying when he had said that Tester had been arrested, Travers at least felt sure of that. And yet some instinct told him that Tester was not the man. How could he have entered the camp that night? If he had contrived to mount the wall, and by means of a pole had propelled himself beyond the masses of coiled wire, he would have landed in a six-foot drift of snow which the first winds had blown up from the north. Had he struggled through the snow, a sentry must have seen him and given the alarm. And after he killed Stirrop, he had to get outside the camp again to where Dulling had picked him up.

Dusk was in the sky and Travers was still working. In the room was not only the first dark but something of fear and vague alarm. Alone with his thoughts in that quiet room, and with the silence of the camp about him, Travers felt the approach of some strange and terrifying disaster, and when the sudden knock came at the door he jumped like a startled hare.

But it was only Sniffy, and then what should he do but be mysterious too. His approach was crab-wise, and his voice a hushed croak.

"Timms said I was to give this to you, sir, and not let anybody know."

Then while Travers stared, Sniffy backed towards the door, and was gone as mysteriously as he had entered. Travers, with a last look at the closed door, picked up Timms's letter.

> Burn this as soon as read. Be in your office at seven o'clock and *on no account stir out*. Burn this.
>
> G. W.

Travers read that note again, then slowly watched it burn, envelope and all. Then the thoughts began once more to whirl like the eddying fragments of charred black which circled and rose from the burnt paper. For a minute or two he squatted there before the fire, then on a sudden impulse left the 'phone to look after itself and made his way across to the Mess.

Pewter, who was O.O., was stretched out in an easy chair before the fire. He scrambled to his feet at the sight of Travers.

"Don't disturb yourself," Travers said. "Seen anything of Superintendent Wharton by any chance?"

"He went out of main gate about ten minutes ago, sir," Pewter said.

Travers pushed the bell. "Join me in a short one?"

"Thank you, sir. A sherry, if I may."

"Here's how," said Travers, and took his tot standing by the fire. All the time he was thinking hard. Wharton, he now knew, had gone to one of two places—to make contact with Lading, or to interview Bertha Dance. He had let her off lightly that morning because he wished to conduct his cross-examination in comparative secrecy. And the reason he wished Travers to stay in his office was for the taking of any 'phone message that might be sent from outside camp.

Somehow the thought eased his mind. The Mess was a change from the oppressive silence of the office, and even the company of young Pewter was for once welcome, so that he stayed on a while. But the time was getting on, and it was about a quarter to seven when he came back to the office again.

A telephone orderly was there. Mr. Ramble, had sent him, he said.

"Where is Mr. Ramble?" Travers asked.

"He did go upstairs with Captain Winter, sir, but he's just gone."

"Well, you make yourself comfortable in Captain Winter's room," Travers said. "If I want you, I'll call."

Then Winter himself came down.

"You're working late?" he said.

"What about yourself?" fired Travers.

Winter smiled. "I'm doing a job of work with Ramble. *For* him, really. I thought I'd do it up in his room so I shouldn't be disturbed."

Off he went again, and once more that uncanny silence settled about the room. Then in an unfortunate moment Travers knew that it was just like that night when Stirrop was killed, except that now there was a strange awareness and that queer sense of things about to happen. Then, as he had done that night, he began to hum to himself and relighted his pipe, and stoked the fire noisily.

He glanced at his watch and saw that Wharton's zero hour was past. At any moment something might happen, and then he smiled to himself, for the only thing that could happen was the sudden ringing of the telephone bell. Then the bell did ring. Travers hesitated strangely for a moment, then picked the receiver up.

"Yes?"

"Main Guard speaking, sir. A closed car, like an ambulance car, just drew up, sir, outside the gate along the road, so I went to investigate. It was a driver from H.Q., sir, and a couple of red hats—military police. They said they had orders to wait outside, and I wasn't to do anything about it. Is that all right, sir?"

"Quite all right," Travers said. "The public highway's free to all. So long as they don't want to come into camp, they can do as they please. Oh, and just a minute. Did Superintendent Wharton come through recently?"

"About half an hour ago, sir."

"Right," said Travers laconically. "Good-bye."

Now his thoughts were really a whirl. Wharton back in camp, and something like an ambulance waiting at the main gate. And Wharton still had that gun!

All at once he found himself at the door, and listening. The camp was still as death itself. The wind lay towards the hutments and there was never a sound, not even of a sentry. A heaviness was in the air, as if a thaw was near, and the night itself was so turgidly black that from earth to sky seemed one impenetrable cloud. A cough came, and the sound was startling in the stillness. Then Travers smiled. It was only the orderly in Winter's room.

He went back to his table and tried to settle to work, and then, all at once, the new silence was shattered. It was a sudden clap, like a gun, and in a flash his heart was racing madly. Then, again, he knew what it was.

"Damn that fellow, Winter! Why the hell can't he shut doors quietly?"

He went through to the orderly.

"Was that Captain Winter who just went out?"

"Nobody went out," the orderly said.

Travers stared. "Then what was that noise upstairs?"

"Sounded like somebody dropping something, sir."

Travers gave a Whartonian grunt, frowned, then went back to his office again. What the devil did it mean? Winter *had* gone out. Then suddenly he was opening the door again, and was making his way round from the back, and looking towards the Mess and listening for the sound of Winter's steps.

Then there was a shot. There was no doubt about it this time. It cracked in the still air, and there followed a wild shout.

"Mafferty! Mafferty!"

It was over at the building, and Travers burst into a shambling run.

Another shot—a louder one—and Travers was frantically trying to open the wire gate. All he could think of was Mafferty. Wharton's voice had called, *and Mafferty, after all, was the man*. The gate opened and was left open, for Travers was running forward towards the dim light of the wire. Something dark lay on the snow by the other gate, and someone was running from the Mess. Voices were coming from everywhere, and behind him the feet of the orderly came pounding.

"What's happened?" Travers paused for breath. "What's been going on? Where's Wharton?"

"Here," said Wharton, emerging from the dark. He was hatless and his coat was smothered with snow.

Another voice came from towards the building, and drew nearer, and in the faint light Travers could see Mafferty.

"Did I get him, sir?"

"I think so," Wharton said, and moved on towards the gate.

Byron was there, and Pewter, and half a dozen men. Wharton pushed his way, and knelt by the thing that lay in the dim light.

"He's still alive. You, whoever you are, run to the gate and tell that ambulance to drive in. Captain Byron, you get him away."

"Clear off, you fellows," Byron said, and as the tiny crowd disposed, Travers found himself alone with Wharton. Then he, too, stooped by the body.

"Good God, it's Winter!"

"Winter it is." said Wharton calmly. "Winter, alias the extra prisoner. Get off back to that office of yours and tell Colonel Caithby to come. Tell him it's all right, and he's to bring the men. Double off quick. There's plenty more to do to-night."

As Travers moved off bewilderedly, he heard Wharton giving orders to Mafferty. Something about the prisoners, and moving them pronto to the first floor.

Ten minutes later a runner said Wharton would like to see Captain Travers at the main building. Colonel Caithby was there, and looking remarkably serious. There was no welcoming smile for Travers, but barely an official nod. Two men were with him, and one was that Sapper sergeant who had been in charge of raising the floors.

"Come on." said Wharton impatiently. "Let's get to work. We've got the prisoners upstairs, so everything's clear. Where's that chap Mafferty?"

Mafferty appeared.

"Extra guards all mounted, sir."

Wharton grunted and led the way to that room where the tunnel had been.

"There you are," he said to the sergeant. "Get those floor-boards up again."

This time the boards came up more easily still. Wharton peered down at the earth where the tunnel had been, and then Ramble appeared, and four men with shovels.

"Right," said Wharton, "Get the earth out and open the tunnel. Throw it anywhere."

The men got to work shovelling out the loose earth. In ten minutes they reported hard bottom.

"There's the tunnel in front of you," Wharton told them impatiently. "Work along it."

An electric light was shone down on a lead, but now only one man could work. Soon two others were in the hole and throwing out the earth he shovelled back.

Then came a muffled sound.

"There's a pipe here, or something. No, it's something else."

Wharton motioned the two out and got down into the hole himself. Colonel Caithby came forward too, and Travers was peering over his shoulder. For days that smell of damp earth was to be in his nostrils, and he would wince at the horror of the thing that followed. First came a bag, yellow with the gravel of the sub-soil, and as Caithby reached down to haul it up Travers suddenly knew.

Wharton's voice came muffled from the tunnel, and then at last he was backing out, and holding the legs of the dead man. Caithby slipped down unhesitatingly, knee deep in loose soil, and lent a hand, while the sergeant stood at the brink, and slowly the body came up. As Travers caught sight of the dead white face, a something rose in his throat, and he was turning his head away.

Wharton and Caithby scrambled out of the hole. Wharton looked down at Lading's dead body.

"Two or three are going to hang for this, sir, or my name's not what it is. You identify him, Captain Travers?"

"Yes," said Travers quietly. "Even with that beard on, I still know he's Lading."

Wharton turned the body over and removed the pullover. There was no need to remove the shirt, for the thrust of the knife had made an even larger rent and the blood had matted.

"And what now?" asked Caithby.

"Get hold of the doctor and have him taken away," Wharton said. "Everything here must be left just as it is."

"A double guard on the prisoners, and this room guarded too," Caithby told Travers, who nodded over to Ramble.

Wharton gave a look round.

"Nothing else we can do here. Better go and do some telephoning."

Outside the building he halted.

"Where was Winter at seven o'clock?" he asked Travers.

"Upstairs in Ramble's room," Travers said. "He told me he was doing a job of work and didn't want to be disturbed."

Wharton moved on without comment, but it was to Winter's room that he went.

"We'll go upstairs," he said. "We ought to see something interesting."

A cold blast met them when the door was opened. Travers switched on the light, and there was a window open. Wharton leaned out, and was hauling in a short length of strong rope.

"That's how he got down without going down the stairs. Now let's see what's here." He gave a grunt of triumph. "Ah, just what I thought."

On the floor behind the door was a wetness that shortly before must have been a pool of water.

"Someone's been standing here," said Travers, staring. "That's what happened when Stirrop was killed."

Wharton shook his head.

"No one's been standing. What you're looking at is Winter's alibi!"

# CHAPTER XVIII
# WHARTON EXPLAINS

THE TELEPHONING had been done, and the three were in Travers's office. It was to Colonel Caithby that Wharton mainly addressed himself.

"It's Captain Travers I've to thank. With him here, and used to me, so to speak, it was just like having an encyclopedia to consult. He used to tell me all I wanted to know." He chuckled. "Though he didn't always know how I used it. And it was not a bad plan, mind you, getting on friendly terms with the camp. I knew where to go for things and who to ask for them, without having to keep running to Captain Travers who was always up to his eyes."

"What gave you the first lead?" asked Caithby.

Wharton pursed his lips. "To tell the honest truth, I don't know. I had a good look at all the suspects Captain Travers gave me, and some I discarded for good. Tester I never liked the look of, and I was glad when I was able to rope him in. All the same, I knew he could never have killed Major Stirrop. Then one day something did strike me.

"The talk was about Stirrop's fractured skull and how it might have been caused by jumping down from too great a height. Remember that word *down*, because it gave me the lead. Then I got to thinking of how he was sandbagged and how the camp had sandbags everywhere. Then I thought to myself why shouldn't a full sandbag have been dropped on his skull? Then I wondered from where, and that led me to that veranda. But it still wasn't good enough. You can't drop a sandbag on a man's skull if that man isn't there, and you've got to be a mighty clever person to do it in the dark even if you know he's there. You've got to drop the sandbag damned accurately, and I told myself it couldn't be done. It would have been too dangerous to miss. Still, we'll come back to all that later."

"Yes, but how'd you get on to Winter?" Travers wanted to know.

"I can't tell you," Wharton said. "The progress was gradual as you'll see. Later we discovered it was his brother who fought with Smuts and who died about four years ago. This brother was also a South African—Weinholst was the real name—but he fought on the other side, and then became an irreconcilable, and a Commie agent. Stirrop ran across him in Burma of all places, in the days when Winter had blond hair and a beard—"

"Good Lord! And I thought it was vanity that made him dye his hair!"

"His hair *was* dyed all right," said "Wharton, "but Stirrop had the idea he'd met him somewhere, and all the time he kept getting warmer, as they say. That's why Winter had to kill him. Then there was that Army Form he had to fill in—"

"B.199A."

"That's it. He didn't fill it in correctly—or a hundredth part correctly—and if he filled it in wrongly, then some smart person might have spotted the mistakes. Another reason why Stirrop had to be got rid of.

"What you don't know, Captain Travers, is that Winter had been living down here for months. He'd got his papers through for his job without too careful scrutiny—"

"I know who gave him a good character," Travers said. "It was the very chap for the purpose. A certain Lord Somebody, whose name I won't mention."

"That's what I thought. And once down here he contacted Tester, and if the two weren't responsible for sabotage, then my name's Robinson. When this last batch of prisoners arrived, he made himself known to Friedemann, but gave him a bad character—as he did Tester—by way of camouflage. He told Friedemann all that was going on, and you bet it was he who gave the orders.

"And now about that extra prisoner business. That was Winter's first plan to kill Stirrop, and it nearly came off. Remember that when you were away. Captain Travers, Winter took over for you, and he had your keys. That explains a lot. Now—to how he planned that murder which didn't quite come off.

"Winter knew that a few prisoners meant easy, and therefore comparative careless, counting, and he knew Ebbing and the two guard officers. So before the evening count he let himself into the store, took off his tunic, and slipped a pullover and trousers over his things, and put on a false moustache, or some other quick disguise, and came out in time to join a room—none too light a room, mind you—for the count. The prisoners didn't all know each other yet, and even if they were wise to what was going on, you bet your life they'd been warned to keep their mouths shut. When the count was over—and wrong—he slipped back to the store and let himself out of the building.

"As for the night when he took that shot at Stirrop, he was too clever. Perhaps he thought someone—Mafferty, for instance—must have heard somebody in the store, so he reported it first, and there were the remains of the snow on his own boots to prove it. And what I want you to remember now is that the existence of an extra prisoner was established. Winter took a risk that night when Stirrop was in charge of the count, but he knew Stirrop and guessed he'd count in his own pig-headed way. Later, as I've just said, he knew that the one person who'd swear blind there *was* an extra prisoner, was Stirrop."

He paused a moment for effect.

"And that's how Stirrop really came to be killed. You will note that once Stirrop was dead, there was no extra prisoner. There was no need of one, and if there had been, then it would have been too risky. Captain Travers had taken too many precautions to have the counts correct. So Winter had to find a new way to kill Stirrop, and he found it." Wharton again paused dramatically. "He found it in the same extra prisoner scheme, and *because he knew Major Stirrop.*"

He rolled himself a spill and lighted his pipe.

"That's better. And now where was I? Oh, yes, at where Major Stirrop was killed. We'll leave that alone for a bit because it comes in later. What we come to next are all sorts of things. What I thought about the dropped sandbag, for instance, and how Winter was in charge of A.R.P., or whatever you call it, and how he discovered sand missing from some of the buckets. Aha! I said to myself, now there's a fine way for someone to have procured a sandbag if he wanted to drop one from the roof or elsewhere. Take an empty sandbag up and fill it with a little from each of scores of buckets. That led me to an examination of that veranda, where I made a certain discovery—namely a stout nail at the head of one of the pillars. Even then I didn't see the whole scheme, though I had ideas.

"Then Captain Travers showed me a paper he'd taken from Major Stirrop's wallet. That did give me ideas, and it also kept me thinking about Winter. He was the one who fitted in best, and that's why I took the trouble, as you know, sir, to get into touch with Colonel Cross. I'd like Captain Travers to have another look at that paper now."

He referred to his notebook and read aloud:

Ring W.O. and see if Harry Cross still B.C. Get 'phone num. . . . (Garrison?) *Weinholst*, and what about beard? Mention Trav.? Two birds one stone. After to-night.

"Well, I did ring Border Command and Colonel Cross *was* still there, and I got the 'phone number from Garrison. Then that bit about Weinholst explained itself, because a long talk on the 'phone with the Colonel revealed that he knew all about the Weinholst brothers. Cross was also a friend of Stirrop, and when he had last seen him they had been comparing notes about things in general, and it turned out that Stirrop had also known the younger Weinholst. Mind you, I still didn't think Weinholst was other than a prisoner. That bit about the beard was what swindled me. You could have knocked me down with a feather when—"

"Is Captain Travers wise to that little trick of ours?" put in Caithby.

Wharton peered quizzically at Travers over the tops of his spectacles.

"I don't think he is. I had to keep all sorts of things away from Captain Travers. You never knew who was listening. But the Colonel Fraser of our inspection was Colonel Fraser Cross. We induced him to come, and he sacrificed a moustache for us, and Winter never spotted him. Why should he? He'd never seen the Colonel in khaki. In fact, he hadn't seen him for years.

"And now the rest of that paper explains itself. Stirrop had remembered who it was Winter resembled, and he wondered if he should mention it to you, Captain Travers. The two birds with one stone were the two things he was going to do that night. One was to test something Winter had promised to prove to him—we'll come to that later—and the other was to consult Captain Travers."

"And then probably take his own view," said Caithby, dryly.

"Well, I didn't know the gentleman," Wharton said, "but I gather you're not far out. And to go on with Winter; as soon as he was on my short list, I went into his alibi. If I couldn't bust that, then he would come off the list. And I did bust it, at least to my own satisfaction. Which brings us to the events of to-day."

Wharton stoked his pipe and gave a shrewd look round.

"We all have to have luck sometimes, and mine was when I could get a good enough hold-on for Tester. Then I announced that I knew he had accomplices, and that I had a scheme, which nobody else knew, mind you, to make him squeal. It was a bluff, but not a risky one—except perhaps for me. Frankly, I didn't expect it to come off, but it did. This afternoon Winter approached me very confidentially, and said he'd overheard two prisoners talking, and they'd accidentally revealed the secret of the extra prisoner. He'd rather I didn't mention the matter to a soul until we'd tested things out, but would I meet him after dark at the entrance to the building. Seven-fifteen was the exact time mentioned.

"That was when I knew for a certainty how Stirrop had been killed. The way, in fact, gentlemen, that I was going to be. When you drop anything down from a height, you can hit your target in the dark if your target's still, and you have some means of letting the object fall plumb on his head. Those pillars are straight up and down. Drop a sandbag from the top of one and it must fall straight down it.'

"There was a confederate?"

"No—and yes." Wharton smiled. "The confederate was a razor blade. Imagine a candle with a flat top. Stick a pin in the top, say a quarter of an inch down. Take a little ball of anything to represent the sandbag and attach it to a length of cotton. Let the cotton go over the pin, leaving the bag dangling. Now attach the length of cotton to another pin at the bottom of the candle." He had been doing it all by way of illustration. "Now I take my knife and cut the cotton, like this. Down comes the bag and I know to the millionth of an inch where it's going to drop. For cotton, substitute stout cord. The candle's the pillar nearest the south-west wall, the pins are nails driven into the brickwork of the wall—the bottom one hidden under the snow—the bag is a full sandbag, and the knife is a razor blade."

Wharton peered at his listeners with a droll kind of apprehension.

"That, gentlemen, was what was in store for me, and I'm no hero. When I began to think of that sandbag falling, I didn't like the idea a bit. In the good old Army phrase, I had the wind clean up. Winter was a stronger man than I, and he'd make sure I didn't move when the bag fell. That's why I took Mafferty into my confidence. And it's why I had an ambulance ready. Someone was likely to get hurt, though I hoped it wouldn't be me. And if nobody was hurt—well, it would do for a black Maria.

"Mafferty was to be on that veranda five minutes before we were due to arrive, and he was to keep a sharp look-out for Winter beforehand. For the sand-bag he was to substitute something reasonably heavy and not dangerous, and I was to put some protection inside my hat. Mafferty was to have his rifle, and I would have the gun. What I expected was that as soon as the bag hit me, Winter would make sure I was dead, and then drag or carry me a few yards away in the dark, out of the reach of wire lighting. When he found I wasn't dead, I'd have to hold him up with my gun. If he shot first, or clubbed me, or stabbed me, then Mafferty would get him."

Wharton shook his head and heaved a reminiscent sigh.

"Only it didn't quite pan out that way. We met—Winter and I—and he said the extra prisoner was hidden in that sort of tower room on the south-west corner. He was due to get out from a window and we were to watch. He placed me plumb under the sandbag, and warned me not to move whatever I heard. Then he said, 'What's that!' and his hand got a good grip of my arm. His other hand went back and the blade cut the cord. There was a kind of swish and before I could even wriggle, something caught me the very devil of a wallop on the skull. I didn't have to sham dead, gentlemen. I went over into the snow and it was a second or so before I got going. And something had gone wrong.

"Mind you, all this happened while you could count ten. Winter, thinking I was a goner, as Stirrop had been, first grabbed the bag, to empty the sand out and hide it under the snow, and make the snow smooth again as he had done the last time. But it wasn't sand, and he knew it. Out came a knife, and he made for where I lay. I let him have a shot and I think I hit him. He turned and bolted for the gate. I hollered to Mafferty who brought him down. All as quick as that."

He shook his old head.

"I don't think I've ever been so seared in my life. I couldn't get that damn' gun out at first, and he was actually on me when I fired. Still, here we are. Sound in wind and limb, as they say. And that I think, gentlemen, is about all."

"But what about that alibi, George?" Travers asked promptly. "I still don't see how he could be listening to all my movements and out there with Stirrop at the same time?"

"It's this way," Wharton told him, "and to-night we've proved it. Winter first acquired a quick reputation for slamming doors. Then he fixed it for you and him to be working in adjoining rooms, and he cut the 'phone so that no message would come to interrupt you. He met Stirrop at a quarter past eight, and he expected to be away for no more than ten minutes to fifteen minutes at the most. Up to that time he took good care to listen to you. He heard you whistling or humming, and he heard you stoke the fire, and he remembered it. Then when he went out he turned off the light and slipped a big icicle under the door, and left the door half open.

"But something went wrong. Perhaps Stirrop argued the point or got suspicious. Then the Orderly Officer was late and came by just when he'd put the body in position. He didn't expect the Orderly Officer at all. The usual procedure is for the O.O. to come from the Company Office, and the Provost from the Sergeants' Mess, and they meet at the back door. It must have been a shock when he came along, and all Winter could do was step on Stirrop's body and crouch behind it in the snow. That's what made the second impression, and why there were no footprints. Then he had to get the snow off his clothes, and dispose of the sandbag. I'd say he did that job last, and it was the experience he gained that made him tackle that job first to-night—before he disposed of me, that is.

"At any rate, it was about a quarter to nine when he got back, and he must have been scared. The ice had melted and the door had slammed, and, luckily, at the most convenient time, for there you were, Captain Travers, turning on the light, and all he had to do was say he had gone to Stirrop's room for the appointment, and he wasn't there. The water on the floor was explained away, and by assuming that while he was away you'd been doing what you'd been doing while he was there, he established his alibi. By offering to establish your alibi to the Brigadier, *he still further established his own alibi*, to which you would have been prepared and to swear on a stack of Bibles. Isn't that so?"

Travers smiled lamely. The old Colonel, who had got to his feet, patted him on the back.

"Never mind, young feller. I'd have thought what you did. And you had a lucky escape. What do you say, Wharton?"

"He certainly did, sir," Wharton said emphatically. "If he had shown any suspicions, he'd have had a knife in his ribs. He'd have been buried somewhere, like poor Lading, and it would have been related how he and Stirrop had had a violent quarrel, and Stirrop had been killed and Travers had bolted."

"I see all that now," Travers said, "but there's one thing I still don't see. When I went into Winter's room, *before he came back*, I picked up a card he had been doing and the ink was still wet. And yet he'd been away best part of half an hour!"

"All part of the alibi," Wharton said, getting to his feet too, and stretching his legs. "Try a little pure glycerine in your ink and see what happens."

Caithby nodded.

"Well, I must be moving. I won't wake the Brigadier tonight, but he'll want to hear all about it in the morning." He smiled and out went his hand to Wharton. "Meanwhile, my own congratulations."

They went to the main gate together. "See you both in the morning," Caithby said. "And I don't know about you, but I doubt if I'll get much sleep. I can't get that poor devil Lading's face out of my mind. A damnable business. And, as you say, someone will swing for it."

"How did you get on to what happened to Lading?" Travers asked Wharton as they walked briskly back.

"It just had to be," Wharton said. "Winter daren't let Lading out of the camp. He waited till you'd gone to H.Q., then spun you that yarn about Lading going in Byron's car. I reckon Lading was already dead."

"It was I who really killed him," Travers said. "If I hadn't let Winter know, he'd have been alive now."

"You're being morbid," Wharton told him. "When Stirrop was dead you had to say something to Winter. It's Friedemann's blood I'm after. He probably did the knifing."

"With Winter at the back of it all."

"Yes," said Wharton grimly. "I don't know if they shoot spies nowadays. I hope they hang them. If they don't, the next thing Winter will have his back against is a brick wall, with his eyes on a firing-squad."

It was about half-past nine the next morning when Colonel Caithby rang.

"Your prisoners are to go away tomorrow," he said. "I've just had advance information. They'll travel under extra escort, but we'll talk about that later. Can you and Wharton be here at ten hours? The Brigadier would like to see you both."

Travers was feeling even unhappier than usual as he and Wharton approached Garrison Headquarters that morning. He had slept badly, and somehow, for all Wharton's pooh-poohing, he could not get out of his mind the idea that in some way he had been responsible for that ghastly business of Lading's murder. But the Brigadier seemed rather less rigid that morning, and the eyes a little less menacing. He invited the two to sit down, and never once did he interrupt Wharton's story, or the deft praises of Travers that the old General managed every now and again to insert.

Yet, in that story, as he heard it for a second time, Travers saw a danger. There was something the Brigadier would be bound to notice. Then when the story was ended and the fear had passed, the Brigadier leaned forward.

"Now, Captain Travers, there's something I have to say to you."

Travers got to his feet, and to attention. Once more he was looking into those steely grey eyes.

"Doesn't it strike you that something was radically wrong in your camp that there was never any suspicion of this man Winter?"

It had come, but somehow Travers found himself prepared to put up a fight.

"May I speak frankly, sir?"

"Why shouldn't you?"

"Exactly, sir." He moistened his lips. "Well, sir, what I must say is this. I never had any suspicions of Winter because he was too clever for me. After all, sir, one doesn't suspect a brother officer who's already been vetted by the War Office. And also, sir, I was adjutant of the camp, not its commandant. If I'd had suspicions they might not have been acted upon."

"I see. Well"—he turned to Caithby—"I don't think I want to detain Captain Travers any longer. Superintendent Wharton, I'd like you to stay for a minute."

"Very good, sir," said Caithby, and smiled across at Travers. Travers saluted, and followed Caithby down the stairs and along the passage.

"Well," he was saying philosophically to himself, "that's torn it. A day or two and I'll he transferred to another camp, or else get fired. And I'm damned if I'll stand for that. I'll put up some sort of fight. I'm back in this ruddy uniform and they're not getting it off me."

"Just come in a minute," Caithby was saying, the door of his room held open. "Make yourself comfortable. I don't expect the brigadier will keep Wharton very long."

"Thank you, sir," said Travers, and sat down as if on the electric chair. Caithby smiled down at him.

"Between you and me, the Brigadier's bark is worse than his bite. I think I told you that once before. I don't think he's dissatisfied on the whole. Anything I can do for you myself?"

"Well, I don't know, sir." His fingers went to his glasses. "What I would like is seven days' leave—when this business is cleared up."

"Good!" said Caithby. "Why not write your application now? If it isn't passed, I can let you know. Leave the date to be filled in later."

So Travers sat down at the table and wrote that he had the honour to request, etc., etc. Colonel Caithby said it read all right, and he thought Travers might count on the leave. Travers was thinking that after that leave he would probably never see that cursed camp again, and would be glad enough of it.

"Something here I ought to have shown you," Colonel Caithby said. "This came in last night, but we knew three days ago."

He handed Travers the W.O. telegram.

P.W. 003/XY42. Reference your S.A.188 appointment Captain Travers Commandant Number 54 P.W. Camp confirmed STOP Repeated Midland Command.

ADVANCING

"I'm to carry on?" asked the staring Travers.

Caithby smiled. "Looks like it. Oh, and here's something else might interest you."

This time it was a copy of Midland Command Orders dated the previous day, and his finger was on para. 993.

Travers saw a list of promotions, headed: *To be Majors.* There, half-way down the list, was his own name.

*Captain L. Travers, with effect from January 23rd.*

Travers shook his head. He wanted to say something but the words refused to come.

"Well, it's not a bad world sometimes," the Colonel said, as if to himself. Then he was cocking an ear. "This sounds like Wharton."

Wharton it was, full of beans and self-satisfaction. Out went his hand to the Colonel.

"Well, I'll say good-bye to you, sir, and thank you for all you've done. If ever you're in town, look me up. Call at the Yard and I'll show you round."

Caithby's eyes twinkled.

"I certainly will. By the way, Travers, you ought to get an adjutant and a new interpreter sometime this afternoon."

"Nothing like working with the top-notchers," Wharton remarked complacently as Travers moved off in the borrowed car. "Not a bad chap, that Brigadier." He swivelled round in his seat. "You're a bit of a top-notcher yourself, so they tell me."

"You know?"

"Know!" snarled Wharton. "I knew yesterday." He gave a second snort, and one of profoundest contempt. "We're supposed to know nothing, we old stagers. The Army's not what it used to be. We get left behind. That's all I've heard since I've been here."

Travers smiled to himself but made no comment. Life at that moment was far too good. For Wharton he had never felt such an affection, and there was Colonel Caithby, too, one of the very best. Even that Colonel Cross who'd done what no other brass hat had ever done in history—shaved off his moustache in the good cause. And there was the camp in sight again. Not a bad spot after all. Many a worse place than P.W. Camp No. 54.

The gate was opened, and then a strange thing happened. As the car passed through, the sentry elaborately presented arms!

"What the devil was he doing that for?" demanded Travers. "There isn't another car behind us, is there?"

Wharton guffawed.

"Aren't you a Major?"

"Good Lord, yes!" said Travers, and smiled sheepishly. "But how did he know?"

"Somebody must have rung up Byron and given him the tip," Wharton said, rather off-handedly, "Perhaps it was some old stager who hasn't forgotten after all. Time may march on you know, but—"

"George, you're a damned old humbug," Travers told him, and drew the car up. "All the same, if you come in the Mess I'll defy Regulations and stand you a drink."

THE END